SHINJI TAKAHASHI

AND THE **MARK** OF THE **COATL**

JULIE KAGAWA

DISNEP • HYPERION

LOS ANGELES   NEW YORK

First Edition, April 2022
10 9 8 7 6 5 4 3 2 1
FAC-021131-22049
Printed in the United States of America

This book is set in Adobe Caslon Pro/Monotype.
Designed by Marci Senders

Library of Congress Cataloging-in-Publication Data
Names: Kagawa, Julie, author.
Title: Shinji Takahashi and the mark of the coatl / by Julie Kagawa.
Description: First edition. • Los Angeles ; New York : Disney-Hyperion,
    2022. • Series: S.E.A. ; book 1 • Audience: Ages 8–12. • Audience:
    Grades 7–9. • Summary: To free himself from an ancient curse,
    thirteen-year-old Shinji Takahashi must team up with a secret
    organization of explorers, find a magical font hidden in the jungles of
    Mexico, and replace a stolen idol.
Identifiers: LCCN 2020057980 • ISBN 9781368068192 (hardcover) •
    ISBN 9781368074537 (ebook)
Subjects: CYAC: Blessing and cursing—Fiction. • Secret societies—Fiction.
    • Animals, Mythical—Fiction. • Magic—Fiction. • Adventure and
    adventurers—Fiction. • Japanese Americans—Fiction.
Classification: LCC PZ7.K117443 Shi 2022 • DDC [Fic]—dc23
LC record available at https://lccn.loc.gov/2020057980

Reinforced binding
Visit www.DisneyBooks.com

TO MARK, KIRAN, AND KIERAN.
WHAT COULD POSSIBLY GO WRONG
ON THIS ADVENTURE?

PROLOGUE

Flames roared and snapped in the night.

The wail of sirens filled the air, lights flashing red, blue, and white as crowds and vehicles surrounded the inferno. Even the rain that fell from the sky could not snuff out the howling flames. The simple suburban home with the quaint picket fence blazed like a fireball against the darkness, drawing the eyes of everyone in the neighborhood. Police officers held back the crowds as firefighters sprayed jets of water onto the roof of the burning house, sending huge billows of smoke into the air.

Unnoticed and unseen by everyone, a large black spider crawled through the window of the doomed house, scuttling away through the wet grass. Firefighters raced back and forth, their booted feet pounding the mud, but the spider deftly avoided being crushed. It paused, hiding beneath an overturned tricycle, as the front door burst open and a firefighter stumbled out of the burning house. Coughing, shoulders hunched, the man held a wrapped bundle close to his chest, shielding it with his body as he staggered into the open. As the spider watched, crouched below the handlebars, two more firefighters hurried forward to help. The first man lowered his arms, revealing the dirty, tear-streaked face of a small boy, dark hair falling into his eyes. One of the firefighters drew in a sharp breath.

"Is he the only one?" The man's voice was low, barely audible over the roar of the flames and the jerky, gasping sobs of the child. "His parents?"

The firefighter holding the boy closed his eyes and shook his head. "They didn't make it."

The other's shoulders slumped. "Poor kid. Well, let's get him to the EMTs. Hopefully he has relatives who can take him in."

They walked away, the boy's sobs fading into the night. The spider crawled out from beneath the tricycle and scuttled off, toward the crowd of people watching the firefighters battle the flames. It scurried around feet and crawled over shoes until it reached the edge of the crowd, where a lone figure watched from the shadows. The figure held a black umbrella, its face hidden in the hood of its raincoat as it gazed at the burning house and the firefighters still rushing around it.

The spider crawled onto the figure's shoe, then scuttled up its leg, vanishing beneath the hem of its coat. A few seconds later, it crawled out from beneath the collar and perched on the slender neck. Mandible waving, it made a faint chittering sound that could not be heard by the normal human ear.

Beneath the hood, the figure's bloodred lips curved up in a smile.

"Excellent," it whispered. "The piece has been found. The game has been set into motion." Turning from the burning house, it began to walk into the dark, though its final words hung in the air. "I will see you soon, Shinji Takahashi."

CHAPTER ONE

Oh, cheer up, Shinji. What could possibly go wrong on this adventure?"

Shinji Takahashi rolled his eyes. His aunt Yui used that word often: *adventure*. As if crawling down the river in the *Good Tern*, her ancient, beat-up trawler, was an adventure. As if poking through a bunch of dusty trinkets, old tools, and cracked clay pottery was an adventure. Even the fact that they were in *Africa*, floating down a river toward a place called Abenge, did not help. Shinji had already been to this village, and many others like it. Half his life was spent aboard this trawler. While most boys his age went to basketball camp and amusement parks and other cool places for the summer, he was stuck here with Aunt Yui, doing business with local artisans for items to sell at her carefully curated store, the Lost River Outfitters. He wouldn't have minded too much if his aunt didn't always try to pass *work* off as *fun*.

Shinji remembered a time when these trips had been exciting. He used to look forward to the end of summer, when the flood of tourists left their little town of Miami, Florida, and went back home. Aunt Yui would close up her shop for the winter, and together they would travel to distant places all over the world. Morocco, Thailand, Norway, New Zealand; every trip was new and exciting, every location full of wonder and awe. But gradually, the long days aboard the *Good Tern* began to wear on him. He wanted to go to regular school. He wanted to play sports with kids his age, hang out at a buddy's house, and do the things normal kids got to do. Aunt Yui had always homeschooled him, and she was a great teacher, but Shinji's only friends were the ones he played online games with. And since his substandard internet plan was always spotty no matter where they were, Shinji would often spend weeks not speaking to anyone but Yui.

"Think of it as a *treasure hunt*, Shinji," Aunt Yui cajoled, making him snort. She said that often, too. And for her, maybe it was a treasure hunt. Standing at the wheel, her dark hair pulled back and stuffed through a baseball cap, a pair of sunglasses perched on her nose, she looked perfectly at home on the water. She *liked* this stuff—going from place to place, meeting with artists and weavers and jewelry makers and designers, searching for *treasures*. She had friends and business partners around the world—like-minded people who wanted to share their cultures with others through their artistry. But Shinji had never seen a woven basket that he would equate with the word *treasure*. "You never know what you might find," she finished.

"I do go on treasure hunts," Shinji argued. "And quests. All the time."

Aunt Yui sniffed. "Those silly online games of yours do not count," she said in disgust. Lifting a hand from the wheel, she gestured dramatically to the trees and the river surrounding them. "These are *real* treasures. Items that tell a real story, not who can kill each other the fastest with a sword that shoots out lightning."

"Really?" Shinji crossed his arms, smirking. "So if you saw a lightning sword sitting next to a bunch of boring clay pots, which one would *you* buy?"

"You should be more interested in the world around you," Aunt Yui went on as if he hadn't said anything. "It is a fascinating, beautiful, marvelous place. There are places we've never seen, sights we never could've imagined. Did you know our ancestors were once the guardians of a sacred shrine in Hokkaido? They were protectors of *real* treasures in the real world; that's something you can't say about your games, is it?"

Shinji rolled his eyes. He'd heard this story all his life;

how his great-great-great-grandfather was the head priest of some kind of sacred temple, and how his ancestors came over from Japan to start a new life in the United States. It didn't change anything now; he was still an orphan, still plain old Shinji Takahashi. There was nothing special about him. "Yeah, you might've mentioned that once . . . or two million times," he told Aunt Yui. "But I still don't have a sword that shoots lightning."

Now his aunt gave him an annoyed look. "Go pull up the fishing lines," she ordered, a surefire sign that she was done arguing with him. "Make yourself useful. We should reach Abenge in an hour or so."

Shinji sighed but turned and left the wheelhouse, wandering to the back of the trawler. Reaching over the edge, he caught a glimpse of his reflection in the muddy river water, a disgruntled-looking thirteen-year-old, dark hair falling into his eyes and a perpetual smirk on his face. Aunt Yui called him a smart aleck and warned that his face would freeze like that if he wasn't careful. Shinji didn't see the problem, but he had promised his aunt that he would work on his "snarky attitude." Especially after that whole incident in Marrakesh. Apparently, a certain Moroccan shopkeeper did not appreciate a child's commentary on his artistic taste.

As he pulled up the lines, dragging a couple of small catfish out of the water, the glimmer of something in the trees caught his attention. Looking up, he spotted something metallic and quick swooping through the branches, like a silver bird or a bat. It was gone in a blink, and though he scanned the trees and canopy for several minutes after, it did not appear again.

Abenge was a medium-size village on the banks of the Zambezi River, and one that Aunt Yui was particularly fond of. She even had names for the trio of hippos that made their home on the opposite bank as you drew closer to Abenge. Lord Henry and his two wives lay peacefully in the mud along the riverbank, looking like enormous round boulders. Aunt Yui was sure to give them a wide berth as they passed; a hippo might look lazy and clumsy, but it was territorial and super dangerous if you got too close. Thankfully, Lord Henry and his entourage were used to the comings and goings of boats and didn't even glance up as the *Tern* chugged by.

A few minutes later, a series of wooden docks appeared on the banks of the river. Aunt Yui maneuvered the trawler close, and Shinji wrapped rope around the pilings until the *Tern* was secure.

As he tugged the final rope tight, Aunt Yui strode past him on the wooden planks and stopped at the edge, grinning widely. "All right, then, we've arrived," she announced, her excitement palpable. "What will we discover today? I wonder. We have some time before we meet with Makena to talk shop. Come on, then, Shinji. Let's go find some treasures!"

With a sigh, Shinji followed her away from the docks and into the village of Abenge. Sheltered by clusters of fig trees, the brick, clay, and thatch huts soon gave way to a large open-air marketplace that always seemed busy, but never in a rush. People milled about with smiles on their faces, wandered around the booths at a leisurely pace, or paused to chat with merchants and fellow shoppers. The smell of cooking meat filled the air, white smoke curling from open grills as food vendors handed out kebabs, ribs, sausages, and other mouthwatering items. The market itself was surrounded by a line of storefronts pressed tightly against each other, selling everything from clothing and purses to whole pigs. The structures were all old, their once brightly painted walls now eroded by weather and time.

Shinji followed his aunt through the crowds, dodging the occasional dog or chicken that wandered into his path, waiting as his aunt stopped at every table selling pottery, baskets, or hand-carved figurines. The afternoon sun beat down on him, and the air was muggy and hot, even in the shade. Sweat trickled into his eyes. He wiped it away with the bottom of his shirt and wished he were in his air-conditioned room playing *Forever Quest II*. When Aunt Yui stopped at yet another stall selling baskets that looked like every other basket Shinji had seen today, he groaned. A bit more loudly than he had intended.

Aunt Yui turned to him, a faint, exasperated smile on her face. "Shinji, my dear, I have an idea," she announced.

"Instead of following me around sighing that the world is boring and unfair, why don't you try to find something yourself?"

Shinji frowned. "What?"

"This will be like one of your online treasure hunts, right?" Aunt Yui reached into her knapsack, withdrew a roll of bills, and handed it to him. As Shinji stared at it in confusion, she raised her hand toward the sky. "I am sending you on a quest, young Shinji," she announced in a grand voice. "To find a treasure worthy of a great warrior like yourself. Search the marketplace, speak to the vendors, and if you find something truly unique and special, you may buy it for your room back in Miami. Find yourself a toy to occupy your time, is basically what I'm saying."

"I don't play with toys anymore," Shinji said, rolling his eyes.

"Then just find something that interests you."

"Wait, really?" Shinji glanced down at the wad of money in his hand, then back to Yui. "You're just going to let me buy whatever? How will I know if it's worth the money or not?"

"Ah, that is the mystery, now, isn't it?" Yui's smile was suspiciously smug. "You find out . . . by asking. Talk to the vendors. See what makes something extraordinary. You'll know in your heart when you find that special item, that what you're looking at is worth it. So, young adventurer . . ."

Her smile grew wider. "Will you accept this quest? The fate of the world may depend on it."

Shinji rolled his eyes. "I know what you're doing," he warned his aunt. "Don't think I don't know. You're not fooling anyone."

"Oh? Well, if you don't think you can shop on your own, I'll just take that money back. . . ."

"Uh, nope." Shinji whisked the roll of cash out of reach. "I didn't say that," he told her, still holding the wad at arm's length. "I'm just not fooled by this whole *quest* thing. This isn't a quest, it's an errand. But I'll do it . . . under protest."

"Mm-hmm." Yui smiled down at him. "Well, you're too smart for me, I suppose. Go on, then, smarty-pants." She waved a hand at the marketplace behind them. "Go find a lightning sword. Oh, and try not to talk back to anyone this time. Important rule of any negotiation: keep the snark to a minimum. Can you do that for me?"

"I'll try," Shinji muttered. Slipping the roll of cash deep into a front pocket, he turned and melted into the crowds of Abenge Market.

For a while, he just wandered, weaving through people and around stalls, not really knowing what he was looking for. He stopped at a couple of booths selling purses and woven blankets but quickly got bored with that and moved on. A table selling various gems and jewelry looked interesting, but Shinji did *not* want to stare at rings and necklaces all afternoon. Besides, they were probably too pricey for him to buy, anyway. After a bit, the sizzle and the scent of cooking food drew him to a central grill, where he bought a goat kebab, figuring Yui wouldn't mind if he spent a few dollars on snacks. Chewing on delicious grilled meat, he wandered past the main stretch of the market, not really looking at anything, until he came to the edges of the marketplace.

Wait a second. I haven't seen this part of the market before, have I?

Shinji paused, gazing around to get his bearings. He had reached a dark little corner of the market, and the faded, blocky buildings looming over him were unfamiliar. Frowning, he scratched his head and stared at the structures, trying to remember if he'd seen them before. It hadn't been *that* long since he'd last been to Abenge.

Something squeaked behind him. He turned to see an ancient-looking wooden sign creaking as it swung over a doorway. The cracked, peeling wood was painted a dingy yellow and read LOOK OUT, TRADERS in blocky black letters. Curious, he edged forward and peered through one of the grimy windows.

"Look out" is right, Shinji thought. He couldn't see much, just a bunch of shelves that were packed with stuff. But maybe this little shop would have something of interest, the "toy/treasure" Aunt Yui wanted him to find.

Pushing aside a curtain of bead strings, he stepped into the shop.

It was cool and dim on the other side of the doorway, a relief from the blazing sun outside. A tiny electric fan hummed on the counter as he stepped into the shop, blowing the smell of incense into his face. As he blinked, waiting for his eyes to adjust, a thin, reedy voice came to him from somewhere in the room's interior.

"Welcome, young man. Do feel free to browse, but try not to touch anything. Wouldn't want your grubby little hands to break something valuable. Everything here is very old."

Including you? Shinji thought as his eyes finally adjusted. The pinched face of an old woman with light brown skin and a crown of gray hair stared at him from behind the counter, lips pursed and eyes narrowed in suspicion. Around her, the counter and shelves of the tiny shop were covered in *stuff*: blankets and baskets, jewelry and figurines, clay pots, seashells, furniture, rusty tools, and a ton of what looked like ancient junk scattered everywhere.

The shopkeeper still glared at Shinji, her beady eyes sharp with distrust, as if he would slip something into his pocket or knock over an ugly but expensive vase. "Can I help you find anything?" she went on, half rising off her stool to peer at him. "Are you lost? The candy and ice-cream store is on the other side of the market. Also, do take note that you're on camera." She pointed to a cam in a dusty corner of the room. Shinji very seriously doubted it still worked. "So I'm watching you."

Geez, calm down, Grandma. I'm not a thief. "I'm . . .
uh . . . just looking around," Shinji said. "Can I do that? I
won't break anything."

"Hmm." The old woman scrutinized him a few moments.
"I suppose it wouldn't hurt, though I've said those words
before and regretted it." She pointed at him with a very shiny
red fingernail. "Don't make me regret it, young man."

Shinji offered his best innocent, get-off-the-hook smile.
"I won't."

"Humph." The shopkeeper sat down again with a huff.
Snatching a magazine from the counter, she flipped it open
and started reading—though she still eyed him over the
pages. Shinji turned and quickly slipped between a couple
of shelf-lined aisles, out of her immediate sight.

For a few minutes, he wandered, gazing at the merchandise crammed onto the shelves. Some of it was stuff he'd
seen before, and some of it was absolute junk: broken clocks,
old dead phones, dolls with no hair, and toys missing an arm
or leg. Like a garage sale from back home; definitely not like
the other vendors in the market. But there were also conch
shells and uncut gems and figurines carved of bone. There
were alligator skulls, antelope horns, and necklaces made of
shark teeth. There were carvings and trinkets and things he
didn't even have a name for. With every aisle Shinji turned
down, he found more wonders and junk, but nothing really
stood out as *the thing* he was looking for.

Shinji.

What? Frowning, Shinji stopped, listening. He was almost sure someone had whispered his name. But it hadn't been Aunt Yui's voice, and she was the only one who would call to him. Gazing down a dusty aisle in the corner, he blinked as he saw two tiny green lights, like glowing eyes, staring out of the shadows at him.

Curious, he walked toward them. The lights disappeared, but he kept walking until he found himself staring at a shelf full of carved animals. Crouching down, he carefully moved wooden elephants and hippos aside, then reached all the way to the back.

Something black and shiny crawled out from beneath the ledge: a massive spider banded in yellow and red. With a silent curse, Shinji yanked his hand back as the huge arachnid scuttled up the shelf and vanished over the top in a flash of chitin and jointed legs.

"Geez." Shinji gave an exaggerated shudder. "Time to clean your shop, Grandma. Ugh." Finding one of those shark-head grabber toys, he poked it under the shelf to make sure no webs or spiders were still lurking out of sight, then carefully reached to the back again. His fingers brushed against something that didn't feel elephant- or hippo-ish. He grasped the object and drew it into the light.

As he turned it over, his heart gave an excited little lurch. For a second, he thought it might be a dragon. Like the creatures in his online games, it had a long, serpentine body and a slender neck reared back into an S shape. A pair of massive wings framed its snakelike form, but these were made of feathers instead of the normal, batlike membranes. After a moment, he realized it wasn't a dragon but a huge winged serpent, a crown of feathers raised around its neck like a cobra's hood. Its eyes, tiny green gems, glittered as he stared at the statue.

"Cool," Shinji whispered.

"Coatl," said a voice behind him.

Shinji jumped, managing not to drop the figurine as he turned around. The shopkeeper stood a few paces away, her mouth pulled into a grim line. How had she snuck up behind him? A lifetime of travel had made Shinji hypervigilant about pickpockets, thieves, and those with not-so-nice intentions. He was usually more alert than that.

The old woman wasn't looking at him, however, but at the figurine he held in his hands. "That," she said in a somber voice, "is the Coatl. The feathered serpent of myth and legend. Very old. Very valuable." Her sharp black eyes slid up to his face. "Far too valuable for you, I'm afraid. If you would kindly put it back on the shelf before you drop it . . ."

Shinji bristled. "I'm not going to break it," he protested. The wood was suddenly warm in his hands, drawing his attention to the statue again. "It's pretty awesome, actually," he admitted, aware that the old woman had stepped closer as if to snatch it up should it tumble from his fingers. The serpent's gem-green eyes glittered as he held the statue up, entrancing him. Suddenly he had to have it. "How much is it?"

"Too expensive for you, boy."

Shinji frowned at her. "I have money."

"Not enough." The shopkeeper's voice was unyielding. She reached out and, in a deftly quick move, plucked the figurine from his hands.

Instantly, Shinji felt a sharp, almost painful stab of loss. His heart clenched, and his insides went hollow as he watched the statue being taken away. The old woman shook her head, then lifted her arm to place the figurine on an even higher shelf.

Suddenly she paused. As she gazed down at the statue, her brow furrowed, and she tilted her head as if she could hear something Shinji could not. Blinking, she gazed at Shinji, then back to the statue, then at Shinji again.

"Interesting." Straightening, the old woman turned her head to stare at him fully, her expression caught between amusement and doubt. "Very interesting. Well, well, that changes things, doesn't it?"

"Um." Shinji frowned, not exactly liking the look the shopkeeper was turning on him now. "What does?"

The old woman regarded him with an eerie little smile. "It appears the idol wants you, boy."

"Huh?" Taken aback, he stared at her, not entirely sure he'd heard her right. "It . . . the statue . . . *wants* me?" The shopkeeper nodded once. "Like, it wants to eat me or something? Uh, you do realize it's a *statue*, right?"

She just gave a faint chuckle and another shake of her head before putting the statue into his hands. "One cannot fight destiny, boy." Her voice was soft, her eyes intense as they met his own. "Even if one did not ask for it. You must be special in some way. The idol calls for you, and you must answer its call. I cannot stand in the way of fate. Therefore it is yours."

Special in some way. Shinji had a fleeting thought of his supposed ancestors and their sacred shrine, then shook his head. *Ridiculous.*

"Really? Just like that?"

"Yes." The shopkeeper smiled, showing off a set of perfectly straight teeth. "For two hundred dollars."

"*Two hundred* dollars?" Shinji gaped at her. Aunt Yui hadn't given him that much cash. "You said the idol was calling to me. That it was destiny!"

"Yes." The shopkeeper's smile didn't waver. "And it is destiny that you give me two hundred dollars for a unique, very valuable Coatl figurine that you found in my shop. It is the only one of its kind, you know. I have to make a living, too."

Shinji scowled. Suddenly all that talk of destiny and fate seemed like a scam, but he *did* want the Coatl. Reaching into his pocket, he pulled out the wad of cash and held it up in front of him. "I'll give you eighty-seven," he countered.

"Done!" The shopkeeper snatched the money from his fingers with a toothy grin. "Lovely doing business with you, young man," she almost cackled. "Do you want me to wrap that up for you?"

Shinji was about to say no, then thought better of it. Walking around the marketplace with a very expensive idol in his hands might be a bad idea. He didn't want to be accused of stealing. "Yes, please," he said.

As Shinji followed the old woman back toward the counter, the door of the shop opened with a creak. Trailing a waft of warm, dusty air, two men entered. One was tall and slim, but powerful-looking, with dark skin and close-cropped hair. The other was pale and blond and built like a tank. They wore expensive-looking suits and dark glasses, and looked like they should be guarding an important celebrity, not browsing novelty shops in Abenge. Taking off their shades, they spotted Shinji and gave him baleful stares, as if silently telling him to get lost.

Shinji crossed his arms and stood his ground. The men's expressions darkened, but Shinji gave them a cheeky grin and turned away. He'd seen all kinds of people on his travels, and men like this always seemed to think their time was worth more than anyone else's.

Sorry, guys. You're just going to have to wait your turn.

The shopkeeper took her time wrapping and bundling the idol, handling it like it was made of gold instead of dark wood. A few minutes later, clutching a plastic bag that said

Thank You above a yellow smiley face, Shinji left Look Out, Traders and stepped back into the blazing sun of Abenge Market.

Man, I hope I didn't get scammed. Now that he was back in the fresh air, away from the dim little shop, the strange old woman, and the eerie, almost reverential feel of the idol itself, blowing all his money on a single figurine felt foolish. *Correction: blowing all of* Aunt Yui's *money,* he told himself as he walked along. *That was dumb. I probably did get conned back there. All that talk of fate and destiny, geez.* He shook his head, disgusted with himself. *One of a kind; yeah, right. This thing probably has a Made in China stamp on the bottom or something.*

"Hey. Kid."

Shinji turned. The two men from the shop were back, and they were walking toward him with twin glares behind their sunglasses. Wariness rose up inside Shinji. Had they followed him? And why were they stalking toward him like a pair of cops closing in on a shoplifter?

Shinji tensed. His first thought was to run, to lose them in the busy Abenge marketplace. He knew the streets and twisty corners of the market pretty well, and he was fast and small. If he took off now, these two goons in suits wouldn't be able to keep up.

But then defiance flickered. Why should he run? He hadn't done anything wrong. He'd bought this statue fair and square and had a receipt to prove it. Planting his feet,

22

Shinji stayed where he was as the two men strode up, their large frames casting a shadow over him.

"Yeah?" Raising his chin, he met their dour glares with a smirk. "What do you want?"

"You bought something in that shop," the first man said, and it sounded like an accusation. "What was it?"

"A statue."

"What kind of statue?"

"Why do you want to know?"

The second man took off his dark glasses and stared at Shinji. He had cold blue eyes that looked both menacing and annoyed, as if he couldn't believe he had to put up with this. "Answer the question," he said flatly. "What did you buy?"

Shinji bristled and held the bag tighter. "Sorry, but I don't see how that's any of your business," he told the first man, whose jaw tightened. "Unless you guys are the statue police, in which case I'm going to need to see some identification."

"Don't be cheeky, brat." The first man squared his shoulders. "I asked you a question, and you'd better answer me if you know what's good for you."

Shinji stood his ground. This was a busy corner, and he'd bought the statue fairly. If these two tried anything, there would be tons of witnesses to see it. "So is this a shakedown?" he challenged. "Are you trying to threaten me into giving away the statue that I bought with my own money? Last I heard, that was kind of illegal."

"Oh, for God's sake." The second man sounded even more exasperated than he looked. "We all know where this is going. Here." He raised his hand, one twenty-dollar bill pinned between two fingers, and pointed at Shinji. "Take it, give us the statue, and get out of here."

Shinji laughed. "Twenty bucks? Are you kidding? You think that's what I paid for this?"

The man's blue eyes went even colder, but he silently added another twenty to the bill in his hand. Shinji snorted. "Nope. Still not even close."

The man lowered his arm, his piercing gaze boring into Shinji like he was a particularly disgusting insect. "Very well," he said in an overly reasonable voice. "What do you want for it?"

"Maybe I don't want to sell it," Shinji announced, feeling stubborn and rebellious under that disdainful stare. "Maybe it's become precious to me."

The other man gave a snort of his own, rolling his eyes. "Don't be ridiculous," he growled. "Take the money. Go buy a bike or a skateboard or whatever kids do with their time these days, and give us the nice, boring statue. It's worth nothing to the likes of you."

The likes of me? Like he was some unworthy, unimportant kid? Shinji set his jaw. That might be true, but he wasn't going to let a couple of snooty hotshot jerks tell him so. And he really didn't take well to being bullied.

"You know what?" Shinji said, and took a few steps back.

"I've made up my mind. The statue isn't for sale. I'm not giving it to you, for any price."

The first man swelled up like an angry bull, nostrils flaring and eyes going wide, but the blond man simply held up a hand, stopping him. "That is a mistake," he told Shinji in that cold, brittle voice. "Think carefully about your next decision, boy. The smart move would be to take the money we are offering. The idol is of great interest to some very important people. You do not want us as your enemies."

"Yeah, you know what? I think I'll take my chances." Shinji backed up another pace, toward the crowds and the bustle of the market, and gave the two men a cheerful smile. "Nice talking to you. You guys have a good day."

He turned and suddenly found his path was blocked by a third man in a suit, who stared down at him menacingly. This one had jowls and pock-marked, tanned skin. A scar ran all the way from his hairline down his cheek and into his dark beard. The first man gave a cold chuckle as all three of them took a step forward, boxing Shinji in. "What makes you think you can just walk away?" the third man asked in a soft, terrifying voice.

Shinji shrank back, tightening his hold on the bag even further. "There are people watching," he told the men. "If you do anything to me, everyone in the market will see it."

The blond man chuckled. "Who do you think they're going to believe?" he asked. "The scruffy street kid or three responsible-looking adults? If I pay someone a hundred dollars to say that you're a filthy thief who stole that statue from a shop, what do you think will happen?"

The men stepped closer, surrounding him, cutting off any escape. Shinji clutched the bag to his chest, breathing hard as they closed in. His mind spun as the blond man leaned down, filling his vision. "Last chance, brat," he warned, his breath hot in Shinji's face. "Give us the statue now, or things are going to get really unpleasant for you."

"Okay, okay!" Shinji cringed back, wrinkling his nose. "Just back off for a second and eat a breath mint. I'll give you the stupid statue already."

"There. Was that so hard?" The blond man straightened, smiling coldly, but he didn't step back. "Smartest decision you've made all day, kid. I really didn't want to have to bruise my knuckles on your snotty face. Now hand over the statue."

"Fine, whatever," Shinji muttered, and held up the bag. "Here. Just take it."

Big hands opening, the man reached for the bag. Shinji waited until his arm was completely outstretched, his fingers inches away from the plastic, before he darted forward, ducked beneath the man's elbow, and took off toward the center of the market.

"Hey!"

Pounding footsteps sounded behind him. Shinji didn't dare look back as he passed a booth selling beaded jewelry and veered sharply to the left, darting between the aisles.

"Hey, watch where you're going!" someone yelled as he

dodged to the side and barely missed running into him. "Crazy kid. Slow down before you hurt someone."

"Sorry!" Shinji called, but he didn't slow down. Instead, he flung himself into the crowd, using his smaller size to dart and weave around buyers and vendors.

Ducking behind a fruit stand, he peeked through the crowd, searching for his pursuers. The three men had split up and were combing the market, angrily shoving their way past vendors and market goers, but they seemed to have lost sight of him. Heart racing, Shinji drew back, melted into the crowd, and went looking for his aunt.

He found her at one of the stalls, bent over and perusing a table of handcrafted leather wallets, belts, and purses. She had a couple of bags dangling from her arm. Shinji hoped neither of them contained a figurine of a winged serpent that looked exactly like the one he'd bought.

"There you are." Aunt Yui smiled as he came up. "That didn't take very long." Her gaze fell to the plastic bag under his arm, and her eyes brightened. "Oh, what's this? Was your quest successful, young knight?"

"We have to go," Shinji said, and grabbed her by the sleeve. "Now. We need to leave this place."

"What? What are you talking about? Hang on." Aunt Yui pulled her arm out of Shinji's grip, then placed both hands on his shoulders, looking down at him. "Calm down, Shinji," she urged in a soothing voice. "Take a deep breath. What happened?"

"Some men are after me," Shinji began. "They threatened me, and when I didn't give them what they wanted, they chased me through the market."

"Threatened you?" Aunt Yui frowned. "Did you antagonize them?" she asked in an exasperated voice. "I told you not to talk back to anyone while we were here."

"No! I didn't talk back to them." *Not until they acted like jerks, anyway.* "Aunt Yui, listen. I bought something in a shop, a statue of some kind. These men followed me outside and tried to make me sell it to them. When I told them no, they chased me through the marketplace."

Aunt Yui's frown deepened. "They chased you?"

Shinji nodded, and Yui's lips thinned. For a second, he held his breath, wondering if she would believe him. He *had* been known to tell elaborate stories, ask misleading questions, and dance around the truth sometimes, but he had never openly lied to her. Finally she straightened with a grim look.

"All right," she told him. "Let's get back to the *Tern*. You can tell me everything that happened there. I will contact Makena and ask if we can meet tomorrow."

Shinji let out a sigh of relief. That was fine with him. Getting back to familiar territory sounded like a great idea. He needed to show the idol to his aunt. Maybe she would know what the winged serpent was and why three men in expensive suits wanted it so badly.

He didn't see the men in the crowd as he and Yui wandered back through Abenge Market, Shinji silently telling his aunt to go faster. As they left the marketplace, he caught that same glimmer of light from the corner of his eye and glanced up quickly.

Through the trees, several yards away, something small and metallic floated in the air. It was sleek and modern, with four propellers that let it hover in one spot. Shinji frowned. A drone of some kind? Was it . . . watching him?

Before he could do or say anything, the tiny machine rose silently into the air, zipped through the trees, and vanished into the greenery. Even more paranoid now, Shinji wrapped the handle of the bag several times around his palm and hurried after his aunt.

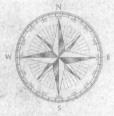

CHAPTER TWO

The sun was hanging low over the Zambezi River, tinting the water red, as Shinji and his aunt made their way back to the *Good Tern*. Shinji kept glancing behind them, searching for men in suits and also for strange glints of metal in the trees. Cicadas buzzed, bullfrogs croaked in the distance, and the waters of the Zambezi sloshed lazily against the sides of the *Tern*. Everything seemed peaceful, but Shinji still couldn't shake the feeling that they were being watched.

"Let's go a few minutes downriver before it gets too dark," Yui said as they climbed aboard the boat. "Then you can have my full attention."

"Yeah," Shinji muttered. "Sounds good."

The engine of the ancient trawler gurgled to life, and Yui deftly slid the vessel into the middle of the river. On the far side of the bank, the dark lump of a hippo, perhaps Lord Henry, raised its head from the water and watched them depart.

Leaning against the railings, Shinji took the plastic bag in both hands, feeling the hard lump of the idol within. Lifting out the tissue-wrapped statue, he paused a moment, then peeled back the paper just enough to see the top of the idol's head.

It looked . . . very normal. A hand-carved statue, intricately designed, of course—the feathers on the serpent's wings were all individually carved—but normal all the same. There was no feeling of magic, no supernatural glow, no sensation of wonder or awe. Even the tiny green gems of its eyes seemed dull and without sparkle.

Why would anyone want this? Shinji thought. *It's just a carving of a snake with wings. Is it really that valuable? I don't see anything special about it.*

But if that was true, why couldn't he stop looking at it? Why did he almost feel . . . connected to this thing?

"All right, Shinji" came Yui's voice from inside the cabin. "I'm ready. Let's see this statue of yours, and you can tell me what happened in the marketplace. From the beginning."

Shinji winced. Tucking the idol into the bag again, he pushed himself off the railing, ready to head into the cabin.

But then, over the rumble of the engine and the slosh of

water against the sides of the boat, he heard a new sound. A strange, high-pitched whine, faint but getting steadily louder. On his travels with Aunt Yui, he'd seen and heard all manner of boat engines, from yachts to Jet Skis, but this was a sound he hadn't heard before.

Puzzled, he walked to the back of the boat to gaze out over the river. The sun had dropped behind the tree line, plunging everything into shadow, and the waters were dark. But he still thought he could hear something, and now he was beginning to see something moving out on the rippling surface.

Suddenly a pair of spotlights flashed on, shining right into his eyes. Wincing, Shinji stumbled back a pace, shielding his eyes and squinting against the sudden brightness. He heard the whine of engines and could just make out two low-slung vessels, black and nearly invisible against the river, speeding toward the rear of the *Tern*. They were very fast, much faster than the *Tern*, closing the distance as if the trawler were bobbing motionless in the middle of the river.

Pirates! Shinji's heart gave a violent lurch. Being attacked by pirates out on the river was rare but not unheard of. Shinji had heard stories of lonely vessels being set upon by marauders looking to loot and steal; he just never thought it could happen to Aunt Yui and him.

"Aunt Yui!" he yelled, spinning around. "Pirates! We're being attacked!"

The vessels pulled alongside the *Tern*, and Shinji could

see dark figures glaring up at him. He whirled and started to sprint toward the cabin, when a pair of hands latched on to the edge of the *Tern* and a black-clad figure hauled itself over the side. Right into his path. The intruder wore a ski mask, so Shinji couldn't see his face, and he lunged at the boy with big, gloved hands.

Shinji ducked, darting beneath the thick arms, and the man grunted in annoyance. Another black-clad figure heaved itself onto the deck, looking around for only a moment before spotting Shinji.

Both men strode toward him, trying to trap him against the aft of the *Tern*. Heart pounding, Shinji backed up until he was pressed against the rails, still clutching the bag that held the statue. Beyond the attackers, he glimpsed yet another pair climbing over the side of the ship and pushing their way into the cabin. A shriek echoed from inside, and worry for his aunt spiked, then the two men cornering him lunged.

Shinji dodged again, twisting away from one pair of arms, trying to duck beneath the second. Hands grabbed for him as he darted by, missing, but thick fingers snagged the plastic bag that held the idol.

With a ripping sound, the bag tore apart. Heart in his throat, Shinji watched the idol fly in a lazy arc through the air before clattering against the side of the ship.

"Get the statue!"

The two pirates leaped for the idol. Shinji scrambled

after it as well. Somewhere in the back of his mind, he wondered if he shouldn't just let them have it. If pirates were willing to attack his vessel because of a statue, why not let them take the stupid thing? But the thought of losing the Coatl made Shinji's stomach churn with anger. It was *his*. It had chosen him; he had to protect it.

Snatching it up, he whirled to face the men who loomed over him. Their eyes were hard behind their masks, and one of them held out his large, gloved hand.

"Give us the statue, boy. Make this easy on yourself."

Setting his jaw, Shinji held the statue tighter, backing up until he hit the railings again. "Not so fast," he told them as they pressed forward. His stomach roiled in terror, but he faced his assailants and forced a defiant grin. "You guys didn't say the magic word."

"You little—" One of the men grabbed for him, and he darted away—though he was running out of space to dodge. The man pressed forward, smiling coldly. "I'm going to enjoy breaking your arms, you little brat."

Shinji's legs shook. Beneath his fingers, the idol was growing warm. A pulse went through the figurine, then another. Almost as if it had a heartbeat. Shinji felt his own heart flutter in response, matching the throb of the statue, and his breath caught. Daring to look away from the pirates, he glanced down and saw the statue's eyes were glowing green, like fireflies in the darkness.

Another scream came from the cabin, followed by a crash. Shinji jerked his head up to see his aunt through the cabin window, fighting with a pair of masked men. Yui held a baseball bat and was swinging it at the heads of her attackers, who barely managed to dodge or duck. But then one of them lunged forward and slammed a meaty fist into her jaw, snapping her head back. She staggered, slumped against the window, then slid down the glass and out of sight.

Aunt Yui!

Shinji screamed. The idol in his hands flared, then exploded in a flash of golden light. Heat rushed through him, searing his veins, filling him with fire and warmth. He opened his eyes and, for a moment, saw the world through a different lens. Everything was brighter, colors sharp and vivid, like it was high noon with the sun blazing overhead. He saw the pirates cringing back from him, their heads turned away and their arms in front of their eyes. Power filled him like sunlight. And gazing down at these small, short-lived mortals, Shinji felt a stab of both pity and anger.

Then the light faded, the rush of power and strength going out like a snuffed candle. Shinji staggered, his vision going fuzzy, as whatever power had been holding him up faded. He fell to his knees, only half-aware of his surroundings, the men closing in around him. Something grabbed his arm, and angry, confused voices echoed in his ears.

"Kid! Where's the statue? What did you do with it?" Something shook him, harsh and desperate, but it barely registered. "Answer me!"

A gasp echoed above him. "His arm, Kraus. Look at his arm!"

The man called Kraus made a muffled sound that might've been a curse. "We'll have to take the kid. We can't return to Frost empty-handed. Grab him and let's go."

"What about the boat? And the woman?"

"Leave them. We can't do anything about it now. Move!"

Shinji felt like he was floating. Sounds and colors swirled together around him, and his head felt disconnected from the rest of his body. He was vaguely aware that someone had picked him up and slung him over their shoulder like a sack of potatoes. Anger flickered, and he raised his head, wanting to fight, to see if his aunt was okay. But the movement caused the shadows hovering at the edge of his vision to flood in, and he knew nothing for a while.

CHAPTER
THREE

He was standing at the edge of a cliff, gazing down on a vast, endless jungle. The breeze blowing across his skin was warm, smelling of dew and wet leaves. Below his feet, water cascaded over the edge of the rocks, falling into the pool of turquoise water far below. A flock of brilliant blue birds with long tails soared over the treetops, filling the air with guttural cries. The canopy of trees seemed to go on forever, a deep green carpet stretching to the horizon.

Unspoiled by man, whispered a voice in his head, alien and yet somehow comforting. *There are still places in this world that have not known the touch of greed or destruction. But mankind's lust for power is infinite. It is up to us—to you—to ensure these natural places are not destroyed. You have become the guardian now . . . Shinji Takahashi.*

Shinji turned. A massive creature waited behind him, silhouetted against the sunlight. Its form was hazy and indistinct, as if he were looking at something through water, but Shinji thought he could make out an elegant, sweeping neck and a pair of enormous golden wings flared to either side.

Beware, young guardian, said the voice in his mind. *The Weaver is watching you.*

Groaning, Shinji opened his eyes.

Fluorescent light blinded him. Wincing, he turned his head away, blinking against the spots of light, waiting for his vision to clear. When he was sure his sight was back to normal and he wasn't staring directly into a fluorescent bulb, he cautiously opened his eyes and sat up.

What in the world? Where the heck am I?

He was lying in a room he didn't recognize. The walls were bare and windowless; the floor, cold white tile. At first, Shinji thought he might be in a hospital room; it had the same harsh, sterile feel. Though hospital rooms didn't usually have metal filing cabinets lining the walls. Or panels with lots of blue blinking lights on the surface. Or a holographic image of himself, floating in the air above a console in the center of the room.

Actually, scratch all that. This didn't feel like a hospital; this felt like a spaceship.

"Finally awake?"

Shinji leaped off the cot and spun around, ready to fight or flee. A girl sat behind one of the strange consoles on the other side of the room, watching him with her chin in the palm of one hand. She was around his age, with a narrow, somewhat pointed face and long yellow hair pulled into a braid over her shoulder. She was dressed in overalls with lots of pockets, and streaks of either grease or paint smudged the denim. Large blue eyes regarded him curiously behind her glasses.

"Hello," the girl greeted with a crooked little smile. As if she didn't smile often and was out of practice. "Jumpy much?"

Instantly suspicious, Shinji narrowed his eyes. Whoever this girl was, he was not in the mood to play games. "Oh, I don't know," he said, crossing his arms. "Maybe I have a reasons to be nervous. Like getting kidnapped off my boat by a squad of masked ruffians, waking up in a place I don't know, and having some strange girl tell me I'm being jumpy."

The smile instantly faded from the girl's face. "Oh no," she said, straightening in the chair. "You didn't come here on your own? Are you serious?"

"About being kidnapped and taken hostage? No, I joke about that kind of stuff all the time." Shinji rolled his eyes. "Of course I'm serious! How do you think I got here? The last thing I remember, I was on a boat with my aunt, floating down the Zambezi River and minding my own business, when these goons climbed over the side and . . ." He trailed off, a stab of worry and fear lancing through his stomach. Where was his aunt? What happened to her after he'd been taken? Was she okay? She was probably worried sick about him.

If she was all right herself.

Shinji glared at the strange girl, clenching his fists. "So, yeah, sorry if I'm a little bit on edge," he snapped. "That's what happens when you get assaulted and kidnapped. Who are you? And where the heck am I?"

"Calm down." The girl stood slowly, holding up her hands. "My apologies. I didn't know what had happened to you. I'm sorry." Despite her appearance, her voice had a mature, cultured edge to it, as if she had spent most of her time around grown-ups who insisted on proper grammar. "My name is Lucy," she went on in a soothing tone, "and right now, you're at the Hightower Corporation."

"The Hightower Corporation?" Shinji frowned. "What's that?"

"It's . . ." Lucy paused, as if she was going to say something and thought better of it. "It's a big company that has lots of money and conducts business all over the world," she went on. "They're very big into . . . acquiring things."

"Really? Is one of their policies 'acquiring' kids off boats, then?"

Lucy shifted her feet uncomfortably, fiddling with the end of her braid. "I don't know," she muttered. "The people who make those kinds of decisions don't tell me anything."

Now Shinji gave her a wary look. Who was this girl, why was she in this room with him, and how did she even get in here? Maybe she was working with the kidnappers, the Hightower Corporation or whatever they called themselves. Maybe she was here to spy on him.

Shinji crossed his arms, narrowing his eyes in the girl's direction. "What do they want with me?" he asked.

"I don't know," Lucy said again, earning a suspicious frown from Shinji. "I really don't," she insisted. "At first, I thought maybe you were a new assistant, a creative prodigy they've sponsored to work on a specific project. They do that sometimes. That's why I'm here, anyway."

"I don't believe you," Shinji growled.

"No, really! I'm telling the truth. Look." Lucy raised her hand, palm up, to one of her many pockets, and made a strange squeaking noise with her lips.

Something in her pocket stirred, and then a tiny metallic head with a pointed nose and muzzle poked out from within. It blinked beady red eyes, twitched its nose, then crawled into Lucy's palm.

It was a mouse . . . made completely of metal. It looked like a real mouse, moved like a real mouse, but its body was robotic, its delicate paws and long tail made of glimmering copper. It sat up in Lucy's palm, whiskers twitching, then scurried up her arm to perch on her shoulder, watching Shinji with glowing red eyes.

"This is Tinker," Lucy introduced as Shinji stared in amazement. "He was a 'pet project' of mine, no pun intended. I work here, or Hightower lets me work here, I guess. I have my own workshop on another floor." She watched Shinji a moment, then smiled. Holding up her hand, she waited as Tinker crawled onto it, then held the tiny creature out in front of her. "Here," she said, meeting Shinji's gaze. "Say hello. He doesn't bite. Or poop, or have fleas, or any of those nasty things real animals have. He is the perfect pet."

Shinji hesitated, torn between wariness and curiosity. He didn't know if he should trust Lucy, but the robot mouse was beyond cool. He wanted to touch it.

Slowly, he raised his arm, turning his palm up for the robotic mouse to crawl into. As he did, however, he froze. As he stared at his forearm, his heart started pounding against his ribs.

Right below his wrist, where there had been nothing a day ago, an image stared back at him. A bright tattoo of blue, yellow, and green: a feathered serpent with brilliant gold wings. The creature's neck was coiled back, the sweeping wings folded behind it, giving the tattoo the vague appearance of a golden football. But the creature's eyes, the same brilliant emerald of the jungle in Shinji's dreams, were staring directly at him.

Shinji drew in a slow breath, turning away from Lucy and grabbing his wrist. "What's happening to me?" he whispered, feeling her concerned eyes on the back of his head. "What is this? I have no idea what's going on."

"Then perhaps, I can explain it to you," said a new voice behind them.

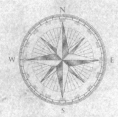

CHAPTER FOUR

Shinji turned. A man stood in the doorway; he was lean, tall, and dressed in a gray business suit and tie. His blond hair was cropped short and slicked back, with not a strand out of place. He smiled as he entered the room, but it was a cold, practiced smile that didn't reach his eyes. The door clicked shut behind him, but before it did, Shinji caught sight of a large man waiting just outside. So, they had a guard watching the room, too.

Not good.

The stranger continued to smile as he crossed the tile floor toward Shinji and Lucy, but it faltered when his gaze landed on the girl. Lucy winced as the man turned his full attention on her, and though his smile crept back across his face, his voice was hard as he spoke.

"Lucy. What did I tell you about sneaking into places you have no business being in?"

"Sorry, sir," the girl replied, ducking her head. "I didn't think—"

"No, you didn't," the stranger interrupted. "And your apologies mean nothing to me. If this happens again, I will shut down your workshop permanently. Do you understand?"

Lucy glanced up sharply, a flash of anger in her blue eyes, but she only nodded. "Yes, sir."

"Good." The man waved a dismissive hand toward the door. "Now take your little toy and leave. I have business to discuss with Mr. Takahashi here."

Lucy gave Shinji a fearful, apologetic look and left the room with Tinker perched on her shoulder. The door hadn't even closed behind them when the man turned to Shinji once more, his smile bigger and colder than ever.

"Shinji Takahashi, wasn't it? My name is Gideon Frost, and I would like to personally welcome you to the Hightower Corporation."

"Uh-huh." Shinji folded his arms across his chest. He did *not* trust this man, not even a little bit. "And is this the part where you explain why your goons kidnapped me off my boat and left my aunt alone on the Zambezi River at night?"

Gideon Frost winced, almost convincingly. "Yes. First

off, I would like to apologize, Shinji," he said. "The incident on the river, while regrettable, was a misunderstanding. Allow me to explain."

"Yeah," Shinji said. "A misunderstanding. I can't wait to hear this."

"The Hightower Corporation is quite invested in acquiring certain artifacts," Frost went on, ignoring Shinji's comment. "Some of these artifacts are old, volatile, and actually quite dangerous. If used improperly, they can bring disaster to the person holding them. We became aware of one such artifact in Abenge Market, being sold as a simple curio in a novelty shop. Obviously, we did not want the idol falling into the wrong hands, so we sent agents to acquire it before it could become a danger to innocent lives."

"You mean Goons One, Two, and Three?" Shinji broke in. "I met them."

Gideon Frost sighed. "Again, you'll have to excuse our agents, Mr. Takahashi," he said wryly. "Their skills do not lie in negotiation. But they knew the danger of the statue, and their mission was to bring it safely back to the Hightower Corporation, at any cost. In their minds, they were only trying to protect you.

"Regardless," Frost went on before Shinji could say anything, "when that failed, we were forced to turn to less desirable alternatives. It is regrettable that the incident on the boat became violent, but believe me when I say our agents were only ordered to bring back the statue. They were not to harm anyone or to cause any damage. I assure you, they will be punished for disobeying orders, but right now we have an even larger concern." He gave Shinji a somber look. "Or should I say, *you* have a larger concern, Mr. Takahashi?"

Shinji frowned. "What do you mean?"

"The idol you took from the novelty store," Frost said, and gestured to Shinji's left arm. "As you have probably discovered by now, it has somehow bonded with you. Curious that it would choose you, considering you are not of Mesoamerican descent." The man narrowed his eyes, studying Shinji from head to toe. "Are you?"

"No. But maybe it chose me because your army was threatening it and I was the only person around who wanted to protect it."

It sounded ridiculous as he said it, but somehow, someway, he also knew it was true.

"Hmph. Well. Be that as it may, the fact that it bonded to you is, of course, of grave concern to us. You see, the idol carries a powerful curse, Shinji Takahashi. Anyone it bonds to is in danger of having their strength, their very life, slowly sapped away, until nothing remains."

Frost walked away from Shinji, moving to the holographic image in the center of the room. Raising a hand, he touched a finger to hologram Shinji's arm, and a golden tattoo flared to life over the image, a twin to his own. "I am afraid you have activated the Coatl's Curse, young Shinji," Frost said, turning back to look at him. "And if we do not find a way to remove the tattoo in time, you will slowly wither away to an empty husk." He pressed a button on the console, and the holographic image flickered once, then shriveled into a mummified figure, gaunt and emaciated. With another flicker, the image became a skeleton before winking out altogether. Shinji cringed, and Frost gave him a somber look. "Unless the tattoo is removed, you will die."

For a second, Shinji couldn't breathe. Grabbing his wrist, he stared at the picture on his arm, at the winged serpent gazing intently back. Was it really killing him? Draining his life until he was nothing but an empty shell? He took a slow, furtive breath, searching his body for weakness, for any signs of sickness or pain. As far as he could tell, he felt pretty normal.

"All I ask," Gideon Frost went on, his voice low and soothing, "is for your cooperation, Shinji. That you remain here, at Hightower, and let us figure out how to get that mark off your arm. Let us try to save you. Once we do, once we have the idol in our possession, you can go home. Return to your aunt and forget this whole unpleasant experience ever happened. That really would be for the best, don't you agree?"

"I . . ." Shinji hesitated. A warning tickled the back of his mind. Something felt wrong here. Frost wasn't exactly lying, but Shinji was smart enough to know the man didn't have his best interests at heart. He remembered the attack on the boat, the fear he felt when Aunt Yui was struck down. He remembered what the men had said just before they left: that they would leave the boat and Aunt Yui floating alone in the middle of the river.

Aunt Yui.

"Where's my aunt?" Shinji asked, turning on Frost. "I want to see her. Where is she?"

For just a moment, Frost's lips tightened, but he forced a smile and shook his head. "I am sorry," he began, "but your aunt is not here. However, she is perfectly fine, I assure you—"

"Prove it," Shinji challenged. "Let me see her. I want to know she's safe."

"That is not a good idea," Frost said, and to Shinji, it sounded like he was trying to think quickly. "We are keeping you and your aunt separated for now, because we feel you could put her in danger without realizing it. At this point in time, the properties of the Coatl's Curse are unknown. It is possible that the curse could spread to someone else, like your aunt. You don't want that, do you?"

"You don't know where she is," Shinji said accusingly. "Your men left her there on the boat, and you don't know what happened to her. All because you wanted the idol." Clenching his fists, he glared at Frost. "So stop acting noble. Your men didn't attack us because they were trying to 'protect me.' You need the statue for some reason, and now that you can't get it, you're trying to 'acquire it' another way. Well, I'm not giving you anything until I see my aunt, so you'd better go find her and hope she's safe."

Frost's face went cold and terrifying, his friendly demeanor dropping in an instant. "You're making a grave mistake, boy," he said in an icy voice. "You have no idea what you're dealing with."

"Maybe you should've thought of that before your agents attacked our boat," Shinji shot back. "Or threatened to hurt us to get the idol. Or knocked my aunt unconscious." Fear for Yui suddenly rose up to clash with the anger. "You want me to cooperate," Shinji said, glaring at Frost. "I want to see my aunt, right now. I'm not answering any more questions until I know she's safe."

Frost stared at Shinji for a long, chilly moment, then smiled. It was not a nice smile. "Very well," he stated. "If this is what it takes to make you see reason, then we will find your aunt. However . . ." His eyes narrowed, and he stepped closer, looming over Shinji. "You *will* give us the idol, Shinji Takahashi," he growled. "The Hightower Corporation will have the Coatl's power, even if we have to separate you from the idol by force."

Shinji's stomach turned, but he stood his ground. Frost stepped back, still smiling coldly. "I suggest you think carefully about your position, boy," he said. "Otherwise we might have to 'experiment' with ways to remove the tattoo. And that might not be pleasant at all."

He turned and started walking toward the door. "I will return tomorrow," he said without looking back. "For your sake, I hope that you decide to cooperate."

The door opened for him, and Frost swept through without slowing down. It slammed shut behind him, the click of a lock echoing through the room, and Shinji was alone once more.

He did a quick but thorough search of the room, looking for vents, loose tiles, hidden windows, anything that might allow him to escape. Unfortunately it was as he suspected. The room was locked down tight. There were no places for him to squeeze into or sneak out of.

Eventually he slumped down onto the cot, angry, exhausted, and, if he was being honest, quite terrified. He had been kidnapped, and he was now a prisoner of this Hightower Corporation. He didn't know what had happened to his aunt, if she was okay, in trouble, or going crazy wondering where he was. And there was a strange tattoo on his arm that might or might not be a terrible curse.

All in all, a pretty sucky day.

Flopping to his back on the cot, Shinji stared up at the ceiling, wondering how he was going to get out of this one. Raising his arm, he gazed at the tattoo across his skin, at the winged serpent that had gotten him into so much trouble.

The Coatl stared back, green eyes seeming to bore into him, and Shinji frowned.

Why does Hightower want you so badly? he thought as he gazed at the mystical creature. *Also, why did you suddenly have to magic or curse or teleport your way onto me? I didn't ask for this. If you had just stayed a statue, this would've been a lot easier.*

The Coatl, if it had answers, did not deign to share them.

CHAPTER FIVE

"P_{sst}."

Shinji stirred. Something was hissing in his dreams. Was it the Coatl tattoo, slithering across his skin to speak to him at last?

"Psst," the voice came again. "Hey, Shinji. Wake up!"

Shinji jerked awake, gazing around blearily. The room he was in was dark and unfamiliar, and for a second, he didn't know where he was. Then he remembered everything and sat upright with a gasp.

A figure stood in the room with him, hovering a few feet away, almost invisible in the shadows. Shinji tensed, ready to demand to know what was going on, but the figure put a finger to its lips before he could say anything.

"Shhhhh," it whispered urgently. Finally he recognized the voice. It was Lucy, the girl who had been here when he first woke up. "It's just me," she went on as Shinji slumped in relief, though he didn't relax completely. She was part of Hightower, and he still didn't know what she wanted. He didn't even know how she kept getting inside his room. Maybe Frost had sent her, either to spy on him or gain his trust. That sounded like something he would do.

"What are you doing here?" Shinji growled. A bleary glance at the clock beside the bed proclaimed that it was 3:15 a.m. Way too early for any normal person to be up and sneaking around. "Shouldn't you be home at this hour? Do you live here or something?"

Lucy moved closer, putting a knee on the edge of the cot. "I heard what my . . . what Mr. Frost told you yesterday," she whispered, ignoring his last question. "I heard what they want, what they're planning to do to you."

"How?" Shinji asked incredulously. "I saw you leave. There was no one else in the room with us."

"There was," Lucy said, and held up her arm, where the robotic mouse perched on the back of her wrist. "I sent Tinker back in. No one ever notices him. He heard everything and transmitted it to me." Shinji gaped in astonishment, but Lucy didn't seem to notice. Her lips thinned, and she shook her head angrily. "I can't believe him," she muttered. "Threatening you like that. Always taking what he wants, regardless of the circumstances. It isn't right. He's gone too far this time. I can't sit back and pretend it's not happening anymore." She looked up at Shinji, blue eyes hard with determination. "I'm getting you out of here."

"What?" Shinji's eyes widened. "How?" he whispered. "The door is locked, and I've searched every inch of this room for an escape. Unless you plan to shrink me down to mouse size, I don't see how I'm leaving."

Lucy gave him a somewhat smug smile. "How do you think I've been getting in here?" she asked mysteriously.

"Uh, I have no idea. Shrink ray?"

"Tinker," said Lucy as the little mouse climbed to her shoulder. "He's not just a silly toy like *some people* think." She rolled her eyes, and Shinji had a pretty good idea who "some people" were. "He's an extremely complicated AI, with a bunch of capabilities that I don't talk about. Including"— she glanced at the heavy door across the room—"the ability to disengage electronic locks. Tinker unlocks the door, we sneak past the cameras, and we're out. So come on. We don't have a lot of time."

"Wait," Shinji said as she stepped toward the exit. "I can't leave," he went on, making her frown. "I need to know if my aunt is okay. Frost said they would look for her if I cooperated. If I leave now, I won't know if they find her or not."

"Shinji." Lucy shook her head, looking pained. "They're not going to look for her," she said. "Frost will tell you what you want to hear, just to secure your cooperation. That's what he does. He's not going to do anything about your aunt, Shinji. I'm sorry."

Shinji's heart plummeted, but he gave his head a stubborn shake. "How do you know?" he asked. "I can't take that chance. If they promised they would look for Aunt Yui, I have to stay."

Lucy sighed. "Here, then," she whispered, and put Tinker on the mattress between them. "Listen to this, if you don't believe me. Tinker, play back what Frost said in the hall."

The tiny robotic mouse sat up on its haunches. His eyes flickered, changing from red to blue, and a tinny recorded voice emerged from his pricked ears.

This is why I hate speaking to children, came the metallic but recognizable voice of Gideon Frost. *They're too emotional. You can't reason with them like you can with an adult.* A pause, and then he added, *If you had just been able to secure the idol in the marketplace, like you were supposed to, this wouldn't have happened.*

My apologies, sir, came another voice, one that made Shinji jerk up in recognition. The same voice that had demanded that he give them the statue, or else. The same voice he'd heard on the trawler right before he passed out. *I didn't expect the little river rat to be such a problem. It won't happen again.*

Be sure that it doesn't, Frost said coldly. *Your family has served us for generations, Kraus, but I have no issues cutting you loose if your skills start to deteriorate. Remember that.*

Yes, sir. Should I gather the team to search for the kid's aunt?

A snort. *No. I will not be blackmailed by a child. Searching for that boy's relative will be a waste of time and resources. We have what we need. He will give us the statue because he will have no choice. I will have the power of the font, and the Coatl is the key to finding it.* Their footsteps began moving away, their voices growing fainter as they did. *Keep that door locked at all times,* Frost went on. *No one goes in or out, do you understand?*

Yes, sir. I'll get Adam on it right away.

The voices faded, and Tinker sat down again. Shinji clenched his fists, anger and betrayal swirling inside him like a storm. *That lying jerk. He never had any intention of finding Aunt Yui. He was just going to use me to get what he wanted.*

"I'm sorry, Shinji," Lucy said again. "But that's why you have to get out of here. Frost won't keep his promise. All he cares about is possessing the statue, by any means possible."

"Yeah." Shinji set his jaw. She was right. He had to get out of here. Even if it meant the tattoo would stay on his arm. Even if there *was* a curse that would slowly sap away his life. He couldn't wait around for Hightower to help him. Frost had already lied; Shinji couldn't trust anything that came out of his mouth. He would find Aunt Yui and get rid of this curse on his own.

Meeting Lucy's gaze, he gave her a grim nod. "So, you said your mouse could unlock the door?"

She nodded, a faint smile creeping across her face.

"Doors, safes, computer passwords. You'd be surprised at what he can get through."

"But there's a guard," Shinji pointed out. "Does Tinker also come with a tranquilizer dart or some kind of sleep ray?"

Lucy shook her head with a strange little grin. "No, but you got lucky tonight. One, Kraus isn't here; I doubt we would have a chance of sneaking out if he was in the building. And two, Adam is on the last shift. He has a huge sweet tooth, but his stomach can't handle it." A small smile played at one corner of her lips. "Earlier this evening, someone might've slipped him a half-dozen jelly donuts, so he's going to be 'occupied' for a few minutes at least."

Shinji's heart beat faster. "Then what, we just walk out the door?" he asked in disbelief. Now that he thought about it, this seemed way too easy. Why was Lucy even helping him? Didn't she work here? If they were caught, he was sure Frost would shut down her workshop for good.

"Yes." Lucy nodded. "We just walk out the door." When he paused, she gave him a scrutinizing look, raising a brow. "Unless you want to stay here."

"No," Shinji said quickly, and stood. He would worry about Lucy, and whether or not she was really on his side, *after* they escaped from Hightower. "I am done with this place. Let's get out of here."

Together, they crept across the darkened room until they stood in front of the door. It looked pretty immovable to

Shinji, and who knew if the guard had come back. Lucy held up a hand and put a finger to her lips again.

With Tinker sitting in her palm, she raised her arm to the door. The tiny mouse sat up, swiveling his round copper ears toward the barrier, his head cocked and whiskers twitching like a real mouse. After a few seconds, he shook himself, turned, and scampered up her arm to vanish into a pocket. Shinji had no idea what communications had passed between the mouse and Lucy, if any, but Lucy nodded once and reached for the door handle.

As she cracked the door open, he held his breath, waiting for a shout of surprise and alarm that would signal the end of their escape. But nothing happened, and after a moment, she eased it open farther and poked her head out, looking both ways before glancing at him.

"Okay, it's clear. Just follow me, and stay close."

They slipped into the darkened hallway beyond and crept down a narrow corridor lined with doors on either side. Shinji guessed they were in some kind of large office building. They turned a corner, and he suddenly found himself facing an enormous glass window that stretched from floor to ceiling. Beyond, the night sky was speckled with stars, and a thin crescent moon hung in the clouds. Far, far below, a blinking carpet of lights stretched away to the horizon.

Shinji drew in a quiet breath. He'd been to a few large cities with Aunt Yui, but this one seemed to dwarf them all. "Where the heck are we?" he whispered.

"New York," Lucy replied, also in a whisper. "Near downtown. This is one of Hightower's . . . um . . . towers. The organization has several all over the world. This is one of the bigger ones, though." They came to another turn in the hall, and she peeked around the corner. "If we can get to the elevators," she muttered, "we're home free. Unfortunately, and of course, they're clear on the other side of the building. We'll have to be careful. There are still security guards wandering around. They don't care about me, but if they see you, we'll be in trouble." She paused a moment, looking around, then gave a decisive nod. "Okay, clear. Let's go."

He followed her down several more identical, confusing hallways, until Lucy suddenly jerked back, bringing him up short. "There's a guard coming," she whispered, backing quickly away. "Hurry, hide in one of the offices."

Shinji jiggled the handle on the nearest door and scowled. "It's locked. Who the heck locks their office door when they go home?" he hissed.

"Shoot, I forgot. They're on a timer," Lucy whispered, moving him out of the way. "Hang on. Tinker should be able to unlock it. Go, Tinker."

She held the metallic rodent up to the door and the key-card swiper above the handle. Tinker sat up, his tiny red eyes turning green as he stared at the door, the tip of his tail flicking back and forth.

Footsteps knocked against the tile floor, getting steadily

closer, and Shinji grimaced. "Hurry up," he whispered, making Lucy frown.

"He's going as fast as he can," she replied, far too calmly.

Shinji danced in place, almost ready to dash off and find his own hiding spot, when there was a faint beep, and Tinker's eyes turned red again. "Got it," Lucy whispered, and pushed open the door. "Come on, Shinji."

Shinji was already moving. Darting across the threshold, he started toward the large wooden desk in a corner, intending to dive behind it, but froze, staring at the wall. Directly in front of him, hovering several feet in the air, was a glowing red hole that led into nothingness. It was tiny, barely the size of his hand, but it pulsed and flickered with an ominous light, seeming to suck in the light itself.

"Shinji, move!" Lucy hissed, jerking him out of his daze. Wincing, he skittered across the room and dove beneath the desk, pulling the chair in. Lucy crouched down behind it, out of sight, as the footsteps paused just outside the door they'd come through. There was another beep, and the door hissed open.

The circle of illumination from a flashlight clicked on, gliding over the walls and floor. Shinji held his breath, watching in fascination as the beam of light slid across the desk toward the tiny black hole in the wall. The light flickered as it passed close, the beam warping and bending as it appeared to get sucked into the hole for a few seconds before snapping out again.

Despite his fear, Shinji couldn't look away. Across from him, Lucy was a statue; even Tinker, perched on her shoulder, had frozen. Not even his whiskers twitched as the flashlight did a careful sweep across the room. Finally, after way too long, the light withdrew, the door clicked shut, and the footsteps shuffled off down the hall again.

Lucy slumped against the desk, and Shinji breathed a sigh of relief. "Thank goodness," Lucy whispered as the mouse vanished into her pocket again. "You cut it a little close there, Tinker. Another second or two and we would've been caught."

Shinji took a slow breath to calm his heartbeat. "Okay, the guard has moved on; awesome. But what the heck is *that*?" he whispered, jerking a thumb at the pulsing gap in the wall. "It almost looks like a portal from some old video game."

"I'm not certain." Lucy rose, dusting off her knees. "I don't know whose office this is, but Hightower has many different experiments going on at any given time. They're always pushing the limits, trying to find new ways to harness magic, science, and technology." She gave the miniature portal a disdainful look, wrinkling her nose. "Always with the goal of making Hightower even more powerful."

Shinji had moved up to the anomaly, watching it flicker and pulse. Almost without him thinking, his hand drifted closer to the glowing hole, feeling not heat, but cold radiating from the center.

"Shinji!" Lucy warned, making him jerk his hand back. "Don't touch it," she said. "It's experimental, so we don't know what it does. You might not have any fingers when you pull your hand out." She looked at the door. "The guard should be gone now, and I already had Tinker cut out most of the cameras, but let's be careful. I don't want to turn a corner and run smack into him."

Carefully they cracked open the door, and when nothing happened, they eased into the hall again. "Elevators are this way," Lucy whispered, taking the lead once more. "We're almost there."

There were no more encounters with the wandering security guard, and Shinji followed Lucy through several more narrow hallways, past huge windows that showed New York spread below them like a carpet of stars, and through an open space with dozens of office cubicles, each one identical to the last. He was both grateful to and suspicious of the girl in front of him. If she hadn't come along, there was no way he could have made it out by himself, not with all the wandering security and mazelike corridors of the Hightower Corporation. On the other hand, he still didn't know why she was helping him. This seemed very risky for someone who supposedly worked here. And what was with that mouse that could open any door in the Hightower offices? How had she snuck *that* little tidbit past Gideon Frost?

Both Lucy and Tinker were a bit of a mystery. Shinji was

glad they were helping him escape, of course, but Lucy was hiding something; he was sure of it.

"Hang on," Lucy said, putting up a hand to stop them. "We're here."

Shinji looked past her arm and saw a trio of elevator doors across the hallway. The corridor was empty, and no one was around the elevator bay, security guard or otherwise. But Lucy still kept her arm out, preventing him from going any farther.

"Why are we waiting?" Shinji wondered. "No one is there. Come on, we're almost out."

"No one is there," Lucy agreed, "but there are *cameras* inside the elevator. And a security desk in the front lobby that sees it all. Just give me a second," she continued, pulling out Tinker as Shinji glared at the elevators in annoyance. Freedom was so close, but of course there had to be one final obstacle to getting out of here. Lucy placed Tinker on the ground, and the little mouse scampered off with the clicking of tiny copper feet.

"He should be able to scramble the feed so that it looks like no one is in the elevator," Lucy explained. "Once that is done, the only thing left will be sneaking around the security desk in the lobby. After we're past that, it's just a short run to the front doors—"

A sudden *ding* interrupted her.

Shinji jumped. The noise wasn't loud, but in the dark, silent corridors, it was like a gong had sounded. Heart pounding, he stared at the wall of elevators again and drew in a sudden breath. The numbers above the middle elevator had lit up and were slowly rising: *14 . . . 15 . . . 16 . . . 17 . . .* Which meant . . .

"Someone is coming!" Shinji whispered, taking a step back. "Lucy, what floor are we on?"

Lucy glanced at the elevator, and her face went pale. "Nineteen," she whispered back. "We're on the nineteenth floor. Tinker, get back here, now!"

The *ding* sounded again. As the bright form of the mouse turned and scurried back to Lucy, the middle elevator doors slid open, spilling light into the dark hall.

Shinji's stomach twisted into a knot. A man wearing a security guard uniform stepped through the doors into the hallway, making no sound at all. Lucy frowned, pressing herself back against the wall, as the man gazed around blankly.

"That's the front-desk security guard—Tom," she muttered. "What is he doing? He's not supposed to be up here."

As if he'd heard, the man looked up, directly at them, and Shinji stiffened. Tom's face was slack, his eyes unfocused, as if he didn't quite know where he was. In that moment, Shinji noticed something wispy and white clinging to his head, like the man had walked face-first into a spiderweb and hadn't bothered to wipe it off. He staggered forward, almost like he was injured, and Lucy gasped.

"Tom?" Before Shinji could stop her, she took a step

forward, her brow furrowed in concern. "What's wrong?" she asked. "Are you hurt? Do you need help?"

Tom's lips peeled back in an animalistic snarl, and he hissed, making the hair on Shinji's neck stand up. Raising his arms, the guard lurched forward, shuffling toward them over the tile like a zombie.

CHAPTER
SIX

Run!" Lucy cried, and they ran, scurrying back the way they'd come. Tom followed, arms outstretched, lurching after them. He didn't make any noise, either to shout or to tell them to stop, which just added to the creepiness as they fled.

Ducking down behind a cubicle, Shinji sucked in air and tried to calm his rapidly pounding heart. Lucy knelt beside him, peering around the edge of the cubicle walls, her eyes wide with fear.

"What . . . is going on?" Shinji whispered. "What's wrong with that guy?"

"I don't know," Lucy answered. "Tom has never left the front desk before, and he's never acted like this. I don't know what he's doing, but I don't want to get caught by him, either." Sinking back, she gazed around the room, her brow furrowed in thought. "We won't be able to get to the elevators this way. We'll have to take the stairs."

Tom lurched around a corner, his head turning from side to side as he scanned the room. His gaze landed on their hiding place once more, as if he knew exactly where they were. Raising his arms, he staggered forward again, moving like a jerky marionette over the tiles.

"This way," Lucy gasped, and she and Shinji took off once more, through rooms and hallways and past office spaces, until they reached a corner with a single door set into the wall. The plaque next to it read IN CASE OF FIRE, TAKE STAIRS, and a green exit sign hung above the doorframe.

Shinji reached out and yanked on the handle, but the door didn't budge. "Locked again," he growled. "Can your mouse open it?"

"Hang on." Lucy stepped forward, holding Tinker out to the card reader beside the door handle. "We need a minute."

Just then, Tom staggered around the corner, nearly running into a wall as he did but managing to stay on his feet. His head snapped up, glassy eyes locked on Shinji and Lucy. Shinji's heart clenched. "I'm not sure we have a minute!"

Tom straightened, then suddenly fell forward onto his hands and knees. His body contorted, bending his elbows until he was crouched down like a giant crab or spider.

Raising his head, he let out another terrible hiss and scuttled toward them.

Shinji's heart nearly stopped. "Lucy!" he yelped, causing her to glance over her shoulder. She squeaked, eyes going wide, but at that moment, the door in front of them beeped.

They pushed the door open and plunged through, then slammed the door behind them, hearing it lock into place again. On the other side, there was a loud thump and a frantic scrabbling sound. Shinji and Lucy fled down the stairs, not bothering to look behind them, until they finally reached the bottom.

Gasping, Shinji leaned against the wall, trying to suck air into his lungs, while Lucy and Tinker worked on the final door. His heart was racing, but at least the creepy spider security guard hadn't chased them down the stairwell. Maybe he'd forgotten his key, or maybe he thought he *was* a spider now, and spiders couldn't open doors. Whatever the reason, Shinji was glad. He'd had quite enough of the Hightower Corporation. The sooner he got away from this place, the better.

"Okay," Lucy breathed as the last door let out a soft beep and clicked open. "We're out."

A rush of warm air, smelling of pavement and car fumes, wafted into the stairwell as she pulled open the door. The space beyond was dark, with a concrete floor and rows of cars stretched out before them.

"Where are we?" Shinji muttered, gazing around.

"The parking garage," Lucy replied. "This way. We really are almost out."

A couple of minutes later, they scurried beneath the metal garage door, ignoring the car that was pulling into the parking lot, and escaped into the streets of the city.

They ran for several minutes, trying to put as much distance between themselves and Hightower as they could. Despite the early hours, there were crowds of people out, moving purposefully down the sidewalks. Cars clogged the roads, taxis and buses honked at one another as Shinji and Lucy wove through the sea of vehicles. A bicyclist swerved around Shinji, barely missing him, and kept cruising down the sidewalk at high speed.

Finally they ducked into an alley, out of the flow of foot traffic, and leaned against the wall to catch their breath. Panting, Shinji closed his eyes and tried to gather his thoughts, which were spiraling through his head like frantic bees. What did he do now? How would he find Aunt Yui? Would Hightower come after him? And what would he do about the tattoo on his arm? The Coatl's Curse, if it was real, was going to suck away his life unless he did something.

I can't worry about that right now, he finally decided. *First, I have to find Aunt Yui. And I have to make sure Hightower doesn't catch me again. They can't just go around kidnapping kids like that. Someone has to stop them.*

Resolved, he shoved himself off the wall and headed back toward the street.

"Shinji," Lucy said, following after him. "Where are you going?"

"To the police," Shinji replied without turning around. Hunching his shoulders, he made his way through the crowd. People parted around him, and a few grown-ups gave him puzzled looks, probably wondering why two kids were wandering the streets in the middle of the night. "I need to contact my aunt," he said over his shoulder. "I need to make sure she's all right. And I'm going to report Hightower and let the police know they kidnapped me."

"Shinji, wait." He heard her scramble to catch up and felt her grab his sleeve from behind. "That's not a good idea."

Scowling, he turned on her, narrowing his eyes. "Why not?" he demanded. "Are you defending them? You know what they did. You heard what Frost told me yesterday. I have to do something; they could be coming after me right now."

"I know." Lucy's voice was still infuriatingly calm. "I'm not defending them," she went on. "I know the awful things they've done. I understand what they're capable of. Which is why I risked everything to get you out of there. But you can't go to the police, Shinji. Hightower is too powerful. They'll twist the truth, pay people to stay silent, make it seem like they've done nothing wrong. I've seen it happen. Somehow you'll end up back at Hightower, right where they want you."

"That's ridiculous," Shinji protested. "What am I supposed to do, then?" He raked a hand through his hair, trying to think. "I have to tell someone. Otherwise Hightower will just come after me again. They won't just give up, will they?"

Lucy hesitated, then shook her head. "No," she admitted reluctantly. "Once they set their sights on something, they won't stop until they have it."

"That's what I thought," Shinji muttered. Turning his arm up, he glared at the marking on his skin, the image of the winged snake staring back at him. "If I could just get rid of this stupid tattoo, they wouldn't have any reason to come after me," he reasoned. "Maybe the police will know someone who can get it off—"

There was a flare of heat through his arm, like a jolt of electricity, searing and immediate. Shinji cried out, grabbing his wrist and falling to his knees, making Lucy gasp.

"Shinji!"

The tingling in his arm and fingers slowly faded, though the meaning behind the sudden jolt was perfectly clear. That had been a warning; whatever force powered the tattoo, it didn't like any plans or schemes to remove it. Breathing hard, Shinji looked up and found Lucy kneeling in front of him, blue eyes concerned as they met his own.

"You okay?"

"Yeah," Shinji rasped. "I think so." Gazing down at the tattoo, he grimaced. "Looks like Frost was right after all. There *is* a curse attached to this thing." Feeling suddenly tired, he slumped back against the wall and sighed, letting his arms drop to his lap. "What am I going to do now?" he muttered.

"Shinji, listen." Lucy sounded hesitant, nervously biting her lip while she gathered her thoughts. "I think we're in way over our heads," she said at last. "Something weird is happening here—your kidnapping, Mr. Frost's obsession with the idol, the way Tom turned into a creepy spider zombie. . . ." She shuddered, and Shinji repressed a shiver of his own. "Whatever is going on, I think it's all because of that tattoo. The police won't help us; if we tell them even half of what we saw, they'll think we're a couple of crazy kids with overactive imaginations. But we do need help, both to find your aunt and with Hightower, and there's only one place I can think of where people might believe us."

"Where?" asked Shinji.

Lucy winced. "The Society of Explorers and Adventurers."

"The . . . Society of Explorers and Adventurers," Shinji repeated slowly. That was a mouthful to say. "I've never heard of them."

"No," Lucy agreed. "You wouldn't have. They're a secret society. A 'members-only' type of club. The Society of Explorers and Adventurers—or SEA, if you don't want to say that big long name every time—is an organization whose members travel all over the world. They know a lot about old artifacts and ancient civilizations. If anyone could tell you more about the idol and that tattoo, it's them."

"But if SEA is so hidden," Shinji wanted to know, "how do *you* know about them?"

"Because," Lucy said, and sighed, "SEA and Hightower are hated rivals. It's a long, complicated story, and one I really don't want to get into right now. But there's a lot of history between them, and a lot of bad blood. As a member of Hightower, I could get into trouble just talking to the Society. They really do not like each other. So"—she gave Shinji a rueful look—"if we do find SEA, please don't tell them that I came from Hightower. They'd probably throw me out and slam the door in my face."

Shinji blinked at her. "You're coming, too?"

"Of course." Lucy grinned at him and stood, pulling him up with her. "How are you going to find SEA without me, exactly? You don't even know where to start looking."

"But what about your job at Hightower? And your workshop?"

Lucy shrugged, looking both uncomfortable and resigned. "I can't exactly go back now," she said. "Tom saw me, even if he's become some weird spider zombie. And once they discover we're both gone, losing my workshop will be the least of my worries." For a second, she looked frightened, like she was doing something she didn't really want to do, but she shook it off. "Besides, I can't just dump you on the streets of New York and leave. What kind of rescue is that? So yeah, I think we're in this together."

"All right." Shinji nodded. She was still hiding something,

but there was no doubt that she had saved both their hides that night. She and her amazing mecha-mouse. "Then how are we supposed to find SEA?"

Lucy thought about it for a few moments. Tinker crawled up to perch on her shoulder, copper ears and nose twitching in the breeze. Finally, she took a deep breath and nodded.

"First, I think we need to get out of the city."

CHAPTER SEVEN

Shinji stared out the window of the Greyhound bus, his cheek and forehead resting against the glass, and watched the endless desert flash by.

California. Lucy was taking them to *California*. Clear on the other side of the country. It had been a three-day trip, sitting on a bus seat with nothing to do, slowly going out of his mind with boredom. Lucy had gotten rid of her phone, saying Hightower would be able to track it, so Shinji had no access to anything online. The bus stopped every few hours for food and bathroom breaks, and Lucy had taken pity on him once and bought him a magazine, but that had been several stops ago. She, at least, seemed to have no shortage of cash, paying for their food and buying them snacks so they wouldn't starve. But the trip was beginning to wear on Shinji, and he had snapped at Lucy once or twice as his patience wore thin and exhaustion gnawed at him.

"Why couldn't we have flown there?" he asked for probably the third time that trip. "This is silly, traveling by bus. We could've been there by now."

"Because plane tickets from New York to California are expensive," Lucy explained, as cool and logical as ever. Shinji had noticed that about her, that the hotter and more riled he got, the colder and more unruffled she became. Probably a side effect from working at Hightower, but it drove him nuts. "Also, the security at airports is much stricter," Lucy went on in that same reasonable voice. "The TSA might question why a couple of thirteen-year-olds are getting on a plane with no parents. Also, trust me when I say that Hightower has eyes everywhere. If they're trying to find someone, airports will be the first place they look. Taking the bus is much more low profile, which is what we need if we want to keep Hightower from finding you."

"Okay, fine." Shinji had raised his hands. "Point taken. And this place we're trying to find, this Society of Explorers and Adventurers, it's in California?"

"Yes," Lucy replied. "At least, that's one of the places their headquarters are located, anyway. I'm just going on what I've heard at Hightower."

"There are more? We couldn't have gone to another location, maybe a closer one?"

"This is the closest one I know of," Lucy said flatly. "I didn't have the money for a ticket to Tokyo or Italy."

Okay, so the other SEA headquarters were out of the question. "California is a big place," Shinji pointed out. "Where in California are we going, exactly?"

"Anaheim," Lucy replied. "According to Hightower, they're located somewhere in Anaheim."

"That's an entire city! How are we going to find a super-secret society in an entire city?"

She looked out the window, and Shinji got the feeling she was tired of talking about it. "I figured we would get there first, without running into Hightower, and then worry about looking for them," she said with the barest hint of exasperation. "If you have a better idea, by all means, let's hear it."

He didn't, of course, and the conversation ended there.

Shinji stirred, raising his head from where he'd been dozing against the window. The bus was slowing, turning into another station. A quick check of the signs told Shinji this wasn't their stop, that Anaheim was still a few hours away. It was, however, the final stop before they reached the city.

Shinji yawned, stretching both arms over his head, eager

to get off the bus. He needed to move, and more importantly, he needed to pee. Glancing out the window, he saw a small crowd of people with tickets in hand, waiting to board. He wondered if any of them were traveling across the country like he'd just done. If they'd asked his opinion, he would've told them to take a plane instead.

Suddenly he straightened, drowsiness forgotten. At the back of the crowd, a pair of large men with dark sunglasses watched the bus pull into the station. Before all this, he wouldn't have given them a second thought; there were lots of men in suits wearing sunglasses, after all. But this pair looked just a tad too familiar, their expressions as they watched the bus pull in a tiny bit too interested.

Lucy sat beside him, slumped against her seat with a book in her lap and her eyes closed. "Hey," Shinji muttered, shaking her arm. "Lucy, wake up."

She groaned, cracking open her lids blearily. "Are we there yet?"

"Not yet," Shinji whispered. "There's one more stop after this, but look out the window. Are those . . . ?"

He paused. The two men were no longer there. They weren't in the crowd or anywhere that he could see. It was like they had vanished as soon as he'd looked away.

"What?" Lucy yawned, sitting up in her chair. "What am I looking at?"

Shinji shook his head. "Nothing," he muttered. "I thought I saw . . . It's nothing. Let's get some food. I'm starving."

"You're always starving." Lucy sighed, but she rose, and together they made their way off the bus.

Shinji left her in a line for burgers while he went searching for a restroom. When he was done taking care of business, he stood in front of a sink, gazing at his reflection as the water ran over his hands. He hadn't changed his clothes in more than three days, or brushed his hair, or had a shower. He was starting to feel a bit disgusting.

"Looking a little rough there, pal."

Shinji jerked up. A young man stood at the sink next to his, scrubbing his fingers with soap and water. Shinji was so out of it, he hadn't even noticed him come up. It wasn't one of the two men he'd seen earlier, he noted with relief. This man was smaller, leaner, and much scruffier-looking. His dark, reddish-brown hair was unkempt, his long coat was rumpled, and he had about three days of stubble across his chin and jaw. A polished cane with a golden parrot head leaned against the sink beside him, an oddly old-school accessory for someone his age.

"Nice tattoo," the man said, gazing at Shinji's hands, where he still held his palms under the stream of water. The Coatl tattoo was clearly visible on his upturned forearm. "I'd say you're a bit young to get yourself inked, but then again, I wasn't much older than you when I got my first one. It's really unique, by the way. Haven't seen anything quite like it."

Shinji's stomach clenched, and he jerked his hands from

the sink. "Thanks," he muttered, quickly turning away. He suddenly wished he had a jacket or sweater to pull down over the mark, but he only had his ratty T-shirt. He stuck his hands in his pockets instead.

"It's a dragon, right?" the man continued, pulling a paper towel from the dispenser. "No, not a dragon, a snake? A winged snake. What are they called?" He wiped his hands, tossed the paper towel in the trash, and glanced at Shinji questioningly.

Shinji backed away. "I dunno," he said, trying to sound casual. "It just looked cool, so I decided to get it."

"Well, from one tattoo lover to another, it is very striking." The man smiled and picked up his cane. "If you want to hide it, however, consider long sleeves, gloves, or even a bandage wrap. People can't notice what they can't see."

He didn't wait for Shinji's answer. With a wink and a salute, he turned and walked away, moving with a slight limp, Shinji noticed. After he left, Shinji quickly toweled off his hands and made his way back to Lucy.

"I met a weird guy in the bathroom," he told her as they sat down at a table, a pair of fast-food burgers and fries between them. "He asked me about my tattoo, then left."

Lucy gave him an alarmed look. "You think he was a Hightower agent?"

"I don't know," Shinji replied. "He didn't seem like anyone from Hightower, but I've only ever met Goons One, Two, and Three. And Frost, of course."

"Hmm." She chewed on her drink's plastic straw. "It might not be anything, but we should be careful, just in case."

When they returned to the bus, Shinji received a shock after he climbed aboard. The strange man was there, parrot-head cane resting on the edge of the seat. He was scrolling through his phone, however, and didn't even glance up when Shinji passed him in the aisle.

"That's him," Shinji whispered to Lucy as they took their seats again.

She blinked. "Who?"

"The weird guy from the bathroom." Shinji jerked his chin at the back of the man's head. "The one who asked me about my tattoo. He's here."

Lucy peeked over the tops of the seats, then relaxed. "That's definitely not a Hightower agent," she said, leaning back. "No one from Hightower would be that scruffy; Mr. Frost would chew them out, then fire them. He's probably just some guy who saw your tattoo and thought it was interesting. People who get tattoos like to admire others', I've heard."

"I don't know," Shinji muttered. For some reason, the man didn't seem like a random stranger. The way he told Shinji to cover up his mark . . . it was as if he knew someone was after it.

Before he could put his thoughts into words, however,

the two men from earlier walked onto the bus, and both Shinji and Lucy jumped.

Shinji ducked low in his seat and glanced at the girl beside him. "Lucy, are *those* . . . ?"

She nodded, her face pale. "Most definitely agents of Hightower," she said, and cast a quick glance at the window, as if contemplating leaping through it. "Should we be running?"

"No." Shinji shook his head and put a hand on her knee. "They know we're here," he said, watching the two men slowly do a scan of the bus. "If we run now, they'll just come after us. They can't do anything now, not with all these people around. When we reach the next stop, we'll get off quick and try to lose them in the crowd."

Lucy gave a fearful nod. Shinji held his breath as the men walked down the aisle, every muscle in his body tense as they drew alongside them. The two men very deliberately stopped right next to his seat, staring down at both him and Lucy. One of them smiled, very faintly, before continuing to the back of the bus.

CHAPTER EIGHT

The final few hours to Anaheim were the most stressful of Shinji's life.

He could feel the glares of the Hightower agents behind him, like laser beams on the back of his head. The agents didn't move. They didn't read newspapers or magazines, or even glance down at their phones. They just sat quietly in their seats, watching him.

Lucy looked even more anxious than Shinji felt, posed rigidly next to him with her hands in her lap. Her face was pale, her lips pressed tightly together, and she flinched every time he leaned in to whisper to her. Clearly she feared getting caught and taken back to Hightower just as much as Shinji did.

The sun had set, and night had fallen when the bus pulled into the final station, and the driver announced that they had arrived in Anaheim at last. As a collective sigh of relief went through the passengers, Shinji bent close to Lucy and whispered, "Okay, when the bus stops, we make a run for it. Try to lose them in the city. You all right with that?"

She nodded shakily, though her face was still pale. "We're so busted," she said. "Once they have a target, Hightower agents never give up the search. They'll keep coming until they catch us."

"Then we'll just have to not be caught. Come on."

He took her hand, and together they made their way to the front of the bus, ignoring the frowns and irritated looks from the other passengers. Shinji dared a glance back once and saw the Hightower agents on their feet as well, staring right at him. His heart thudded in his ears, and his stomach felt like a nest of writhing snakes as he pushed his way toward the front of the bus, with Lucy right behind him.

"Whoa, whoa, whoa. Slow down, you two."

Abruptly, the strange man Shinji had met in the bathroom rose and, with surprising speed, stepped into the aisle and put a hand on both their shoulders. Shinji jumped, and Lucy let out a squeak, but the stranger only chuckled. "Relax," he said, squeezing their shoulders in a gentle but warning manner. "I know it's been a long trip, and you're eager to see everyone. But the last thing I need is you two rushing off without me and getting lost. Just hold your horses, and we'll all leave together."

Shinji twisted in the stranger's grip, gazing up at his face. The man smiled cheerfully down at him, but there was a hint of warning in his eyes. "Trust me," he said, and jerked his head, very slightly, toward the back of the bus. "We don't want you running into people that you shouldn't. Oh, and here," he went on, and handed Lucy his parrot-head cane. "Hold on to that for me, would you? I'll let you know when I need it back. Ready, kiddos?" He grinned as the bus doors opened with a hiss. "Here we go."

The stranger kept a light but firm grip on their shoulders as they left the bus, smiling cheerfully as he steered them through a mostly empty bus station, their footsteps echoing over the tiles.

"Who are you?" Shinji asked in a low voice without looking back. "Are you with Hightower? Where are you taking us?"

"Patience, Mr. Takahashi," the stranger said, startling him. "All questions will be answered in good time. Right now, though, your friends from the bus are following us. I suggest we keep moving until we can speak freely. . . . Oh, hello."

Shinji looked up and saw the two men standing casually

in front of the exit doors. They looked like they were speaking to each other, but he knew they were staring right at him. How they had gotten in front of Lucy and him, Shinji had no idea, but there they were.

"This way, then," the stranger said easily, steering them in another direction. "Well, it's going to be harder to lose them than I thought," he mused. "Let's see if we can't find another way out."

This routine went on for several more minutes. Each time they found an exit, the Hightower agents would already be in front of it, forcing them to go another way. It felt to Shinji like they were being herded somewhere, like sheep being driven by a pair of border collies.

"They're good," the stranger mused as the Hightower agents appeared in front of yet another hallway. "They've done this thing before, I'd bet. They know we don't want to draw attention to ourselves and that causing a scene would be bad for us."

"What are we going to do?" whispered Lucy.

"For now, we go along with it," the stranger said. "They can't keep this up forever. However, if I do say run, both of you run and don't look back. Find a place with lots of people; they won't try to grab you there. Understand?"

Shinji's heart was pounding, but he nodded. "Yeah."

"Look," Lucy pointed out. "There's an exit. It doesn't look guarded this time."

The stranger raised his head. "Hmm, to the parking lot," he muttered. "I think I see where this is going, but maybe we'll get lucky."

They left the building and headed into the parking lot, walking between rows of vehicles and moving farther away from the lights of the station. The parking lot was completely deserted; except for the three of them, no one was around.

So it didn't surprise Shinji when a Hightower agent slid out from between two vans and stepped up to block their path. Shinji half turned and saw the second Hightower agent round a car and step up behind them, boxing them in.

The stranger sighed. "Well, I was hoping to avoid this," he said, still sounding unconcerned. "Persistent, aren't they? I guess we'll have to deal with this little problem now, or they'll harass us the whole time we're here."

"What are we going to do?" Shinji asked, giving the Hightower agents fearful looks. As one, the agents began walking forward, making him tense.

"*You* aren't going to do anything," the stranger replied easily. "Just stand there and keep out of the way. Don't run," he warned Shinji with a frown. "I don't want to spend the whole night tracking you down again. I'll take that, thank you," he told Lucy, plucking his cane from her limp hands with a smile. "Now, if you would both take maybe four steps that way," he said, indicating the direction with an open hand. "Thank you. This should be over in a minute."

Shinji and Lucy huddled against a yellow Jeep, watching as the stranger turned and took a couple of limping steps toward the first approaching Hightower agent. Lucy was shaking; Shinji felt her trembling as the two men drew closer.

"They're going to hurt him," she whispered. "They're not going to ask questions or talk. They're going to beat him up, and then they'll come after us. We should run, Shinji. Or we're just going to be dragged back to Hightower."

Shinji clenched his fists. He knew Lucy was right, but he didn't want to leave the stranger to these thugs. He wished there was something he could do.

"Evening, gentlemen," the stranger said as the first man strode up. The Hightower agent was tight with coiled muscles, but the other man's posture was completely relaxed. "What can I do for you this fine—"

The agent swung a fist at him. A big, meaty fist aimed right at his face. Lucy gasped, and the stranger gave a yelp of surprise. Shinji jerked his head back, and by some miracle, the blow missed his nose by centimeters. At the same time, he spun to the side, lashing out, and the golden beak of his parrot cane struck the back of the man's knee. The agent grunted and crashed to the pavement, and the stranger winced as he backed away.

"Oops, sorry, sorry! I didn't mean to do that. You okay there, pal?"

The first agent bounced upright with a snarl. The second

stalked toward the stranger, head and shoulders lowered like an angry bear. The stranger grimaced, holding up the cane with both hands.

"Guys, come on," he pleaded. "We don't have to do this. We could all shake hands, go home, eat cookies; no one has to get hurt. Violence isn't the answer."

One Hightower agent lunged, fist drawn back to strike. The stranger cringed away with a yelp, throwing up his cane, and somehow, the parrot's beak struck the agent's wrist as it was coming down. There was a pop, and the agent let out a howl of pain, staggering back and cradling his arm. The second agent barreled toward the stranger with his head down and his arms spread, as if to tackle him like a linebacker. At the last second, the stranger twisted out of the way, and somehow the hooked parrot beak caught the agent's pant leg as he sped by. The agent tripped, pitched forward, and crashed headfirst into a truck. He slumped to the ground with a groan, holding his skull, and didn't get up again.

"Ouch. That didn't look pleasant." The stranger winced, giving the other Hightower agent a pleading look. "I don't suppose you want to call this a draw, do you?" he asked. "Your friend would probably appreciate a cold compress in a few minutes."

The Hightower agent glowered, then reached into the back of a pickup truck and withdrew a tire iron, swinging it before him like a sword. Before the stranger could say anything, the agent charged.

"This really doesn't seem necessary!" the stranger said, backpedaling and swinging furiously with his cane as the Hightower agent bore down on him. The clacks of wood on iron echoed through the night, and Shinji's stomach clenched as the stranger was forced back, barely seeming to block each swing of the agent's weapon. Still, none of the blows were getting through. Every swing was blocked, parried, or dodged, and though the stranger winced each time his opponent smacked the stick aside, he wasn't getting hit at all.

Finally the agent gave a furious roar and lunged, stabbing at the stranger's face. The stranger pirouetted like a dancer, and the golden parrot head struck the agent in the back of his skull as he passed. The larger man stumbled, swayed on his feet, then slumped onto the hood of a sports car. Sliding down the metal, he collapsed to the pavement.

The stranger took a deep breath, tipping an imaginary hat to his fallen foes. "Terribly sorry about that, boys," he said. "I wish we could've come to an understanding. I suggest an ice pack and a bottle of rum when you wake up. You gentlemen have a good rest of the night."

Lucy's mouth was open as the stranger joined them again, his limp more noticeable than before, Shinji saw. "Oh wow," she whispered, gazing at him with slightly starry eyes. "That was incredible. You're amazing."

"What? What are you talking about?" The stranger gave a painful grimace, rubbing the back of his head. "That was luck, pure and simple. I abhor violence. I am unashamedly a giant coward at heart." Tucking his cane beneath his arm, he dusted off his hands and gave the unconscious Hightower agents a wary look. "That was unpleasant, and I am terrified. Shall we get out of here before our friends wake up and are very angry at me?"

"Hold on." Shinji crossed his arms. He was in awe of the stranger and grateful that he'd saved Lucy and him from Hightower, but he still didn't know anything about him. "You never answered my question. Before we go anywhere with you, who are you, and how do you know my name?"

"Ah, Shinji. Such a distrustful lad. Not that I blame you; I can only imagine what you've been through with Hightower." The stranger scratched the side of his face and grinned. "Very well, let me answer your questions. We know about you, Shinji, because we've been looking for you. Or, rather," he went on, and tapped the end of his cane against the inside of his own wrist, "we've been looking for *that*. The legend of the Coatl's Curse is something we've only ever heard about. Now that it's activated, the Hightower Corporation will stop at nothing to acquire its power for itself. Even if it means sacrificing you. Which is something we cannot let happen."

"You keep saying *we*," Shinji pointed out. "Who's *we*? Who are you?"

The stranger smiled.

"Allow me to introduce myself," he said, and gave a very flashy bow. "My name is Oliver Ocean. Part-time voyager, retired pirate, all-around scoundrel, and a member of the Society of Explorers and Adventurers."

CHAPTER NINE

Oliver Ocean didn't have a car.

"I can't drive," he told them in the back seat of an Uber. "Never learned how. All those pedals and dials and buttons; it's too much to remember. Boats are much easier; plus, when you're out on the open water, you don't have to worry about getting hit by a bus or run over by one of those food-delivery bicycles."

Shinji and Lucy exchanged a glance. Now that the relief of escaping the Hightower agents had faded, Shinji was back to being suspicious and wary. He'd asked Oliver where they were going, but the man only told him it was a secret, which did not help mitigate his distrust. Who was this person, really? Sure, he might've saved them from Hightower, but what did they really know about SEA? Maybe the Society just wanted to use him, since they knew about the Coatl's Curse, too. Maybe the Society of Explorers and Adventurers was just as bad as the Hightower Corporation.

"You both still seem a bit unsure." Oliver's voice and expression were perfectly serene; he leaned easily against the side door, watching them with a faint smile. "Am I that scary?"

"Maybe," Shinji muttered.

"We just don't know anything about you," Lucy added. "Or SEA."

Oliver shrugged. "Not much to say, really." He seemed unconcerned about being overheard. Up front, the driver had been listening to a show on the radio and was paying them no attention. "I've been a member of the Society all my life," Oliver went on. "My grandmother Mary Oceaneer was one of their most important members way back when. She sailed around the world with her parrots, discovered new places and treasure, and basically made a huge impression on me as a kid. I wanted to be just like her when I grew up." One corner of his mouth twisted in a wry smirk. "Though you can be sure I changed my last name to *Ocean* as soon as I could. Bad enough that I was named Oliver. But Oliver Oceaneer?" He rolled his eyes with a snort. "So ridiculous.

"Anyway," Oliver continued as Shinji bit back a snicker of his own, "that's a little bit about me. If you want information about the Society, well, I'm not one to explain it. I will say that we are the good guys, or we *try* to be the good guys. Some of us more than others." He gave Shinji a grin. "A few of us find ourselves neck-deep in trouble no matter how hard we try."

Shinji almost smiled in return. He still didn't know anything about SEA, but Oliver Ocean seemed all right. Maybe even somewhat of a kindred spirit. Shinji wanted to like him, but something held him back. In his travels with Aunt Yui, he'd seen too many things go bad to let down his guard that easily. Grown-ups, as he'd learned the hard way, couldn't be trusted.

Shinji swallowed hard. He hoped Aunt Yui was all right. He hoped he wasn't wasting his time with SEA when he should've been trying to find her instead. If SEA couldn't help him, he didn't know what he was going to do.

"Here we are," Oliver announced as the car slowed and then pulled alongside a curb. Shinji opened the door and stepped onto the sidewalk, looking up and down the narrow street. There weren't many people around, and the storefronts lining the sidewalk were old and faded. Directly in front of them, an open door sat beside a tinted store window that was too dark to see anything through it.

"The Discovery Trading Company?" Lucy asked, gazing at the flickering sign above the single door. "What is that?"

"Exactly what it sounds like," Oliver said, striding past them with a grin and a wink. "It's a store that caters to globe-trotters and adventurers of all types. If you ever need rhino repellent or a patch for your hot-air balloon, this is the place to get it."

The Discovery Trading Company. Shinji felt a pang in his chest as Oliver ducked into the store ahead of them. Rhino repellent and hot-air balloons? This was exactly the odd, quirky type of place Aunt Yui would've loved.

Intrigued despite himself, Shinji stepped through the doorway. Beyond the frame, the store itself was tiny and cluttered and smelled faintly of cigars. For a second, he was uncomfortably reminded of the shop in Abenge where his troubles all began. But the merchandise here was very different. Bowie knives and machetes hung on the far wall, along with hatchets, bows and arrows, a couple of boomerangs, even a strange, flat metal ring that looked like a throwing weapon of some kind. A pup tent stood in the corner behind an entire fort of backpacks, rucksacks, bedrolls, and duffel bags. The basket from a hot-air balloon hung from wires on the ceiling, surrounded by swarms of model planes.

But the weirdest merchandise lay scattered throughout the shelves, alongside perfectly normal, everyday items. Shinji found the bottle of rhino repellent (guaranteed to work!) behind cans of mosquito spray. A few shelves down was the "sidekick aisle," where boxes of monkey chow, parrot pellets, doggy backpacks, and tiger bowls sat side by side. There was an entire shelf of parachutes, a corner filled with camera and film paraphernalia, and a whole display dedicated to various charms and good-luck items: rabbits' feet, lucky dice, four-leaf clovers in glass, even rusty horseshoes. Stranger, less recognizable items sat there, too. Shinji saw a huge metallic-green beetle, a white cat figurine with one paw raised, a varnish-covered acorn, and a strange bronze knife with a human face etched on the handle all scattered throughout the display.

It was like an army-surplus store had collided with an outdoorsman's warehouse before both smashed face-first into a novelty and joke shop. Shinji figured he could spend several days in here and not see everything there was to see.

"Lucy, check this out," he muttered, and held up a tiny orange backpack. "So your monkey partner can carry his own supplies through the jungle."

She shuddered and took a rather large step back from him. "Monkeys are disgusting," she said. "They eat bugs they pick off other monkeys and throw their own poop at people. That backpack is probably full of fleas."

In the next aisle, Oliver chuckled. "Not much of an animal lover, are you?"

"Animals bite," Lucy said. "And drool, and shed, and carry around parasites." Her hand strayed to her pocket, where Shinji would bet Tinker was hidden. "Machines are far less dirty."

Oliver gave another chuckle and shook his head. "You're going to love Kali, then," he said ominously.

At first, the store seemed abandoned. There were no

employees in the aisle and no customers browsing the merchandise. There didn't seem to be any security cameras watching from dark corners or hidden crannies, either. Shinji was starting to wonder if the store was even open, when a door he hadn't noticed before creaked back and a woman stepped behind the counter. She was small and slight, with large leather gloves and a greasy leather apron. Her hair, a bright, shocking orange, stuck out like a flame atop her head.

"Oliver Ocean." The woman's voice wasn't exactly welcoming, and she gave the man leaning against the counter a wry look. "I see you're back, ye scoundrel. And you didn't have the decency to get scuppered away by a kraken like I'd hoped."

"Aw, Molly, it's good to see you, too." Oliver grinned. "Is everyone here? I found the boy, like I said I would."

Molly sighed. "Aye," she muttered, nodding to the door she'd come through. "Off with you, then. She's waiting for you."

Oliver turned and beckoned to both Shinji and Lucy. "This way," he urged. "Follow me."

Shinji glanced back at the orange-haired woman. "Isn't she coming with us?"

"Molly? She's the store owner, actually. Knows all about SEA and is kind enough to provide a front for our little operation, but she's really not the adventuring type." Oliver gave a shrug as he hurried forward. "Come on, then. We have a meeting with some very important people, and if we're late, we might get fed to jaguars."

"He's joking, right?" Lucy whispered as they trailed Oliver through the back door. "He has to be joking."

"Probably," Shinji muttered, gazing around. Beyond the door was a small, dingy-looking break room with an ancient sofa and a battered wooden bookcase against the far wall. A table with a few fold-out chairs sat next to a soda machine, and Shinji guessed that was where they were going to meet these "very important people."

But Oliver didn't walk toward the table. Instead, he moved to stand in front of the bookcase, scanning the shelves. "Where is it?" he murmured as Shinji peered around him. "I can never remember the right title." His fingers traced the book spines as he murmured, *"Primates of the Caribbean, Shades of Khaki, Left at the Falls* . . . aha!"

Reaching up, he hooked two fingers at the top of a spine—*The Jungle Book*, Shinji read—and pulled.

There was a *clunk* behind the wall, and then the entire bookshelf swung inward. Shinji's eyes widened, and he heard Lucy's sharp intake of breath as a hidden passageway was revealed behind the shelves. The hallway was long and narrow and stretched off into the darkness. Oliver grinned at Shinji's and Lucy's expressions.

"Here we are, then. After you?" He gestured to the dark corridor, smiling as neither Shinji nor Lucy moved. "No? Okay, everyone follow me."

They stepped through the door into the hall, and the bookshelf groaned shut behind them. It was not, as Shinji had expected, completely dark; sconces lined the walls every dozen or so feet, giving off a soft orange glow. Instead of dingy tile, the floor was velvety red-and-gold carpet, and small alcoves held stands with marble busts, vases, flowers, and other decorations.

"Wow," Lucy murmured, gazing down the elegant-looking corridor. "I wasn't expecting this."

Oliver chuckled as they started down the hallway, their shoes making no sounds on the plush carpet. "One of the primary rules of having a secret organization," he told her. "The best ones are in the places you'd never expect—"

A deep growl cut through the darkness, raising the hair on Shinji's neck. Oliver froze, his mouth open midsentence, as a pair of dark, beady eyes appeared in the shadows ahead.

"Oh no." He sighed as the eyes came forward, and a huge, shaggy creature stepped from the darkness to block their path. Its pitch-black fur blended into the shadows of the corridor, its shoulders and paws were massive, and powerful muscles rippled beneath its dark pelt. Rearing onto its hind legs, the black bear opened its mouth and roared, flashing fangs as long as Shinji's fingers.

Lucy let out a squeak and cringed back as Oliver swiftly stepped forward, his arms raised as if to shield them.

"Shinji, Lucy," he snapped, his voice hard, "get behind me, now."

The bear roared again and bounded forward, plowing toward them like a falling boulder. Shinji yelped, and Lucy screamed as the huge animal reared up and collided with Oliver, driving them both to the ground.

"Oliver!" Shinji looked frantically around for a weapon; maybe he could distract the huge predator long enough for Oliver to get away. Stepping to the wall, he yanked a vase from one of the alcoves and spun, ready to hurl it at the bear.

"Shinji, wait!" Lucy held up her arm, stopping him. "Look."

Shinji looked. The bear lay on top of Oliver, jaws open and huge paws pinning him down, but it wasn't biting him. And Oliver . . . was laughing, Shinji realized. Laughing and playfully grabbing the shaggy cheek ruffs, while the bear made growling noises and tried to lick him.

"Yes, hello, Kali, I missed you, too. I did." Oliver tried holding the predator's head away as it squirmed and pressed forward. "But I don't need bear spit up my nose—argh." He grimaced as the bear finally broke free, its wide pink tongue slapping his face. Lucy gave a violent shudder and turned away. "Good. Great. That's just what I wanted. Ugh."

"Kali," called a new voice. "Good girl, but that's enough. Let him go, please."

The bear sat up. With a last playful growl, she clambered off Oliver, making sure to step on his stomach, and padded toward a figure standing at the end of the hall.

A woman stepped forward, smiling as the bear circled

around, then came to stand beside her. She was quite tall, with long black hair, dark eyes, and a very firm, no-nonsense mouth. One slender hand rested on the bear's head as she gazed down at Oliver, a small smile playing on her lips.

But then her gaze traveled to Shinji, and the smile grew even wider. "Shinji Takahashi," she said, making him stiffen. "You're here. I am so glad that you're all right. And that our buffoon of a pirate was able to find you in time."

"Was there any doubt?" Wheezing, Oliver struggled to sit up, grabbing his cane from where it had fallen when the bear attacked. The woman ignored him, her attention focused solely on Shinji.

"My name," she told him, "is Priya Banerjee. And I am the chairwoman of the Society of Explorers and Adventurers, just arrived from our outpost in India to greet you. I know you have many, many questions, and I will try to answer them now. So . . ." She turned away, raising an elegant hand to beckon Shinji and the others forward. "If you and your friend would follow me; we've been expecting you."

CHAPTER
TEN

SEA's headquarters turned out to be quite vast, Shinji discovered. Following Priya and her black bear down the hall, they passed through a doorway flanked by antique suits of armor and stepped into a large, lavishly decorated room. Plush, antique-looking sofas sat against the walls, which were lined with maps, postcards, letters, and pictures of locations around the world. The ceiling rose above them, hung with chandeliers and intricately painted with creatures both real and imagined. A jade dragon with extremely long whiskers soared over the heads of a herd of elephants, their trunks raised as if in greeting. A panda sat in a bamboo grove, while a white buffalo gazed stoically at a sunset.

Peering at the mural above him, Shinji gave a start. A familiar snakelike creature lay coiled up in one corner of the ceiling, feathered wings tucked to its back. It was a different color from the tattoo on his forearm; this serpent had rainbow wings instead of gold, but it was definitely the same creature.

In the center of the room sat a large, battered wooden table that looked like it had come straight from a castle or Viking hall. Three people sat around it, all watching Shinji's approach with mild to intense curiosity. Kali loped over to a nearby couch and clambered onto the cushions, covering the whole couch with her body as she lay down.

"Shinji, Lucy, please have a seat," Priya instructed, gesturing to the table. Oliver flopped into a chair and put his boots up on the table, earning an annoyed look from the rotund little man beside him. Shinji gingerly took the seat across the table, next to a slight woman in a wheelchair. She peered at him from beneath a shock of electric-blue hair and gave him a cheerful smile. He returned it cautiously.

Priya came to stand at the head of the table, facing them all. "Thank you for coming," she said, nodding to the faces around the table. "I'm glad you all could make it. Since we all know why we're here, let me first start with introductions for our young friends. Shinji Takahashi and Lucy Smith," she went on, glancing at their side of the table. "I would like to welcome you both to the Society of Explorers and Adventurers."

"The West Coast branch, anyway," Oliver broke in.

"Yes," Priya agreed with an annoyed look at the speaker. "This isn't all of us," she continued, "but the rest of our members are in different parts of the world at the moment. Let me introduce you to the ones here. The man next to Oliver is Professor Roberto Carrero Rivas, our primary expert on Mesoamerican artifacts."

The man smiled at Shinji and bobbed his head, making his gold-rimmed glasses flash in the light. "You may call me Professor Carrero."

"Sitting beside you is our tech wiz, Zoe Kim," Priya went on, and the blue-haired girl winked at him. "You might've seen her drones flying around Abenge before all the craziness started."

Shinji jerked up. "Those were yours?"

"Yep!" Zoe grinned. "I love my drones; they let me be in places I'd never get to otherwise. By the way, good job in standing up to those Hightower goons. I saw those men following you through the market." She snorted. "Such a classic Hightower move: wave money in someone's face till they give in. And if that doesn't work, bully them until they get what they want." She gave him a friendly arm punch and another smile. "Props for sticking to your guns, kid. Not many people will stand up to Hightower like that."

"Thanks." Shinji blushed, pleased but trying not to show it. He could sense Lucy's unease beside him. She was remaining very still in her seat, as if afraid to draw attention to herself—to clue them in to the fact that she, too, was one of those greedy Hightower people. He wanted to turn and say something, let her know that it was going to be okay, but he didn't want to give SEA any reason to be suspicious.

"And finally," Priya went on, nodding to the other end of the table, "we have Maya Griffin. One of the best explorers, trackers, survivalists, wilderness experts, tomb finders, and all-around adventurers in the business. She has been to all corners of the world and has experienced more things than most people will see in several lifetimes."

"Hey," Oliver protested. "What am I, chopped liver? I've been all around the world as well. What can she do that I can't?"

"Make a halfway decent pot of coffee, for one" came a voice from the other end of the table.

Shinji followed the voice. The woman whom Priya had identified as Maya Griffin lounged in the last seat, one leg dangling over the armrest, turning a knife in both hands. A little flutter of awe went through him. She looked like a character in a video game, right down to the khaki shorts, the laced-up boots, and the leather belt sheath at her waist. Dozens of individual braids were pulled behind her head, and the tooth of some large predator hung from a leather cord at her neck. Her dark eyes gleamed as she met Shinji's gaze with a smirk.

"You came in with Oliver, huh?" she asked Shinji. "Good for you. I'm surprised our ex-pirate was able to get you here in one piece without losing you along the way."

"*One* time that happened," Oliver began, "and it's not my fault the guy didn't—"

"Thank you, Oliver," Priya interjected loudly, bringing the attention back to her again. "Now that we have introductions out of the way, I'm sure that Mr. Takahashi has questions. I will answer them as best I can, Shinji, but first let me tell you a little about us. About the Society of Explorers and Adventurers, our purpose, and our mission. We are a society dedicated not only to exploring the wonders of the world and the hidden places therein but to preserving and protecting what we find. You see, long ago, when the Society was first getting started, we had the unfortunate tendency to collect whatever we found. When an ancient tomb was uncovered or a lost relic unearthed, we would simply take whatever was there. Without permission. Without thinking of how our actions might affect the people and the civilizations the objects belonged to. In the past, this course of action got several of our members into trouble. One of our most influential members acquired an artifact called the Balinese music box, and his manor was nearly destroyed after the box was opened by his pet monkey, unleashing its magic. And of course, there is the tragic story of Harrison Hightower and the disaster that befell him that night so many years ago."

Shinji sat bolt upright in his seat, his eyes going huge. "Hightower?" he repeated.

"Yes." Priya nodded gravely. "Harrison Hightower the Third, founder of the Hightower Corporation, was once a prominent member of the Society. Like so many of us, he wanted to explore the world and all its hidden gems, but he also had an insatiable thirst for artifacts and relics of other cultures. If he could not buy what he wanted, he would resort to other methods. Including threats, bribery, and outright theft. He was also rich and arrogant, and thought money could get him whatever he desired. He scoffed at the idea of preservation, saying that artifacts were meant to be possessed and admired, not stuck in a forgotten tomb doing nothing.

"This desire would ultimately be his downfall," Priya went on. "In 1899, Harrison Hightower was on an expedition to Africa when he obtained a statue of the trickster god Shiriki Utundu. Or, I should say, he stole the sacred idol belonging to the Mtundu tribe and fled with his prize back to New York."

Shinji stole a furtive glance at Lucy, but she wasn't looking at him. Her gaze was drawn to the table in front of her, her lips tight and her body tense, as if bracing herself for what was coming next.

She knows this story, he realized. *Why didn't she tell me?*

"On New Year's Eve 1899," Priya continued, unaware of Shinji's realization, "Harrison Hightower threw a press conference and a party in his hotel to boast about his latest find. When one of the reporters asked if the rumors of a curse on the idol were true, Hightower laughed and had him thrown out. He didn't believe in curses and openly mocked anyone who did.

"Hightower decided to retire early to find a spot for the idol in his penthouse. It is said he was stopped at the elevators by his personal valet and warned to show the idol the proper respect. Hightower's response was to sneer and extinguish his cigar on Shiriki Utundu's head before heading into the elevator.

"That was the last time anyone saw him."

Shinji drew in a quick breath. "What happened?" he asked, hanging on every word in the story now.

"No one really knows," Priya said. "Witnesses reported seeing a green flash of light and hearing the echo of laughter at exactly midnight, just before the elevator in the Hightower Hotel plummeted from the top story to the very bottom of the shaft. A terrible tragedy, of course, but the strangest thing was, though he had entered the elevator and no one saw him leave, Harrison Hightower's body was never found. Rumors are, he still haunts his hotel, tormented by the very spirit he mocked in life."

Shinji felt a chill run from the bottom of his spine all the way up his back. Harrison Hightower had found a mysterious statue, just like he had done. If the curse of Shiriki Utundu had been real, the Coatl's Curse could be real as well.

"So," Priya concluded, "that is the story of our most

infamous member, and his strange and tragic end. It is the reason why we at the Society of Explorers and Adventurers have made it our mission to preserve the past and the wonders of ancient cultures, not exploit them. We are not innocent about the things we have done. Like Hightower, the Society is guilty of taking artifacts that don't belong to us. But we have realized our mistakes, and through the years, we have attempted to restore and return these artifacts to the places where they rightfully belong.

"Which brings us to you, Shinji Takahashi," Priya said. "A few days ago, the Society became aware that a certain idol had appeared in Abenge Market. We suspected Hightower would be looking for it as well, which was why we had Zoe monitoring the area. Unfortunately Hightower moved faster than we anticipated. They were already in Abenge when you stumbled upon the Coatl statue. I do apologize, Shinji. Maybe if we had acted sooner, you and your aunt would not have become embroiled in this mess."

Aunt Yui. Shinji jerked up. In all the talk of curses and magic and trickster gods, he had nearly forgotten why they were looking for SEA in the first place. Yeah, he wanted to get the tattoo off his arm and Hightower off his back, but first . . .

"I need to find my aunt," Shinji said, gazing up at Priya. "Please, will you help me? She was hurt fighting Hightower on our boat. I don't know what's happened to her, but I have to make sure she's all right."

"We've been looking for her, Shinji," Priya said softly, and Shinji's stomach dropped to his toes. "After what happened in Abenge, I sent Maya to track her down. She found the trawler, but there was no sign of your aunt anywhere. We've been searching, trying to contact Yui Takahashi ever since, but to be honest, it's as if she's vanished."

Shinji went numb. "Vanished?" he whispered.

"I am sorry," Priya told him. "I know that's not what you wanted to hear. But we will keep looking, I promise. We have people out there searching right now, and they won't give up until they find her."

"I want to help," Shinji announced. "She's my only family. What can I do?"

"We are doing everything we can," Priya assured him. "When we find her, you will be the first to know. What I need from you, Shinji, is for you to trust us."

Shinji slumped back. Aunt Yui was missing, and no one, not even the Society of Explorers and Adventurers, knew where she was. He didn't know what to believe, or whom to trust. Priya said they were doing everything they could to find her, but Gideon Frost had promised that as well, and he had lied. Could he really trust the Society any more than he could trust Hightower?

"Shinji, please, listen to us," Priya went on in a gentle voice. "I know this is distressing, but there is more. Your aunt is not the only one in danger. You see, the statue you found in Abenge did not belong in Africa. It originally came from the deep jungles of Mexico. And, like the idol of Shiriki Utundu, it was rumored to have a powerful curse attached to it."

"The Curse of the Coatl," Professor Carrero broke in, as if he could not contain himself any longer. He leaned forward, his eyes bright behind his spectacles. "My apologies; I have been studying idols and artifacts for many years now, and the legend of the Quetzalcoatl, or Coatl for short, is a particular favorite. Do you know anything about the Coatl, young Shinji?"

Shinji eyed him suspiciously, then shrugged. For now, he really didn't have any choice but to trust these people. Yes, he wanted to find his aunt, but there was also the problem of the tattoo on his arm and the curse that had come with it. "Not much," he replied. "Only that it's a big snake with wings."

"That it is," agreed Professor Carrero. "In fact, *Quetzalcoatl* in the Náhuatl language means 'feathered serpent.' Though the Aztecs didn't portray the creature with wings at all. Oh, forgive me," he continued at Shinji's confused frown. "I'm getting ahead of myself. Let me start from the beginning. Long ago, there was a civilization known as the Ximalli. It is said the Ximalli existed at the same time as the ancient Aztecs, and might even have shared a common ancestor, but because they were a secretive society, and because the Aztec empire was so large, not much is known about the Ximalli. We do know that they revered the

Coatl, the mighty winged serpent that was a sign of fertility, abundance, and riches. But there is a condition to the serpent's blessings in that you must work tirelessly for such things. The Coatl represents tenacity, not giving up until you achieve your goals. But it is also a protector, a guardian defending its territory from intruders and people who wish to exploit the natural world."

"Okay," Shinji said, suddenly remembering part of a dream where he stood at the top of a waterfall and gazed down into a jewel-green valley. "So what does that have to do with me?"

"Do you believe in magic, young Shinji? Real magic?"

Shinji blinked. Up until a few days ago, he would've said no. Magic shows and magicians were cool and all, but he knew they weren't real. In his travels aboard the *Good Tern*, he'd heard lots of stories. Stories of ghosts and monsters, of creatures lurking in the woods, strange lights in a swamp, a voice calling your name from the darkness. Normally he was skeptical about supernatural happenings. Not like Aunt Yui. She believed all the ghost stories, urban legends, and local superstitions, but Shinji tended to rely on what he saw or felt himself. But that was before the idol of a winged serpent somehow grafted itself onto his skin. That was before he'd seen a black hole hovering near a wall in a New York City office building. And it was before he found himself sitting in the middle of a secret society, talking about curses, magic, and mythological creatures. Now he didn't know what to believe.

"I . . . don't know," he told Carrero. "Maybe? I guess we're not talking flying carpets and pulling rabbits out of hats, are we?"

"Not exactly," said Carrero. He couldn't seem to stop his excitement now, gesturing with both hands as he spoke. "You see, young Shinji, there are certain places in the world where magic bubbles to the surface. It is unseen and invisible; you cannot see the magic, but you can feel it. We call these special places fonts, and everything touched by them takes on a little magic of its own. If you build on or near a font, strange and wonderful things can happen. In fact, one of the largest fonts in the world was discovered right here in Anaheim. We are not sure if the owner was aware of the presence of the font or not. But in 1955, a man named Walt Disney built his dream upon this magical font, and the rest, as they say, is history."

"Okay, but I still don't get what this has to do with me," Shinji said. "Or the Coatl tattoo."

"Typically," Professor Carrero answered, "these fonts of magic have powerful guardians protecting them. Mythical beasts and places of legend hidden from human eyes, defending the few remaining bits of magic in the world. I believe the Coatl is one of these guardians of a font, and that the idol—your tattoo, young Shinji—is the key to finding it.

Hightower knows this, too, and a font of magic, unclaimed and untouched, would be irresistible to them."

"Hightower would use the power of the font for themselves," Priya said. "That's why they wanted the idol so badly. That's why they are now after you."

"So how do I get them to stop?" Shinji asked. "I can't keep running from Hightower my whole life. I still need to find my aunt. And I have to get *this* thing off my arm before it kills me."

For the first time, Maya Griffin spoke up.

"Simple," she said, her voice low and confident. She tossed the knife she was holding into the air and caught it by the handle as it came down. "We do what the curse wants us to do: return the idol to the font. Once the idol is returned, the Coatl should be satisfied and the curse will fade."

"But I don't have the idol anymore," Shinji protested.

"You do, dear boy," said Professor Carrero. He pointed to Shinji's forearm, at the tattoo emblazoned across it. "It's right there. Typically these types of ancient curses are activated when someone takes something from a tomb or sacred site that does not belong to them. In this case, the statue of the Coatl. Once we get the bearer of the curse—in this case, you—back to where the artifact was stolen, the idol should materialize, and you can return it to its proper place."

"Hopefully before it kills you," Maya Griffin added, balancing her knife on two fingers. "And before Hightower uses you to reach the font themselves."

Priya gave the other woman a dark look before turning to Shinji again. "Yes," she agreed. "I'm afraid that is the same conclusion we have all reached. We cannot allow Hightower to find the font. They would only exploit its power for their own gain. Nor can we allow the curse to consume an innocent boy. Therefore the solution is obvious. We must find the font, return the idol, and free Shinji from its curse. Are there any questions?"

Yeah, Shinji thought. *I have questions. Why me? I wasn't looking for this magic font. I didn't ask for any of this. Why did I suddenly get stuck with an ancient curse?*

But he didn't want to sound ungrateful or whiny, especially when the Society was offering to help him remove the tattoo and find his aunt. Beside him, forgotten by everyone, Lucy stirred and raised her head.

"Um, I have a question," she said quietly. "Actually, it's more of a request. I would like to come along with Shinji and the rest of the expedition. I won't get in the way, but Hightower is after me, too. And I don't have anywhere else to go."

"I don't know about that, my dear," said Professor Carrero, frowning slightly. "Bad enough that we are going to be dragging one young person into danger. I don't like the idea of putting another child at risk."

"I'm not helpless," Lucy argued. "I know a lot about tinkering, and a little bit about magic, too. I wouldn't be a burden, and I know how to take care of myself."

"That's not the concern I have." Surprisingly, it was Oliver Ocean who spoke. He still lounged in the chair with his feet up on the table, but his fingers were steepled against his chin, and he was staring at Lucy with narrowed, appraising eyes. "I don't doubt this girl's abilities," he said, "but she did come from Hightower. I found her and Shinji on the run together, but what if Hightower planned this from the start? What if she's a spy sent to infiltrate our organization? It's not beneath Hightower to use kids to do their dirty work."

Lucy bristled. "I'm not—" she began. But before she could say anything, Shinji stood up.

"She comes," he said firmly. "End of story. I wouldn't have gotten out of Hightower if it weren't for her. She's not a spy." He glanced at Lucy and received a grateful smile before he glared at Oliver. "I'm not leaving her behind. If Lucy doesn't come with us, then I'm not going, either."

"Nice ultimatum, kid." Oliver smirked at him, undisturbed. "But I'm not the one with the cursed snake tattoo on my arm. Do you have a way of getting yourself across the continent to the Mexican rain forest? Or reaching the font on your own?"

Again, Shinji glared at the ex-pirate. "I'll find a way."

"Find a way right into Hightower's clutches, you mean."

"Oliver, enough." Priya's cool, unruffled voice broke through the tension. "Shinji, please sit down. I know you've been through a lot, and that this has come at you all at once. If you can vouch for your friend, that is good enough for me." She leveled a hard stare at Oliver, which only caused him to shrug and lean back with his hands behind his head. "The more important issue," she went on, "is how we are going to find the Coatl's font. There's not much information concerning the Ximalli, and we might not have a lot of time. I'm sure Hightower is searching for Shinji at this very moment."

"I think I can help with that," Maya said. She tossed the knife once more, caught it, and stuck it in her boot. "I have a contact in Mexico City," she went on. "He happens to be an expert on the ancient Ximalli culture. If anyone can point us in the right direction, he can."

"Perfect." Priya nodded. "Then let's get an expedition together quickly. Maya, you'll be at the head. Professor, I think we'll need your expertise on ancient relics and curses. If you're interested in joining."

"Of course!" Professor Carrero exclaimed. "What kind of 'explorer and adventurer' would I be if I were not? To see potentially undiscovered Ximalli ruins amid a tale of an ancient curse? It's the stuff we all dream about."

"Zoe." Priya looked at the blue-haired woman. "I unfortunately cannot come on this expedition, but I would still like to see what is going on once they reach the jungle. Can your drones track them, keep an eye on what they're doing from the sky?"

"Oh, sure!" Zoe nodded enthusiastically. "Yeah, there's no way I'm missing this."

Oliver Ocean gave a loud yawn and stretched, dropping his boots from the table with a thud. "Well, you've convinced me," he declared as they all stared at him. "I was going to sail down to the Keys this weekend, but I think I'll tag along with the expedition. It's been a while since I visited Mexico City. I wonder if Rosa is still working at La Clandestina. . . ."

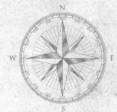

CHAPTER ELEVEN

The Society of Explorers and Adventurers didn't waste any time. Once they determined who was going on the expedition, Priya announced that they would depart for Mexico City the next day at dawn. That sent everyone in the room scurrying off in different directions to prepare for the trip, leaving Shinji and Lucy alone with Priya.

"Let me show you where you can stay," Priya told them as the bustle from the other adventurers finally died down. "This way, if you would."

On the couch, Kali immediately hopped down and padded across the room, passing right next to Shinji. He was tempted to reach out and pet her; the predator's shaggy black pelt looked very soft, and he had never been this close to a real bear. But then he remembered the huge teeth from when she had tackled Oliver and thought maybe he shouldn't press his luck. She could probably tear his head off without even trying.

With Kali lumbering ahead, Priya led them down red-and-gold-carpeted hallways, heading deeper into SEA's headquarters. Pictures of strangers in exotic locations lined the walls: A man in a safari helmet posed before a waterfall, an orangutan reaching for his camera. A woman stood at the top of a snow-covered peak, gazing down at the clouds far below. Strange items hung on the walls or sat in alcoves between pictures. Wooden masks, carved figurines, clay pottery, necklaces strung with beads or turquoise or bones.

Priya must have caught him looking, for she gave him a faint smile. "Many of these were gifts," she told him, nodding to a long-handled pipe resting on a stool. "Today, more than ever, we try to be conscientious about whose land we are visiting. That wasn't always the case," she continued, a slight frown crossing her features, "but we're trying to correct the mistakes of our past. There are still hidden wonders and undiscovered places in the world. We have to make sure they'll be there for future explorers to discover."

She stopped at a door that said GUEST QUARTERS in gold letters above the frame. Pushing it back revealed a cozy room with a couch, a small kitchenette, and a flat-screen TV above a stone fireplace. More maps, pictures, and odd paraphernalia covered the walls, and a spiraling wooden staircase led up to a balcony that overlooked the chamber.

Shinji gazed around curiously. He'd never been in a place like this; the tiny huts and cheap hotels he'd stayed in with Yui didn't even come close. A large map on the wall caught his eye; it looked like something a pirate would use, hand drawn, with pictures of sea serpents and tentacled monsters in the corners. As he stared at it, he was almost certain he saw some of the creatures move. Below the map, a narrow shelf held a scattering of gold coins, a music box, and a small silver compass. Shinji picked it up to look at it more closely, wondering if it did anything weird or special. But it seemed like an ordinary compass.

"The guest rooms are up the stairs," Priya told them as Shinji reluctantly put the compass back on the shelf. "Dinner will be in the main dining room tonight, and you're welcome to join us," she went on. "Otherwise, someone will be here to collect you both tomorrow at dawn. That will be five a.m., for those who wish to set an alarm." She smiled at Shinji's grimace, then drew back and half closed the door. "Rest up, and I will see you soon."

The door closed, and Shinji and Lucy were left alone. For a few seconds, an awkward silence filled the room. Then Lucy gave Shinji a faint smile.

"Thanks," she said quietly.

Shinji frowned. "For what?"

"For standing up for me. For saying I had to come, too."

Lucy fiddled with the end of her braid. "I thought once they knew I was from Hightower, they would just toss me out or send me back. But I get to come along after all, so . . . thanks again."

"No problem." Shinji gave a careless shrug, but a tiny, ugly doubt nagged the back of his mind. A dark *what if* haunting his thoughts. What if Lucy *was* a spy? What if Tinker had been in her pocket, recording everything they had said? All she had to do was send one message to Hightower and the mission would be over before it even got started.

"But look at this, Shinji." Lucy turned, craning her head as she stared at the room around her. "We're in the middle of SEA headquarters, one of the most secretive, mysterious societies in the world. How many people have stood where we're standing right now? How many people even know this is here?"

Shinji flopped down on the plush sofa before the fire-place. "As long as they can help me get rid of this curse so I can go home," he muttered. "And find Aunt Yui so I have a home to go back to." He sighed, leaning back against the cool cushions. Everything suddenly felt very surreal. A few days ago, his life was normal, and now it was very . . . not.

Why me? he wondered again. *I'm not that special. The statue could've attached itself to anyone. Why did it pick me?*

"Don't forget Hightower," Lucy said. "We don't want them to get the statue, either. Or the font."

"Yeah," Shinji muttered, and snorted. "You'd think that after what happened to that one guy with the idol, Hightower wouldn't want anything to do with cursed statues."

"Well, that's the problem with Hightower," Lucy said. "They're greedy. If they see something they want, they just take it. No matter the consequences or how many people are hurt because of it."

Shinji frowned and sat up, remembering something that had happened during the meeting. "You knew that story," he accused. "About Harrison Hightower and the idol. You'd heard it before."

Lucy's smile was grim. "Everyone in Hightower knows that story," she said. "To them, Harrison Hightower's disappearance is not a warning or a threat. It's just proof that great magic—great power—exists in the world. And if they can learn to harness it, they would be unstoppable."

Shinji was getting a headache. His brain spun, still trying to process all the information he had just received. Magic, curses, idols, and secret organizations. It was a lot to take in. "I still can't believe magic really exists," he said. "And that there are these spots just lying around, spitting it out. Why doesn't everyone know about it?"

"Think about it, Shinji." Lucy put Tinker on the back of the couch, where he scampered up and down the cushions with happy squeaking sounds. "If everyone knew about magic, everyone would want it. Say you were a fisherman, and you knew of a super-secret pond that always had the best fish. Would you share that knowledge? Would you want other people to know about it?"

"Why not? It's always better to share, right?"

"Not according to Hightower." Lucy gestured to an imaginary lake stretched out before them. "What if you told other people about this special pond, and they told all their friends, who told all *their* friends? What if they all came and caught better fish than you? Those fish could have been yours if you hadn't said anything. And then, what if they fished the lake dry, so that there was no fish left for anyone else?"

"These must be super-special fish. Do they make you fart rainbows or something?"

"I'm just saying." Lucy shrugged. "That's how Hightower thinks. The greedy don't want other people to have what they have. And for the people who *are* aware of it, they don't want the greedy to come and take it away. So the fonts stay hidden. Probably better that way."

"I guess."

"Besides," Lucy went on, sitting down on the other end of the couch with him. "It's not like you can use the magic to shoot fireballs or make yourself fly. That's not how it works."

"Really?" Shinji slouched against the armrest, which was quite comfortable. He was suddenly very tired. The shock, stress, and confusion of the past few days were hitting him all at once. "How does magic work, then? If you can't use it to shoot lightning from your fingers, then what's the point?"

Lucy rolled her eyes. "The point," she told him, "is that the magic affects the world around it in subtle ways. Maybe a long time ago there were those who could use the magic for flashy stuff, but most people have lost their affinity for it. There are those who *can* manipulate the magic in small ways, but they're few and far between." She sounded sad for a moment, then shook her head. "Anyway, you can't just march up to a font, stuff some magic into a water bottle, and walk off with it. It's not a physical thing. But if you build something on or around the font, the magic affects it. People get stronger or happier. Plants never die. And businesses prosper."

She fiddled with the end of her braid and chewed her lip, as if debating with herself whether or not to say something. Finally, she shrugged. "That's the secret of Hightower's wealth," she admitted. "It's how they got so powerful so fast. A long time ago, Hightower discovered a font and built a hotel on it. The organization has been reaping the benefits of the magic ever since."

"How do you know all this?" Shinji asked, trying to sit up again. It was hard. The cushions were soft, and his eyes felt full of sand. "I mean, no offense, but you're just a kid, like me. Why would Hightower tell you all these crazy company secrets?"

"Because," Lucy said, and sighed, "I . . . am one of those people who can manipulate the magic."

Shinji's eyes widened. Suddenly he was no longer sleepy. "You can use magic? You never told me that."

"What do you think Tinker is?" Lucy went on. She held out her arm, and the tiny mechanical mouse scurried up to perch in her palm. "He's not just a super-intelligent robot; it actually took a little bit of magic to bring him to life. That's my talent, I guess. I can blend science and magic together in small ways. Like inventing useless gadgets or cute mechanical pets. Nothing big or earthshaking."

"Can you show me?"

She gave him an almost disdainful look, then sighed, gazing around the room. "I thought I sensed a couple of magical artifacts in here," she murmured. "The map has a very old magic clinging to it, but it's not tech, so I don't think I can do anything with it. Hang on." She closed her eyes, as if listening for something Shinji couldn't hear. Or sensing something he couldn't feel. "There *is* something, and it's close."

"The compass?" Shinji suggested quietly, not wanting to break her concentration. But Lucy shook her head and opened her eyes.

"The music box," she said, glancing toward the shelf. "It's old, but I can sense the magic inside. Go get the music box and bring it to me."

Shinji complied, walking to the shelf and grabbing the

music box from where it sat next to the compass. It didn't look like any music box he'd seen before. For one thing, it was cylindrical instead of square, fitting easily in the palm of his hand. The polished outer shell was made of copper and brass, with intricate designs woven throughout. A tiny golden windup key stuck out of the side.

Shinji returned with the box and handed it to Lucy, who studied it in silence for a few seconds. "So," he ventured as she turned the box over in her hands, "how does this work, exactly? I've never seen anyone do real magic before."

Lucy ran her fingers over the top of the music box. "I have to have a source of magic," she explained. "I can't pull it from the air or conjure it from nothing. The Hightower building we escaped from sits on a font. It's a small one, but it's enough magic for me to tap into for my creations." She held up the box, causing it to glimmer in the dim light. "Artifacts like this one were created using a source, so they have a bit of that magic inside them, like Tinker. This is pretty old, but if I concentrate, I might be able to . . ."

She trailed off, closing her eyes. Shinji held his breath, watching the box in her hand. For a few moments, nothing happened. Neither Lucy nor the box moved, and nothing could be heard except the ticking of a cuckoo clock on the wall.

Shinji had just started to fidget when there was a click and the windup key on the side started to turn on its own. He blinked, watching it rotate once, twice, and then the lid on the music box opened. A faint, tinkling melody filled the air as a tiny porcelain ballerina rose up, arms over her head as she spun with the music.

Okay, Shinji thought. *That's pretty cool, I guess. But making a music box play on its own isn't really that—*

He froze, as the ballerina suddenly turned her head and smiled at him. Stepping off her pedestal, the porcelain figurine twirled once, then with a graceful hop, she started dancing around the edge of the platform.

Shinji's mouth dropped open. The ballerina moved like a real person, dancing and twirling elegantly around the stage. Shinji couldn't look away, fighting a very real urge to reach out and poke the dancer with a finger. He continued to watch, entranced, until the song came to an end. The ballerina smiled up at Shinji and dropped into a deep curtsy as the lid of the music box closed, hiding her from sight.

Lucy let out a breath and slumped back against the cushions. "Sorry," she panted, lowering her arm. Her face was pale, and her forehead was slightly sweaty. She dabbed it with the back of her sleeve. "Manipulating any magic, even for short periods, takes a lot out of me. I can only do it for a little while."

"That was awesome," Shinji breathed. Reaching for the music box, he flipped open the lid, only to find the ballerina was a lifeless porcelain figure once more. Feeling slightly dazed, he returned the music box to the shelf. Real magic.

It actually existed, and Lucy could do incredible things with it. Shinji felt like his head would explode with everything he'd learned today.

"So what else can you do?" Shinji wondered, walking back to the couch. Lucy was playing with Tinker, as if to assure the robot mouse that he was still first in her affections. "If the Hightower building sits on a magic font, you must be able to invent all kinds of cool stuff."

"That's what Hightower would like us to believe." Lucy withdrew her arm, letting Tinker climb onto her shoulder. "I've learned that the magic, whatever it's used for, is always subtle. But Hightower wants more. They want me to invent these grand, complicated things that will benefit the company, and I haven't been able to do it." She slumped farther into the cushions, a bitter smile crossing her face. "So far, I guess I'm a disappointment."

"Hey," Shinji said, suddenly angry at Hightower again. "Are you kidding? Tinker is freaking amazing. We would never have gotten out of Hightower without him. Besides, I don't know anyone else who can do real magic, and I've been lots of places. If the Hightower people can't see that, then that's their loss."

Lucy smiled and looked away, her ears going slightly red. "I'm kind of tired," she announced, rising from the couch. "I think I'll go upstairs to check out my room. Do you care which one I take?"

Shinji shook his head. "Nope, I'm gonna stay right here for a while," he said, relaxing against the armrest. "Not moving anywhere right now sounds like a great idea."

Lucy nodded, then turned and walked up the stairs to the balcony. Shinji settled back against the couch and tried to relax, but it was hard. His mind spun with everything he'd seen and heard tonight. Magic and curses and fonts and ancient temples; it was a lot to process. Eventually, though, exhaustion finally caught up to him, and he dropped into a restless sleep.

He was standing on the vine-covered steps of an ancient temple, gazing up at the soaring wall of stone and rock. Overhead, the jungle canopy shut out the sun, with only a few thin streams of light creeping down to mottle the floor. Birds shrieked in the trees, and monkeys howled in the branches, adding to the ruckus.

He made his way up the crumbling steps, feeling the eyes of the jungle upon him. His wrist and forearm throbbed, as if there were a pulsing flame trapped beneath his skin. At the top of the stairs, he could see the entrance to the temple, a pair of thick stone doors that looked like they hadn't moved in a thousand years. He could see the image carved into the middle of the doors, a familiar coiled serpent with wings outstretched, staring right at him.

Beware the Weaver, something hissed in his head.

He reached the top step. The burning in his arm was growing hotter, and the eyes of the carving were glowing with intense green light. He could feel something on the other side of the stone, calling him without words. He reached for the door, stretching his hand toward the image of the winged snake. But as he did, it vanished, dissolving in the air like mist in the sun. He was left staring at a blank wall, though the burning in his arm did not fade.

"Shinji," a familiar voice whispered behind him.

Shinji turned. Aunt Yui stood at the bottom of the steps, gazing up with a dazed look on her face. His heart jumped, and he started down the stairs toward her, but her body suddenly jerked like it was attached to strings. He saw wispy white ropes stuck to her arms and back just as she was yanked up into the trees, and vanished into the branches overhead.

Heart pounding, he raced the rest of the way down the steps, peering into the canopy for any trace of his aunt. He called her name, but only the monkeys and birds answered him.

And then something dropped from the branches, jerking to a halt a few feet away. Shinji stared at it in horror. It was Tom, the security guard who had chased him and Lucy through the Hightower building that night. The guard dangled a few inches from the ground, covered in the same wispy white ropes that made him look like a giant marionette. He swayed there a moment, motionless, his chin resting on his chest. Shinji wondered if he should help him but then saw something that made his blood run cold.

A shiny black-and-yellow spider, its legs as thin as needles, crawled onto the man's shoulder and sat there a moment, staring at him. Then, lightning quick, it darted up the guard's neck and scuttled beneath his hat, vanishing from sight.

Tom stirred and raised his head. His eyes, glassy and empty of reason, blinked once, then fixed on Shinji. His mouth opened, and a voice emerged that wasn't Tom's voice. It was high and breathy and filled with anger.

Give me the heart, it hissed. *Return what is rightfully mine. Restore what your kind stole from me, or I will make everything you hold dear vanish right before your eyes.*

More bodies dropped from the branches, bouncing to a halt before they hit the ground. All held up by those sticky white threads. He saw Priya and Kali dangling motionless in the air. He saw Oliver Ocean and Professor Carrero bound together in one cocoon. And hanging by herself a few feet behind them was Lucy, eyes closed, swaying gently in the breeze.

Shinji was frozen with horror. He wanted to run, but his feet wouldn't listen to him. *You cannot escape me,* the voice hissed through Tom's mouth. *I am the weaver of fate, the one who has controlled your destiny from the beginning. You will find the fountain and give me the heart, or I will cut the threads of your existence from the world!*

Above him, the branches rattled, hundreds of leaves rustling all at once. He looked up to see hundreds of spiders dropping from the trees on silken threads. Now he tried to run but found he couldn't move. White ropes had wrapped around his wrists and ankles, holding him in place like a puppet.

As he was slowly pulled into the air, struggling like a fly caught in a web, the sibilant voice chuckled in his ear. *Fight me all you want, little fly. I have woven your fate, and you will give me what I need. It is only a matter of time.*

A spider crawled onto his forehead, black mandible waving, and Shinji screamed.

"Shinji! Hey, wake up!"

Shinji jerked awake with a gasp. Above him, Lucy took a step back, her eyes wide with alarm. Gasping, Shinji gazed around, trying to remember what had happened. The room was dim, the only light coming from a chicken-footed lamp in the corner.

"Shinji, it's me," Lucy said, taking a step forward. Tinker peered out of her pocket, wire-thin whiskers and ears catching the lamplight. "Calm down, you were dreaming."

Shinji relaxed, finally remembering. He was still in the headquarters of the Society of Explorers and Adventurers. He had fallen asleep on the couch and, according to the clock on the wall, had slept through the evening and into the next day. It was nearly five in the morning.

"I thought I would wake you before Priya got here," Lucy told him softly. "Last night, she came to take us to dinner, but you were completely out, and she didn't want to disturb you. I grabbed you some leftovers; they're in the fridge if you want them."

Shinji's heart continued to race. He could still see his aunt dangling in the air before being pulled out of his reach. The spiders everywhere. His hands shook, and he took a deep breath to calm down.

"Shinji?" Lucy cocked her head at him, her expression concerned. "You okay?"

"Yeah," he rasped out. "It was just a dream."

"Shinji? Lucy?"

There was a soft tap on the door before it clicked open to reveal Priya standing in the frame with Kali beside her. The bear's blocky muzzle wrinkled as she sniffed the air, as if sensing the remnants of Shinji's dream. Tinker, peeking out from Lucy's pocket, instantly darted back and vanished.

"Are you two almost ready? Everyone is waiting."

A few minutes later, they followed Priya into a smaller but no less elegant room, where maps and more strange paraphernalia were scattered about. A battered ship wheel hung on the far wall; the brass plate below it read: THE M.S. SALTY IV. A yellowed newspaper—the *Daily Gnus*—sat behind a glass case, the headline proclaiming the famed explorer Dr. Albert Falls still missing. Another case held an enormous curved talon, longer than Shinji's hand. At first, he thought it was a dinosaur claw, until he looked closer and saw that the plaque below it read EUROPEAN DRAGON TALON, SOUTH WALES. 1862.

The four members of the Society were crowded around a table, talking with one another in low but excited tones. A map lay spread across the surface, held down by two donut boxes and several full coffee cups. Save for Zoe, all of the Society members were dressed for travel. Oliver Ocean still wore his long coat, but Professor Carrero was dressed in khaki shorts, boots, and a round safari hat. Across the table, Maya wore a similar outfit, but unlike the professor, who looked like he was ready for a Halloween party, it looked perfectly natural on her.

"Hey there, Shinji. Lucy." Oliver grinned at them around half a powdered donut. "We took the liberty of raiding the Discovery Trading Company last night," he told them. "Those two backpacks over there are yours. They should have everything you need for a trek into the jungle." He gave a wink. "Just go easy on the monkey repellent. Pretty potent stuff. Not only will it keep monkeys away, it'll keep your party members away as well."

Shinji picked up the backpack, which was different from

the normal canvas backpacks he'd taken to school. This was more like a hiking pack, with lots of pouches, zippers, and places to store things. It was heavy, but not unbearable, and he slid it over his shoulders easily.

A soft, high-pitched squeal made him look back. Lucy was standing next to Zoe Kim, Tinker perched on her palm as she held it up. Zoe had both hands in front of her mouth and was grinning at the robot mouse in utter delight.

"Ah, he's adorable!" she squeaked. "And so intricately designed. May I?"

She held out her hand, and Tinker hopped into her palm. "Oh man, he weighs practically nothing," Zoe crooned as the mechanical mouse sat up on his haunches, twitching his copper ears at her. "I'm gonna have to pick your brain later; I'd love for my drones to be a little lighter."

"What alloys do you use for the frames?" Lucy asked, and Zoe launched into an explanation that made absolutely no sense to Shinji. Oliver saw where he was looking and rolled his eyes.

"You should've seen them last night at dinner," he told Shinji in a low voice. "Like two peas in a pod. Once Zoe gets talking about tech and wires and fancy gizmos, there's no stopping her. Makes my eyes glaze over. I'm glad she found a fellow geek, even if it is someone from Hightower."

Shinji's heart lurched, and he looked up sharply. Oliver gave a lazy shrug. "I'm not an idiot, kid," he said easily. "I've been around, and your friend doesn't exactly scream *normal upbringing.* I knew she was from Hightower the second I saw her."

Shinji swallowed. "Then why let her come?" he asked.

"Better the enemy you can see than the one you can't," the ex-pirate replied, and held up a hand as Shinji started to protest. "I'm not saying she *is* an enemy," he said quickly. "I'm being cautious, that's all. Frankly, I don't see how *you* can be so certain. I know you're a smart kid, and from what I've heard, you've been around a bit as well. You know how the world can be." He glanced to where Lucy and Zoe were still deep in conversation, their heads nearly touching as they cooed over Tinker. "Just be sure your desire to have a friend isn't keeping you from the truth," he warned. "Now, if you'll excuse me, I need at least three cups of coffee in my system before the start of any excursion, and so far I've only had two. My caffeine levels are not where they should be."

Oliver walked away, leaving Shinji struggling with doubt. *Was* he being stupid? Oliver was right: people could be shady and dishonest and untrustworthy. He'd seen it over and over again in his travels with Aunt Yui. In fact, she often depended on Shinji to let her know when something seemed off, when a deal was too good to be true. Aunt Yui was good-hearted and tended to take everything at face value. Shinji, as she'd told him herself, was a cynical smart aleck who always saw the glass half-empty.

Shinji set his jaw. Lucy was his friend. She'd gotten him out of Hightower and all the way across the country to find

SEA. She couldn't be a Hightower agent. He was going to believe that until she proved him wrong.

"The car is here," Maya announced, looking at her phone. "And Scarlett is waiting for us at the airport." She gave them a serious look that was all business. "Let's get this adventure started."

They drove to the airport, cruising past the crowded lots and main terminal to a lonely trio of hangars on the far side. A single plane, tiny and red, waited for them as they piled out of the car. Lucy took one look at it and blanched.

"We're flying to Mexico in *that*?"

"You say that like you don't think he's safe." A woman strode around the front of the plane toward them, smiling. She wore a leather jacket, gloves, and a pair of flight goggles atop the brightest red hair Shinji had ever seen.

"Scarlett!" Oliver stepped forward. "You haven't changed much. Still chugging along in that rust bucket you call a plane? I would've thought the wings would have fallen off by now."

"Careful, Oliver." The woman gave him an evil smile. "If you hurt his feelings, he might act up out of spite." Shinji smirked, thinking she must be kidding, but when Oliver didn't laugh, his grin faded. After everything he'd seen, maybe the plane *did* have a mind of its own.

The red-haired woman glanced at Shinji and Lucy and brightened. "Are these our new adventurers, then?" she asked. "I swear, they get younger every year."

Professor Carrero cleared his throat. "If you'll allow me, Miss Blauerhimmel," he said. "Shinji, Lucy, this is Scarlett J. Blauerhimmel, an *excellent* pilot and a member of the Society of Explorers and Adventurers."

"*Rhett* and I have been all over the world," the woman told Lucy, jerking a thumb at the plane behind her. "He may be old, but he's more reliable than any of those fancy little jet planes zipping about. Don't worry, you'll be perfectly safe with Scarlett J. Blauerhimmel. We've only almost crashed twice in the last five years."

Oliver winced. "Weirdly enough, that does not inspire a lot of confidence," he muttered as the woman turned away. Shinji gave him a puzzled look.

"Are you afraid of flying?" he asked the ex-pirate.

"Flying? No." Oliver looked a bit pale as they made their way toward the little red plane. "*Falling*, yes. Falling and crashing. In a plane that is basically put together with duct tape and rust. Ships never have this problem."

"Don't ships sink?" Lucy asked.

"Exactly," Oliver said. "They sink. They don't plummet from the sky in a blaze of fire and smoke, and all you can do is cling to your seat belt and wish you'd brought that extra parachute lying on your bathroom floor."

"Here we are!" Scarlett announced cheerfully, wrenching

open the back door of the plane with a grinding squeak. Inside was a tiny area barely big enough for five people, with seats welded to the walls and a metal floor covered in rust. Oliver groaned and ran a hand down his face.

"Scarlett, I love you. You know I do. So please don't take offense when I say I wish this thing would come to life and fly itself into the side of a mountain. Without you in it, of course."

"Shh." Scarlett reached out and patted the side of the plane. A few bits of rust flaked off and drifted to the ground. "Don't listen to him, *Rhett* baby. He doesn't mean it."

The plane creaked as they all crowded inside, taking their seats along the wall. Lucy paused a moment to pull a towel out of her backpack and drape it across the seat before she gingerly sat down. As Shinji fastened his seat belt, pulling it tight across his lap, he noticed a parachute hanging on the wall across from him. Only one parachute. Oliver caught where he was looking and grimaced.

"Sorry, kiddo. But if we go down, you're gonna have to fight me for it."

"Everybody ready?" Scarlett called back from the pilot seat. The plane coughed once and shuddered to life. "On to Mexico City! Great choice, by the way. Dancing, food, nightlife, everything you could want in one place."

"This isn't a vacation, my dear," said Professor Carrero. "We are on the trail of a hidden font that has a nasty curse tied to it. There is no time for sightseeing. The life of this young man could be at stake."

"I'm just saying. There are worse places in the world to visit." Scarlett flipped a few switches, then pushed a lever slowly forward. "All right, here we go. No one think heavy thoughts. I'm just kidding! Next stop, Mexico City."

Oliver sighed and scrubbed a hand over his eyes. "This is going to be a long flight."

CHAPTER TWELVE

It wasn't a very long flight, but it *was* a bumpy one.

At times, Shinji felt he was on a roller coaster. A really noisy, shaky roller coaster. The whine of the engine was so loud, it was impossible to talk to someone without yelling. And the plane jerked, swooped, dropped, and bounced its way through the air, making him grip his armrest until his knuckles turned white. Beside him, Lucy's jaw was set, and Professor Carrero had his eyes closed for most of the trip. Oliver's face had taken on a sickly green tinge, and Shinji hoped he wouldn't hurl his powdered donuts all over his shoes.

The plane suddenly dropped several feet in the air, and

Lucy let out a squeak, closing her eyes. Shinji wondered if she had ever been in an airplane before. While he and Aunt Yui often traveled by boat, sometimes they had to fly places as well. Shinji had never been on a plane quite like this one, but he had flown enough not to be bothered by it. Usually.

The plane shuddered again, and Lucy pressed her lips tightly together, looking like she would rather be anywhere else than here. Remembering something his aunt told him once, Shinji leaned close to be heard over the drone of the engines. "It'll be okay," he told her. "Aunt Yui told me planes don't just fall out of the air. Even if one of their engines dies, they can still land safely."

"I am sure that's true for normal planes," Lucy said through gritted teeth. "But I don't have a lot of confidence that this one meets the standard safety regulations."

Shinji couldn't really argue with that. "Well, if the worst does happen," he said, "I'll be sure to throw you the parachute before Oliver can steal it."

"That is terrifying, but I appreciate the thought."

After a harrowing touchdown that jolted Shinji's whole body and clacked his teeth together, the plane finally came to a shuddering halt at the end of a lonely runway. The groan of relief that went through the cabin when the engine clicked off was audible.

"Never again." Oliver was the first one out of the plane, closing his eyes and taking a deep breath when he hit the ground. "That's what I keep telling myself every time, and yet every time, I keep getting on that flying death trap. Why do I do this to myself?"

Maya smirked at him as she climbed out of the plane. "Aren't you a part of the Society of Explorers and *Adventurers*?" she challenged. "Your sense of adventure seems to be lacking today."

"Hey, I've sailed all the seas, played hide-and-seek with sharks, been dropped into the ocean while tied to an anchor, and been chased through the Amazon rain forest by people with spears. I have a very healthy sense of adventure . . . on the ground."

"You kids have fun now!" Scarlett called, lifting an arm as they made their way across the runway. "*Rhett* and I will be waiting when you need us."

"Can't wait," Shinji muttered, earning an appreciative snort from Oliver. Suddenly the thought of sailing back to the United States in a nice, steady barge seemed very agreeable. He would never complain about the *Good Tern*'s speed again.

"So where did you say your contact was meeting us, my dear Maya?" Professor Carrero asked, lengthening his stride to keep up with her. "Dr. Ramos Rojas was his name, I believe? I think I've heard of him before. He's not part of the Society, is he?"

"No." Maya shook her head. "Dr. Ramos doesn't get out much anymore. You'll see when we get there. About a year ago, I was his guide while we were searching for a lost temple in Yucatán. There was . . . an incident, and now he refuses to dig around old ruins in the middle of the jungle. But he is an expert on the ancient Ximalli and their civilization, culture, and practices. If we're going to find this font, we need to understand the curse that is tied to it. The Coatl and the kid are obviously the keys to tracking it down. Dr. Ramos might be able to point us in the right direction."

A few minutes later, Shinji was sitting in the back of a taxi, staring out the window at the amazing sights of Mexico City: the bustling crowds, milling people, and streets full of traffic. They passed an enormous building that looked like a palace, with white marble walls and a golden domed roof. Peering up at its impressive walls, Lucy sighed.

"I wish I had my camera," she murmured. "I know we're not on vacation, but I've never been to a place like this. My dad was always too busy to take me anywhere."

The longing and bitterness in her voice was audible. Shinji thought back to his travels with Aunt Yui, of visiting small towns and villages, of sailing down a river to spots all over the world. His throat felt tight. Suddenly he wished he could be with her right now, on the *Good Tern*. He wondered where she was and if he would ever see her again.

At last, the taxi turned into a parking lot and pulled to a stop in front of a massive white building, an enormous flag of Mexico fluttering beside the entrance. Shinji peered out the window and saw a fountain with a blocky stone statue sitting in the center. Below it were the words MUSEO NACIONAL DE ANTROPOLOGÍA.

"The National Museum of Anthropology," Lucy read, peering over his shoulder. Shinji blinked at her.

"You know Spanish?"

"A bit. Enough to understand if someone talks slowly." Lucy shrugged. "I also know French, German, and a tiny amount of Italian. My dad . . . insisted I learn."

"Really?" Shinji asked. He knew a little Japanese, mostly from his grandmother before she died. Kasumi Takahashi insisted he greet her in her native language and seemed disappointed in Yui for not making him speak Japanese one hundred percent of the time. She was also the reason Shinji had a traditional Japanese name and not something like Rick or David. He couldn't imagine having to learn three different languages at once. "Wait, so you had your workshop *and* you had to learn all that? What about school and homework and stuff?"

She looked out the window, suddenly evasive. "I've never gone to school," she muttered. "I've had private tutors my whole life."

"Oh." Well, that made sense, though it did widen the status gulf between them a little more. Shinji and Aunt Yui had never been poor, exactly, but they'd never had the wealth Lucy's family must have possessed. "Say something in French, then," he challenged.

"*Tú es un idiot,*" Lucy replied in a flat voice, and got out of the car without bothering to translate what she'd said.

Shinji was pretty sure he knew what it meant.

The National Museum of Anthropology was enormous and sprawling. Following Maya through the glass doors, they passed exhibits of stone carvings, statues, paintings, and murals, some of which were really cool, though Maya gave them no time to pause and look around. They trailed her across an outdoor area where a fountain sprayed water into a pond, through even more buildings and exhibits, and down a series of winding hallways, before she finally stopped at a simple wooden door.

"This is Dr. Ramos's office," she said in what sounded like a warning. "He can be a little eccentric, so be prepared. He hasn't really been himself since . . . well, I'm sure he'll tell you all about it." And she pushed open the door.

The room beyond smelled like dust. Shinji coughed, seeing streams of sunlight filtered through the blinds behind the desk. Books lay everywhere—stacked on the floor, on the desk, crowding the huge bookcases around the room. Statues, masks, and other artifacts were scattered here and there among book debris, but these items had been hung carefully on the wall or placed in a box instead of being carelessly strewn about. A framed picture over the desk caught his eye, the painting of a strange, terrible beast with a wolf body, a ratlike head, and a clawed appendage that looked like a hand on the end of a long, skinny tail. It didn't look like any animal Shinji had ever seen.

A thin man with dark, frizzy hair and a thin mustache peered up from behind a huge book, his eyes widening as the visitors came in. When they saw Shinji, they widened even more.

"Cursed!" he cried, slamming the tome shut in a billowing explosion of dust. Shinji and everyone except Maya jumped. "You are the cursed one. I can see it on your face. I can see it in your eyes. You cannot hide it from me, I know you have been cursed!"

Maya sighed. "Shinji," she said, sounding faintly exasperated and apologetic at the same time, "everyone, this is Dr. Gabriel Ramos Rojas, one of the premier experts on Ximalli culture and society. And, Dr. Ramos, you know about the curse because we discussed it on the phone. This morning."

"Irrelevant." The thin man waved his hand like he was shooing away a fly. "I would've known he was cursed the moment he stepped through my door. I can smell it now, you know." He tapped the side of his nose. "Only a person who has already been cursed can sense it in another."

Shinji drew in a sharp breath. "You've been cursed, too?" he asked.

"Oh, yes!" Dr. Ramos shuffled around his desk, knocking over a stack of books as he did. Oliver managed to catch one before it tumbled to the floor. "A most terrible curse, in fact. Do you want to know what happened? Of course you do." He snatched the book from Oliver's grasp and plunked it back on the desk. "My expedition and I were exploring the lost temple of Tezozomoc," he began in a dramatic voice. "There were warnings, of course, rumors that it was cursed. But we were not afraid. I was in an underground hall when the ground suddenly gave way beneath me. I fell, and I think I struck my head, for I don't remember much after that. When I woke up, I was surrounded by skulls, hundreds of them, all staring at me with their empty eye sockets." Dr. Ramos's voice trembled, his eyes going wide as if he were seeing the skulls in front of him once more. "I heard voices in my head, telling me I was doomed, that I had angered the gods. I fled, of course. Somehow, I found my way outside and returned home to Mexico City. But it was too late; I knew I had been inflicted with a terrible curse."

"What kind of curse?" Shinji wondered.

"A terrible one!" Dr. Ramos insisted. His eyes darted to the corners of the room, as if he expected things to leap out at him. "Even now, I'm waiting for it to manifest," he admitted in a hushed voice. "Sometimes I don't want to cross the street or even leave my house. What if a bus runs me over? What if a lion escapes from the zoo and attacks me? I've become paranoid about the curse's retribution, but at the same time, the waiting is driving me insane."

Shinji furrowed his brow. Leaning against one of the bookshelves, Oliver rolled his eyes. "Are you sure it was a curse?" Shinji wondered. "It just sounds like you had a bad experience in the ruins, and now you're scared to go back."

"Excuse me?" The doctor's mustache bristled. "And what do you know of curses and Mesoamerican ruins, boy?" he demanded. "Have you studied the history of Tlaxtcha? Can you tell me all the phases of the Ximalli calendar and how they relate to the sun and moon? I bet you cannot even give me the names of the three city-states that made up the Triple Alliance."

"Calm down, my dear sir, calm down." Professor Carrero stepped forward. "The boy meant no offense. He is under a curse himself, we believe."

"I know that!" Dr. Ramos snapped. "I told you that. Didn't you hear me? I said I could sense it on him. Well, let's see it, boy," he demanded, turning back to Shinji. "Show me this curse of yours."

Shinji held out his arm, wrist up. Dr. Ramos's eyes got huge, and he grabbed Shinji's wrist with long, cold fingers.

"The guardian of the font," he whispered, making Shinji start. "You are under the Coatl's Curse."

Shinji felt his stomach twist. Everyone stared at them, their concern now apparent. Lucy's eyes got big and wide, and a grim look appeared on Oliver's face. Dr. Ramos looked around and smirked, pleased at the reaction. "Well, *now* everyone believes me, do they?"

"What do you know of the curse?" Maya asked into the startled silence.

"Ohhh." The doctor shook his head and backed away, giving Shinji a look of pity. "I know the boy is in a terrible predicament," he said. "A dreadful curse, that. A fate far worse than mine. Do you know the story of the Coatl's Curse, boy?" he asked, and when Shinji shook his head, he gave a grim smile. "Let me tell you the tale, then. Long ago, the Ximalli discovered a place of power, a great font of magic in the middle of the jungle. It was protected by a guardian, a beast of legend, the mighty feathered serpent. The Ximalli built a temple atop the font to honor the great serpent, and in return, the Coatl gifted the Ximalli with a special idol, the heart of the jungle. As long as the heart remained within the temple, the font would be protected and their empire would thrive.

"But, as I'm sure you can guess by now, the idol did not remain in the temple. As kingdoms rose and fell and humankind spread across the globe, magic waned. The great serpent slept as its temple was forgotten, and as it slept, a thief crept into the temple and stole the heart of the jungle from its sanctum. What happened to the thief, and the idol, no one knows. They vanished, and were both lost to history for many, many years.

"Until now," Dr. Ramos finished, and grabbed Shinji's arm again. His fingers felt like clammy spider legs, wrapped around his wrist. "Because *you* have somehow found the idol and activated the curse attached to it. This"—he lifted Shinji's arm to show off the Coatl tattoo—"is the heart of the jungle. It has chosen you to take it back to the temple and return it to the font. If you do not . . ." He raised his other skinny hand and clenched it into a fist. "The curse will suck away your life, your memories, everything that makes you who you are, until there is nothing left. You will start to hallucinate, to see and hear things that aren't there. There might be voices in your head, telling you things that aren't true. Soon, you might not know the difference between who is a friend and who is an enemy. If the idol is not returned to the temple, there will be nothing left of this boy but an empty husk. When the dreams begin"—Dr. Ramos looked right at Shinji, his mouth set in a grim line—"the end is near."

Shinji yanked his arm back, rubbing the cold spot on his skin. *When the dreams begin.* Did that mean he was going to die soon? He didn't feel any different than he'd always felt, but beside him, Lucy looked horrified, and the rest of the team wore grave expressions.

"We know we have to return it to the font," Maya said at last. "But do you know where the font is, Dr. Ramos? Where we can find it?"

"I don't have its exact location, no." Dr. Ramos stepped back. "However, in regard to the Coatl's temple, there are rumors. Legends." He turned to his desk, shuffling through the mess of papers and books. "There are hints that the Ximallitlaca built a hidden temple deep in the Lacandón jungle. Vague rumors, you understand, but I might have a map of the area. It was going to be my next expedition, after . . . *the incident.* Darn it, where is that map?"

He moved a stack of papers, and there was a blur of yellow and black as a spider scuttled out from beneath and vanished over the edge of the desk.

Shinji jumped. "Spider!" he yelped. The doctor blinked at him.

"What?"

"Didn't you see that?" Shinji pointed at the desk. "The spider? When you moved those papers, this big yellow-and-black spider jumped out."

"I didn't see a spider."

Shinji frowned. "How could you not see it? It was huge."

"Ah." Dr. Ramos gave him a sympathetic smile. "Oh dear. I see what is going on." He shot a worried look at the other explorers and shook his head. "Remember what I said about the effects of the curse? The hallucinations have already started."

"What? No, there *was* a spider," Shinji insisted, pointing more emphatically at the desk. "I've seen that kind of spider before, in . . ." He faltered. *In my dreams.*

Dr. Ramos's smile widened, as if he knew what Shinji was thinking and the very idea of it—of Shinji losing his mind—was intriguing to him. "I'm afraid time is very much of the essence," he said, glancing up at Maya and Professor

Carrero. "The boy does not have very long before the curse begins taking its toll. You will need to find the font and return the idol as soon as you can. Here."

He drew a faded piece of parchment from a drawer behind the desk, then held it out to Maya and the professor. "I've circled the general area in which I believe the temple could be located," he told them, ignoring Shinji completely now. "I can't tell you the exact location, of course, but if you search this section of the map, I believe you'll have a good chance of finding it. Do be careful, though," he added as Maya reached out and took the parchment. "This is a dangerous, vastly unexplored part of the jungle. There have been a few reports that people who enter this area don't come out again."

"We'll be careful," Professor Carrero promised, though Shinji saw a gleam of excitement cross Maya's face. He shot a glance at Oliver and saw he, too, was smiling. The thought of tromping into the dangerous, unknown places excited them, he realized. Probably why they were part of the Society of Explorers and Adventurers. You'd be a pretty awful explorer if you didn't want to go exploring.

What about you? asked a voice in his head. *You always wanted a real adventure, and now you're on one. How do you feel about that?*

Honestly, Shinji didn't know what to think.

"Thank you, Doctor," Maya said, nodding to the smaller man. "You've been very helpful. Are you sure you don't want to come with us? The anthropologist I knew would've jumped at the thought of a discovery like this. He wouldn't have let anything stop him."

"Back into the jungle?" Dr. Ramos blanched. "Into another ancient ruin? With skeletons and curses and giant bugs? Ah, well . . ." He scratched the back of his neck as Shinji and Lucy exchanged a wary look. "M-maybe next time," he said. "I'll let the Society do the exploring for now. Go save this young man; I'll be with you in spirit. Unless you die or get cursed. Then I'll be safely in my office."

CHAPTER THIRTEEN

Well, that was enlightening," Oliver announced as they left the National Museum of Anthropology and walked back across the parking lot. "And we get to hike through a dark, unexplored part of the jungle, full of snakes and monkeys and mosquitoes the size of tennis balls. And we need to do it soon before Shinji starts seeing giant blue flying pigs." He gave Shinji a sympathetic grin. "Hallucinations can be fun, but not when they're about spiders." He shuddered and shook his head. "Spiders are never fun, real or imagined."

"I didn't imagine it," Shinji muttered. "I really did see a big spider." But he wasn't certain anymore—of anything. He didn't know if anything he'd seen or remembered was real.

Lucy nudged his arm. "I believe you," she whispered. He gave her a grateful smile, glad that one person at least thought that he wasn't going crazy. "Did you see how dusty that place was?" she went on. "No wonder there were bugs living there. Probably mice and roaches, too. Ugh." She shuddered, then glanced down at her pocket, where a faint squeaking could be heard. "No, I'd never think that about you, Tinker."

Oliver yawned. "Well, real or hallucination, we're not going into the jungle tonight," he announced, glancing at the horizon, where the sun was starting to set. "And, like all the best cities, Mexico City really is better when the sun goes down. And I hear the street vendors calling my name. So . . ." He rubbed his hands together. "Who wants tlacoyos?"

Shinji frowned. "What's a tlacoyo?"

"Only the best Mexican street food ever made," Oliver replied with a grin. "C'mon. I'm starving."

After another quick taxi ride, Oliver led the way to an outdoor food court filled with small tables and delicious smells, where a roaming guitarist serenaded customers wandering through the dozen steaming food stalls. The sounds of sizzling meat and veggies filled the air. Shinji and Lucy sat on a rickety wooden bench, Lucy having draped a towel over it first, while Oliver approached a stall and returned with two paper plates. Tlacoyos turned out to be blue corn tortillas stuffed with beans and meat and cooked on a grill.

They were shaped slightly like a football, which Shinji would've found amusing if he wasn't starving. They were also delicious, and he wolfed down three before he thought about stopping.

"Whoa, slow down, kid," Oliver warned as Shinji shoved a fourth tlacoyo into his mouth, barely stopping to chew. Professor Carrero and Maya had wandered to different parts of the food court, one to get pastries and the other to get beer, so it was just Shinji, Lucy, and Oliver. "Keep eating like that and you'll get heartburn. Save room for churros later, eh?"

Shinji had never had a churro, either, but he wasn't a picky eater. In his travels with Aunt Yui, he'd had to eat a lot of different stuff. His aunt would often tell him: "Try anything once. If you don't like it, that's fine, now you know. But if you don't try it, you might miss out on something amazing." Thanks to Yui, Shinji had quite the extensive palate. He had only refused to eat something once, and that was a fried tarantula. Snakes, fish, and reptiles were fine, but he drew the line at giant arachnids.

Lucy, who had been strangely quiet and nervous all evening, suddenly put down her food. "Um. Where's the restroom?" she asked.

Oliver jerked his chin at the far side of the food court, where a faded restroom sign hung next to a short hallway. "Be careful," he warned as she stood up. "This is a very touristy part of town, but you still need to be smart. Don't talk to strangers, and don't give anyone your phone number, even if they're cute guitar players who will promise to write you a love song and serenade you at your window tonight."

"Ew," Lucy said, wrinkling her nose. Picking up her towel, she started walking toward the bathroom signs. Oliver watched her until she disappeared into the hallway; then he turned to Shinji.

"So, Shinji," he said when they were alone. "What did you think of our good Dr. Ramos?"

Shinji shrugged. "I dunno. He seemed all right."

"Did he, though?" Oliver raised a skeptical eyebrow. "I've been all over, kid. From shady markets to rough-and-tumble harbors to tiny little back alleys. I admit, I've gotten into some pretty hairy situations. But I always come out on top because I follow one rule. Always trust your gut. Your senses can be fooled, but your gut is never wrong. And you're a smart kid; I knew that the second we met. Streetwise, fearless, and kind of a smart aleck, like me when I was your age. So . . ." He crossed his arms, watching Shinji with a shrewd, appraising look. "What is your gut telling you?"

"That . . ." Shinji paused, chewing his bottom lip. "That he was hiding something," he finally said. "Or he knew something and wasn't telling us."

Oliver nodded slowly. "Which could mean any number of things," he said. "But at the very least, I think we need to be extra careful on this trip. For all we know, Hightower is still after you. They'll use anyone and anything they can to get what they want. Even Ramos. Even your little friend Lucy. We still can't be one hundred percent sure she's not an undercover Hightower agent. Until that tattoo is off your arm, the curse is lifted, and the idol is back in the temple, you can't take anything for granted."

"Yeah," Shinji muttered, gazing down at the Coatl tattoo. "I get it."

Oliver drained the last of his cup, tossed it into a nearby overflowing bin, and yawned. "Well, I promised you dessert, didn't I? And you can't visit Mexico City without having a churro; that would just be blasphemous." He pushed himself off the bench and grinned. "Wait here. Don't go anywhere. I'll be right back."

Shinji watched him walk away, toward a vendor cart at the edge of the food court, and looked around for Lucy.

When he spotted her, she was standing near the bathroom hallway on the other side of the food court, and she wasn't alone. A man in a suit stood in front of her, gesturing with his hands. He was too far away for Shinji to hear, but Lucy shook her head vigorously, crossing her arms.

Hightower! Shinji stood up, taking a breath to call for Oliver, but then the man abruptly stepped back, turned, and walked away down the street, disappearing around the corner of an old building. Lucy watched him until he was gone, then hurried back to the bench.

"Who was that?" Shinji hissed as she rejoined him. "Was he Hightower? Do we need to get out of here?"

"No." Lucy quickly sat down, shaking her head. "It wasn't anyone from Hightower," she assured him. "He was . . . um . . . just lost. He wanted directions to some restaurant I've never heard of."

Shinji narrowed his eyes. She wasn't looking at him when she spoke, instead staring straight ahead at the crowd. Was she lying to him? "Are you sure?"

"Yes. It wasn't Hightower." Lucy glanced away, still not meeting his gaze. "We're not in any danger. Don't worry about it, Shinji."

"But—"

"Here we go, kiddos." Oliver strode up, holding a paper napkin wrapped around a bouquet of pastry sticks covered in sugar. "Authentic handmade churros. Get 'em while they're warm. Who wants one?"

"Me," Lucy said, and immediately reached for the dessert sticks, leaving Shinji's doubts unanswered.

Shinji. Shinji, wake up.

Shinji stirred and opened his eyes. The hotel room was still dark, and the glowing green numbers of the clock beside the bed proclaimed it 2:13 a.m. He could still hear cars and foot traffic outside the window, though; it seemed Mexico City never went to sleep.

In the other bed, Professor Carrero snored softly, a sleep

mask pulled down over his eyes. After they had checked in that evening, Oliver announced that he was going out again and told the professor not to wait up for him. He still hadn't come back, but Shinji suspected the ex-pirate might be out all night. Nothing seemed weird or strange; the door was still locked, the chain still slotted in place. But Shinji was certain something had woken him up on purpose.

His forearm itched. Glancing down at the tattoo, he stiffened in surprise. The Coatl image had moved. Instead of staring straight at him, the winged serpent's eyes were now turned to the side, gazing at the door.

"Okay," Shinji muttered, pushing back the covers. "Now the tattoo is moving. Great. That's perfectly normal." He waited, blinking several times to be sure his eyes weren't deceiving him, that he wasn't seeing things like Dr. Ramos had suggested. But the Coatl tattoo remained where it was, its eyes on the door to the hall. "This is a long hallucination," Shinji whispered. "Unless I'm dreaming again."

He frowned. What if it wasn't a hallucination? What if the tattoo was trying to warn him of something? Careful not to wake the professor, he rose and crept across the room to the door, standing on tiptoes to peek through the eyehole. For a second, all he saw was the door on the other side of the hallway. A room-service tray had been left out, the skeleton of a half-eaten fish making him wrinkle his nose. *Gross. At least cover it up again.*

Then Lucy strode past the eyehole, walking down the corridor. Alone.

Shinji jerked up. *Lucy?* he thought in surprise. *Where is she going?*

Curiosity gnawed at him, mingled with a terrible suspicion. He *wanted* to trust her. He wanted to believe she wasn't a Hightower spy, but after their evening in the food court, as well as what Oliver had told him, he was plagued with doubts. Silently, he slid back the chain, unlocked the door, and stepped into the hall. The end of Lucy's braid vanished down another hallway as Shinji eased the door shut, and he hurried after her.

He trailed her through the halls, peeking around corners to stay out of sight. She moved quickly, leaving the corridors of hotel rooms and moving past the lobby. Shinji watched as she moved to a pair of conference room doors, hesitated as she took a deep breath, then slipped through into the dark.

Shinji hurried to the doors, pushing them open a crack to peer inside. Round tables with white tablecloths filled the space, a stage with a podium sitting against the back wall. Lucy stood in the center of the room, holding Tinker in one upraised palm. Her face was nearly impossible to see in the shadows, but Shinji thought she looked grim. Carefully, he slid through the doorway and ducked behind one of the covered tables, peeking over the cloth.

Lucy lowered her arm, letting Tinker crawl off her hand

onto a table. She scratched him on the head with the tip of one finger, then rose and took a step back, crossing her arms.

"All right, Tinker," Shinji heard her mutter. "Connect us."

The mechanical mouse sat up, nose twitching, and then two thin beams of bluish-white light came from his eyes. They flickered and pulsed as they grew, eventually turning into the holographic image of a person. A man Shinji recognized.

Gideon Frost of the Hightower Corporation looked around the room, then gazed down at Lucy with a chilly smile. "Well," he began in a tight voice, "I'm glad to see you haven't completely lost your mind."

Lucy's sigh sounded annoyed, which was not like her at all. "What do you want, Dad?"

What? Shinji almost burst out of his hiding place. Stunned, he stared at the girl's back with his mouth hanging open. Gideon Frost of the Hightower Corporation was Lucy's *father*?

"What do you think I want?" Gideon Frost asked impatiently. "I want my daughter to see reason. I want her to stop this foolishness immediately. What were you thinking, running off with that boy? Going to *the Society* for help? Do you know what you've done?"

"I did what I thought was best," Lucy said, matching his iciness with her own. "I stepped in before you could show him how ruthless and power hungry the organization really is. When will it be enough? All we do, all Hightower has ever done, is take and take, and I'm tired of it."

"That boy is vital to the plans of Hightower," Gideon Frost said coldly. "As are you. You have the gift, Lucy. Do you know how special you are? The talent for blending science and magic only comes to a handful of people, and you would throw away your future for a worthless nobody?" His hologram loomed over her, indignant and furious. "We trained you," Frost went on, pointing with an accusing finger. "We gave you everything you needed, taught you how to harness that talent and shape it to your will. I spent a fortune tracking down tutors for you, flying them in from around the globe, and this is how you repay me? This is how you repay the organization that made you what you are?"

Lucy didn't answer. She had shrunk back with both arms around herself and wasn't looking at the hologram anymore. Frost took a deep breath and sighed, running a hand down his face.

"Lucy," he said, and his voice was calmer now, almost soothing. "I'm not angry with you," he said, and Shinji had to bite his lip to keep back a snort. "I'm disappointed, and I'm worried that my only daughter is surrounded by strangers on the other side of the world. You don't know the Society of Explorers and Adventurers like I do. You think these people are altruistic heroes, that they have your best interests at heart?" He chuckled, shaking his head. "Do you know what they really are, Lucy? Mercenaries. Criminals.

Pirates. People who live on the edges and the fringes of society are often those who reject the rules and live by their own code. They can't accept how the world is, so they make up their own. Misfits, every one of them. Including that boy. A river rat. Floating aimlessly around the world, scrounging for junk. You are so much better than that. You actually have a future."

Shinji clenched his fists. He'd *had* a future. He hadn't been planning on running the Lost River Outfitters for the rest of his life, but even if he had, what was wrong with that? Sailing around the world, discovering new places, looking for treasure? He'd been to more countries and seen more things than most kids his age would even dream of. *Misfits, every one of them*, Frost had sneered. *People who live on the edges and the fringes of society are often those who reject the rules and live by their own code.* Like Oliver Ocean and Scarlett Blauerhimmel.

Like Aunt Yui.

A lump caught in Shinji's throat, and his chest felt tight. All those times aboard the *Good Tern*, he hadn't realized what he had. He wished he could talk to his aunt now, to tell her how he really felt.

"Just think about it, my dear." Frost was still talking to Lucy, his voice as low and smooth as oil. "Give me the location of the font and the idol, and all will be forgiven. You know it is the right thing to do. The magic of our font is drying up. We need a new source of power soon, or

Hightower's magic, and everything that depends on it, will fade. All those projects and toys and inventions you dream about?" He made a dismissive gesture. "They will never happen. Without a font, your workshop is dead, and you are nothing but a normal girl. No magic, no inventions, nothing special about you."

Lucy cringed. Frost held out a pale, long-fingered hand to her, his expression both severe and cajoling. "It is time to stop these childish games," he said in a low voice. "You are the heir to Hightower; the blood of our founder, Harrison Hightower the Third, flows through your veins. It is time you accept that."

"I . . ." Lucy's voice trembled. She stood in front of the hologram with her fists clenched at her sides and her head bowed. Frost loomed over her, a smug, triumphant smile on his ghostly face.

"You know I'm right," he crooned. "Do what you are supposed to do, Lucy. Tell that mouse to turn on its tracking device and let our agents find you. It will be over in a day, and you can come home. You can return to your workshop and forget this ever happened."

Gideon Frost is Lucy's dad. Crouched behind the table, Shinji shook his head in anger and disbelief. *She lied to me, to all of us. Oliver was right all along.*

Lucy took a deep breath and raised her head. For a moment, her expression was haunted, but then her eyes hardened. "Tinker," she whispered, and Shinji tensed, every muscle in his body coiling in preparation for betrayal. "Disconnect, now."

"No—"

The image of Gideon Frost flickered, then winked out like someone had flipped a switch. Lucy stood there for several moments, her brow furrowed and her face dark, as if she didn't know what to do. Tinker, sitting on the table, gazed up at her, making puzzled squeaking sounds. Lucy sighed.

"I don't know, Tinker," she muttered. "He's impossible." Tinker chittered sympathetically, and she scrubbed a hand across her face. "And if I don't follow orders, he'll probably disown me. What am I supposed to do now?" She sighed again, and her thin shoulders slumped. "I suppose we'd better get back to the room before anyone notices we're gone—"

Shinji stood up, and Lucy jumped a foot in the air. "Shinji!" she exclaimed as Shinji stared at her, his jaw set and face tight. "When did . . . ? How long have you been there? Were you . . . spying on me?"

"Spying on *you*?" Shinji exploded. "Look who's talking! I think I should be asking you that same question." He took a step forward, narrowing his eyes. "You didn't mention that Gideon Frost was your *father*," he accused. "That seems like a big thing to leave out. And that you're the wonder kid of the Hightower Corporation, their super-special prodigy. When were you going to tell me? Or were you just waiting for the right time to sell us all out to Hightower?"

"How can you say that?" Lucy snarled back. "Weren't

you listening? Didn't you see what just happened? My dad and I have never gotten along. And ever since Mom died, he's been even more unbearable. He wants me to be like him, willing to do whatever it takes to benefit himself and Hightower. For years, I watched him step on people and use completely ruthless tactics to get what he wanted. I don't want to do that." She clenched her fists, a haunted look again crossing her face, as if she were remembering all the terrible things she'd seen. "I'm not like him, and I never will be."

"But you're still part of Hightower," Shinji insisted. "He's your father, and you didn't tell us. You've been sneaking around, hiding things this whole time. How can we trust you? All you'd have to do is tell Tinker to send Hightower our location, and they'd know exactly where we were."

"Shinji." Lucy's voice trembled, sounding equal parts angry and hurt. "I wouldn't do that. Why would I help you escape Hightower just to sell you out now?"

"The font." Shinji jerked up. "So that I would lead you to the font, of course. Hightower's magic is fading, and you can't make any of your inventions without it. So when I showed up with the curse, you knew that I would eventually have to go find the Coatl's temple and the font."

"Shinji . . ."

"Everything makes sense now." Shinji was on a roll, ignoring the bleak look that crossed Lucy's face. "You were the one who 'helped' me escape from Hightower, because it would look like you were on my side. You were the one who suggested we go to the Society, because they had the resources to discover where the temple was. Everything we've done up until this point has been because of you. Now all that's left is to wait until we find the temple and the font. One message from Tinker to Hightower, and it's all over."

Throughout all this, Lucy had stood rigid in front of the table. Tinker crouched next to her, whiskers twitching as he watched Shinji pace. Now, as Shinji turned on her with a grim look, Lucy shook her head with a smile.

"You have everything all figured out, don't you?" she asked in an icy voice.

Shinji crossed his arms, though his chest felt tight at how much she sounded like Gideon Frost right then. "Prove me wrong," he challenged.

He hoped she would. His throat felt sour, a sick, heavy weight sitting in the pit of his stomach. Lucy stared at him a moment longer, her expression flat except for the faintest trembling of her bottom lip. Finally, she nodded.

"All right," she whispered, and turned her head to look at Tinker, sitting beside her on the tablecloth. "If this is what it takes. Tinker," she went on, the quaver in her voice growing more pronounced, "emergency shutdown mode, now."

Tinker jerked. His tiny body went rigid for a moment, then started to spasm. Threads of electricity crawled over him like strands of lightning, flickering blue-white in the darkness. Then, with a final flash, the little mouse collapsed onto the table. His glowing eyes flickered once, twice, and blinked out.

Lucy stifled a sob, turning her head away and closing her eyes. Shinji felt cold as he looked up at her. "What did you do?"

"I shut him down." Lucy looked up at him, and her eyes were glassy. "He can't . . . do anything now. He can't receive messages, or send them, or open doors, or move around, or anything. He's just . . . a hunk of metal and wires now. The magic that kept him alive is gone."

"Can't you just . . . turn him back on again?"

She shook her head. "It doesn't work like that," she said. "I need a magic source to revive him, and there's none around here. Without magic, I can't bring him back." Her voice shook, and the tears gathering in her eyes grew brighter, though they didn't spill down her cheeks. "Hightower won't be receiving any messages, at least not from me. Happy now, Shinji?"

"I . . ." Shinji's stomach churned at the look on her face. "You didn't have to do that," he told her.

Her eyes flashed, but she didn't answer. Turning her back to him, she gently gathered Tinker to her, cradling the limp body in her palms. The mechanical mouse lay crumpled in her hands, bright copper tail dangling limply over her pinkie. Tenderly, she put him in her pocket, brushed past Shinji without a word, and began walking away.

"Lucy," Shinji began, "wait. I didn't . . . I'm sorry."

She didn't answer, and she didn't stop. Crossing the room, she opened the door and ducked through the frame without looking back. It swung shut behind her, and Shinji was left in the darkness alone.

CHAPTER FOURTEEN

Lucy still wasn't speaking to him the next day.

"Somebody is in a mood this morning," Oliver remarked at breakfast. The hotel's complimentary food bar had offered a sprawling selection of pastries, fruit, eggs, and other breakfast-y items, but Shinji barely tasted them. Lucy's eyes were red and puffy; like him, she probably hadn't slept much. But she maintained a frosty silence when Shinji tried talking to her, and took her plate to the other side of the table, joining Maya and the professor. Her tone, posture, and the look in her eyes very clearly stated: *Leave me alone.*

"Brr," Oliver commented with an exaggerated shiver. "Is it cold in here, or is it just me?"

"I don't know what you're talking about," Shinji muttered, stuffing a lemon pastry into his mouth. Oliver had been the one who first mentioned that Lucy could be a spy. He was the one who had put the idea into Shinji's head. Not that Shinji had anyone to blame but himself for what had happened between them, but he certainly didn't want to explain last night to the ex-pirate.

"Uh-huh." Oliver took a sip of coffee, then leaned closer to Shinji and lowered his voice. "Take it from me, kid," he murmured. "I've seen a lot of angry people. And, no matter what, if someone is giving you the cold shoulder, you can be sure that they're not happy with you. So . . ." Sitting up, he gave Shinji that lopsided smirk. "Whacha do?"

"I . . ." Shinji looked down at his water cup, guilt a poisonous lump in the pit of his stomach. "I just . . ."

Abruptly, Maya stood, startling them all and saving Shinji a reply. "Dr. Ramos is here," she announced, glancing up from her phone. She sounded as surprised as Shinji felt. "He's waiting for us in the lobby. It seems he's decided to come along after all."

"Hello, my fellow cursed warriors," Dr. Ramos greeted, raising a hand as Shinji and the others met him in the airy hotel lobby. He was dressed in khakis and wore the same round safari hat as Professor Carrero. A large green duffel bag sat beside him. "All ready for your trek into the deep, dark jungles of Mexico?"

"I thought you weren't coming," Shinji said as the frail-looking man turned a beady eye on him. "You said your curse kept you from wanting to go anywhere near ancient ruins again."

"Ah, well . . ." Dr. Ramos stroked his thin mustache. "It occurred to me that I might be able to break this terrible curse if only I confront it head-on. Like Nanahuatzin facing the flames that would turn him into the sun, I must face my own fears and walk into the fire. Only then will I emerge victorious."

Shinji glanced at Oliver, who raised a skeptical brow. *Trust your gut,* he was saying. Oliver didn't believe Dr. Ramos, either. But then again, Oliver hadn't trusted Lucy and had suggested that she could be a spy. So his gut couldn't be right all the time, because Lucy wasn't a spy.

She was just . . . Gideon Frost's daughter, and the descendant of Harrison Hightower himself, which sounded far worse. Shinji was suddenly very confused. Dr. Ramos took advantage of his hesitation and stepped around him, smiling broadly at the others.

"Come, then," he urged. "Aren't you the Society of Explorers and Adventurers? Let us be on our way now. Adventure beckons, and the boy does not have a lot of time. Do you have the map I gave you?" he asked Maya.

Maya frowned. She, too, seemed wary of this sudden

change of heart, but she pulled the rolled piece of parchment out of her backpack and held it up. "Right here."

"Excellent!" Dr. Ramos strode forward and snatched it out of her fingers, making her scowl. "Don't take it personally, my good adventurer. I just don't want you to suffer trying to decipher my messy handwriting. Well?" He turned to give the others a shallow smile. "Shall we go? Adventure awaits."

Maya and Oliver exchanged a look. "Someone's had a lot of coffee this morning," Oliver muttered.

One harrowing plane ride later, Shinji found himself in the back of a Jeep, bouncing down a muddy, unmarked road toward a line of trees on the horizon. Oliver and Professor Carrero sat beside him, with Lucy, Maya, and Dr. Ramos in a second Jeep up ahead. After the plane had touched down, Shinji tried to talk to Lucy again, but she'd seen him coming and immediately walked away. Climbing into one of the Jeeps, she slammed the door shut, locking it behind her.

So she still didn't want to speak to him.

He considered telling Oliver or Professor Carrero what he'd overheard the night before, that Lucy was Gideon Frost's daughter and that Hightower was still out there, looking for them. But the guilt of how he'd treated Lucy gnawed at him; all she had done from the moment they'd met was help, and he'd let his own fears and suspicious nature get the best of him. Shinji just hoped she would stop being mad long enough for him to apologize.

A couple hours later, the Jeep came to a halt, and Shinji found himself at the edge of a dark, tangled jungle, the canopy of trees stretching away as far as he could see. Around him, birds squawked, insects buzzed, and in the distance, he thought he could hear monkeys screaming back and forth. He couldn't see anything moving, but the jungle was definitely alive.

Shinji's heart pounded, and the tattoo on his arm felt hot. He could sense something out there, almost calling to him, waiting for him in the deepest parts of the jungle. The Coatl on his arm pulsed softly, like a heartbeat against his skin.

"Impressive, isn't it?" Dr. Ramos mused, suddenly appearing beside Shinji. "And just think, somewhere in that damp, spider-infested mess is a temple that guards one of the last sources of magic in the world." He glanced down at Shinji and smiled, but it was a strangely empty smile that didn't reach his eyes. "You must be terribly excited to find it."

"Uh . . . yeah." Shinji edged away from him. "I am."

Dr. Ramos turned back to the jungle. "You feel it, don't you?" he whispered. "The call of the temple. The curse is responding to it; it knows how close we are. If you listen carefully, it might lead us right to the temple's doorstep. That would be good for you, wouldn't it?" He turned and gave Shinji another of those creepy, empty smiles. "The sooner we find the temple and the font, the sooner you can be free of the curse."

"Yeah, I know." Shinji suddenly didn't want to be around this person anymore. Turning away, he looked for Lucy and the others. Oliver and Professor Carrero were gazing into the jungle together, probably discussing the upcoming journey. Lucy stood next to Maya, who had placed a small briefcase on the ground and clicked open the top, revealing a small drone. As Shinji watched, the small machine stirred, propellers flaring to life, then rose smoothly into the air. The tiny screen at the front of the drone blinked on, and Zoe Kim's grinning face flickered into view.

"Can you see us, Zoe?" Maya asked.

"Yup!" The drone whirled, dancing in place, then spun in a slow circle, taking everything in. "Oh wow, you guys are out in the middle of nowhere, aren't you? Guess I'll have to work doubly hard to make sure you don't get lost. Oh, Lucy!" The drone dropped down to hover in front of the girl. "How are you doing? These hooligans treating you okay?"

Lucy smiled at her. "Most of them."

"Good! I'll be scouting ahead and keeping track from the air, so don't worry about getting lost. Not that you would with Maya," she added as the other woman shoved a knife into her boot and checked the machete at her hip. "But just in case something goes wrong—someone gets bit by a snake, a monkey steals your pack, you stumble onto an ancient burial site full of angry spirits—I'll be there to get you out quickly. So don't worry about a thing."

"Thanks, Zoe."

"No problem. I wouldn't miss this for anything." The drone rose into the air, then swooped over to Oliver and Professor Carrero. "Hey, boys!" Zoe called, making Oliver grin back. "Ready to start this adventure? I just want you to know that, while you're hacking your way through thorns and slapping away mosquitoes the size of your head, I will be experiencing everything from the safe, air-conditioned comfort of my office. Don't be jealous or anything."

Maya gave her hatchet an expert flourish and hung it on the other side of the machete. "Everyone ready?" she called, and Shinji watched the rest of the group straighten and take deep breaths, preparing themselves for the journey. "Time and curses wait for no one. Let's get going."

The jungle was never still. Birds darted overhead, bright streaks of color against the green. Insects buzzed through the air, whining in Shinji's ears before he slapped them away. Branches rustled, and every so often he saw something move out of the corner of his eye. But when he turned his head, nothing was there.

It was slow going. The air was damp and humid, making him feel like he was hiking through the jungle draped in a heavy blanket. Several times, the way ahead became blocked with vines and undergrowth, and they had to pause while Maya hacked a way through with her machete. As the morning lengthened into late afternoon, Shinji lost all sense of direction. The canopy overhead blocked out the sun, and every gnarled tree, vine, and rock they passed looked the same as all others before them. His backpack felt like it weighed a hundred pounds, but Shinji set his jaw and trailed Oliver in dogged silence, refusing to fall behind.

Lucy struggled. Shinji would often check behind him to see where she was, and she looked exhausted every time he did. The daughter of Gideon Frost had obviously never gone hiking through a damp, mosquito-infested jungle. She probably had never done anything more rigorous than climbing a flight of stairs. But she never complained, which Shinji thought was admirable. He wished he could talk to her, but he was afraid she would just ignore him again.

Lucy suddenly stumbled on a vine, nearly falling to her knees. Oliver grabbed her arm, holding her upright. "Whoops, careful there. You okay?"

She nodded, and he helped her toward a log sitting beside the path. "Right. Sit there for a second. I think it's time for a break."

"No." Lucy shook her head, though she was breathing hard. "I'm fine," she panted. "I can keep going. Don't stop on my account."

"It's not for you, kiddo," Oliver said as Maya turned to see what was going on. "There's a rock in my boot that's been bothering me the past two miles, and I think I need some stronger bug repellent. The mosquitoes are just laughing at this one. That okay with you, fearless leader?" he asked Maya.

Maya glanced at Lucy, then nodded. "Take a break," she called to the others. "Fifteen minutes, then we head out again."

Lucy sat down on the log with a sigh, without even draping a towel over it first, Shinji noted. She looked tired, and hot, and generally uncomfortable. Sweat streaked her skin and plastered her hair to her forehead. Shinji felt the same, but he was used to sweat and heat and mosquito-infested wilderness. Pulling out her water bottle, she gazed mournfully at the tiny swallow of water that was left, then downed it in a single gulp.

Shinji hesitated, gathering his nerve, then edged up to Lucy and offered his own mostly full canteen. A peace offering, one he hoped she would accept. *I screwed up*, he thought at her, hoping she would at least sense his remorse. *I should have trusted you. I'm sorry, can we please be friends again?*

Lucy glared at him stonily. For a moment, he thought that she would turn away and continue to ignore him. But then she sighed and reached for the canteen. Unscrewing the top, she took a couple of deep sips, and Shinji's stomach unknotted.

"Thanks," Lucy muttered, handing it back to him.

"No problem." He slung the canteen over his shoulder

and perched gingerly beside her, a little unsure about how to proceed. Now that she was talking to him again, he didn't want to mess it up. "You okay?"

"Just . . . hot." Lucy swiped a sleeve across her brow. "It feels like I'm walking through a sauna. A noisy, buggy sauna where every mosquito alive wants to eat me."

"Yeah. Welcome to the jungle."

"The jungle sucks. I'd say it can bite me, but it already has."

He snorted a laugh, then sobered. "Sorry that I didn't trust you," he said quietly. "Oliver got into my head, and . . ." He trailed off. That just sounded like an excuse, blaming someone else. He hesitated a moment longer, then took a quiet breath. "My parents died when I was really young," he said, surprising himself with the confession. Lucy's eyes widened as he pushed on. "In a fire. I know it wasn't their fault, but . . . I used to get angry at them for not being there. And . . . it was hard to trust anyone after that, you know? I mean . . . what if they left me, too?"

"Shinji." Lucy's voice was horrified and sympathetic. "I didn't know. I'm so sorry."

He shrugged, feeling a lump catch in his throat. He had never told anyone about his parents. He didn't even talk much about them with Aunt Yui. "It's fine," he murmured. "It happened a long time ago. I barely remember them now." He felt a light touch as Lucy put a hand on his arm and had to blink rapidly until his eyes were clear. "Anyway," he added, taking a quick breath, "I don't think you're a spy. And I'm really sorry about . . ."

He nodded toward the pocket where she kept Tinker.

"It's okay," Lucy was quick to reassure him. "He's not gone forever, just until I can find another magic source." She chewed her lip, then sighed. "And I wasn't entirely honest, either. I'm sorry I kept things from you. Thanks for not telling the others who I really am. SEA hates Hightower, but they hate my family in particular. If they knew I was a direct descendant of Harrison Hightower the Third . . ."

Shinji nodded. "I won't tell them," he promised. "Though really, shouldn't this tattoo be attached to *you*? I mean, your family is the one with a history of curses and stuff."

She gave a very un-Lucy-like snort. "*I* know not to go around picking up strange idols."

Shinji smiled back, but at that moment, there was a bright flash of metal as Zoe's drone swooped down through the branches and hovered in front of the group.

"We've got trouble," she announced as they all looked up quickly. "There's a group of about a dozen people following us, and at least half of them have guns. They're a few miles behind, but they're moving fast. One even took a shot at me as I flew by!" Both her voice and the drone trembled, either from fear or indignation. "I don't think they're a group of tourists on safari, guys."

"Hightower." Maya leaped upright, grabbing her pack and the machete she'd stuck in the earth. "They're after the kid. We need to go, now."

"How did they even find us?" Oliver demanded as Shinji's stomach twisted itself into a knot. "We are literally out in the middle of nowhere. No one knew we were in Mexico City, unless . . ." His dark eyes went to Lucy, and narrowed to slits. "Someone here tipped them off."

Lucy paled. "I didn't," she whispered, and shot a desperate look at Shinji. "It wasn't me, I swear."

"Really?" Oliver crossed his arms, clearly unconvinced. "You're the only one here who came from Hightower. And you were talking to some strange fellow back in Mexico City. Don't think I didn't see that." He gave her a hard smile. "If you're not the mole, who is?"

Shinji scrambled to his feet, but Oliver swung that cold smile on him. "Hey now, don't go jumping to her defense again, kid," he warned. "I was leery about bringing her along in the first place, but I let it slide. Now we're in the middle of the jungle, Hightower is after us, and no one else knows where we are. You put the pieces together."

Lucy stood. "It wasn't me," she said again, and held up her hand. "Look."

Tinker's tiny, mechanical body lay in her palm, glimmering in the late-afternoon sun. Shinji felt his stomach roil seeing him like that, but Lucy stood firm in front of Oliver, her jaw set. "I shut him down so there'd be no way I could contact Hightower," she said. "Or for them to contact me. I didn't tell them anything."

The ex-pirate hesitated, and Maya turned on him with a scowl. "Oliver, there is no time for this!" she snapped, and pointed the end of her machete into the jungle. "Everyone, move! We can figure this out later, but there's only a few hours of daylight left, and we need to put as much distance between us and Hightower as we can. Let's go."

"Fine." Oliver snatched up his pack but still shot a warning glare at Lucy. "I'm watching you," he told her. "The truth will come out eventually. It always does."

They hurried into the jungle, moving much quicker now. The trees seemed to close around them, getting even more tangled. Vines and undergrowth clogged their way, making passage all but impossible. When the path was blocked, Oliver pulled his own machete from his backpack and started hacking through plants and undergrowth with Maya.

Shinji and Lucy watched the two explorers clear the way, their blades slicing through tough vines and branches. Shinji clenched his fists, wishing he could do something to help, but he didn't have a knife and he didn't want to get *too* close to those swinging blades. Lucy was tense, her arms around herself, blue eyes darting about as if she feared Hightower would crash through the jungle into their midst at any moment.

"I wish Tinker was here," she whispered. "He could do something to help. I feel so useless right now."

Shinji brushed her elbow, making her start. "I don't think it was you," he whispered as her fearful gaze landed on him. "For real this time. I'm not sure how Hightower found us, but I know you didn't send them anything."

"Thanks, Shinji," Lucy whispered back. "I know I'm the most likely suspect. Oliver is right to be suspicious; I don't know how Hightower found us, either."

"Maybe someone else tipped them off." Shinji glanced around at the rest of the Society. Maya and Oliver stood shoulder to shoulder, hacking at vines. *Not Oliver,* Shinji thought. *He hates Hightower as much as anyone.* Shinji didn't know Maya very well, but it was difficult to imagine the professional, matter-of-fact adventurer betraying them to their enemies. Professor Carrero stood under a tree, panting and dabbing his blotchy face with a handkerchief. He, too, seemed unlikely to sell them out.

Zoe? Shinji thought. It would be easy enough, with her speed and mobility, to fly down to Hightower and give them information. But that made no sense; if it were true, why would she warn them all that Hightower was coming?

His gaze suddenly landed on Dr. Ramos, standing a little apart from the others. The feeble-looking man caught his eye, but he didn't look away as Shinji expected. Instead, a faint smile slid across his face, making him look sinister. Almost menacing. But it was gone in a blink, and Dr. Ramos returned to looking frail and shaken.

"Almost through!" Oliver announced from up ahead,

where the stubborn tangle of undergrowth had blocked their way forward. "Just a few more vines and . . . uh-oh."

That didn't sound good. Shinji and the others hurried to where Oliver and Maya had sliced through the tangle of vines and branches. Pushing their way past the trees, they suddenly found themselves at the edge of a ravine, the ground dropping sharply away into empty space. The gorge stretched away in either direction, looking endless. Gripping a sturdy branch with tight fingers, Shinji leaned forward to gaze into the chasm. There was no water at the bottom of the ravine, no white river gushing over sharp rocks, but it was a *long* way down.

"Well, that is not ideal," Professor Carrero commented, looking pale as he peered over Shinji's shoulder. A strong wind rushed out of the crevice and nearly blew the hat from his head. "Oh my. Oh goodness. Can we go around?"

"No time," Maya said, appraising this new obstacle as if contemplating how best to conquer it. "And we can't double back, either. Somehow, we're going to have to cross it."

"Well, that's easy . . ." Oliver began, and Maya turned on him.

"Oliver, if you say something like *we just have to grow wings and fly*, I am going to throw you into the chasm."

"Aw, Maya, you know me too well." The ex-pirate grinned, and jerked a thumb down the ravine. "But I was just going to point out that there's a bridge over that way."

Everyone looked up. A few hundred yards down from

where they stood, an ancient-looking rope bridge spanned the chasm. It wasn't a modern structure; the railings were made of thick woven rope, not cable, and the planks were simple wooden boards. Shinji could see lines dangling from it, snapped bits of rope just swaying in the wind.

"Oh, great," he remarked as they hurried toward it. Gusting wind from the chasm tugged at their hair and clothes as they walked along the edge of the drop. "That looks perfectly safe. And not at all clichéd. It's certainly not going to snap when we're all out in the very center of it."

"Shinji, my dear boy," Professor Carrero panted, keeping well back from the edge of the ravine as they hurried forward, "you've been hanging around Oliver far too long."

"Um. Thanks?"

"It was not a compliment."

A blast of wind howled up from the chasm as they reached the bridge, causing the whole thing to sway and the ropes to creak loudly. Gazing over the bridge, Shinji felt his insides twist. The thick ropes spanning the space were frayed in places, and several of the planks were green with moss and lichen. It did not look safe. At all.

With a whir of propellers, Zoe's drone swooped down to hover in front of them. "Hightower is closing in," she warned. "They're moving fast, following your trail. You guys need to get moving or they're gonna catch up."

"Come on," Maya ordered, and strode fearlessly out onto the bridge. The ropes groaned, and the planks creaked under her weight, but the bridge held. After a moment's hesitation, Professor Carrero followed, then Dr. Ramos, his withered frame barely making the planks squeak. Zoe's drone swooped overhead in a flash of metal, and Shinji envied its ability to fly.

"All right, kids." Oliver smiled and motioned Shinji and Lucy forward. "Your turn. Don't worry, I'll be right behind you. Also, remember the first rule of crossing a rope bridge over an endless ravine: Never ever look down."

Taking a deep breath, Shinji walked out onto the bridge. Boards groaned beneath his shoes, the ropes shuddering as he left solid ground and stepped out into open space. A pair of colorful birds soared by beneath him. Clutching the railings in a death grip, he started across the chasm.

Don't look down, he told himself. *Just don't look down.*

The bridge swayed horribly when he reached the middle. Wind gusted up from the chasm and made the entire thing swing and groan in the breeze. Shinji's knuckles were white as he clutched the railings. He kept his gaze fixed on the other side of the bridge.

Don't look down, he repeated, a mantra to keep him going. *Don't look down, just don't look—*

Something small moved in the corner of his eye; he glanced down to where his hand gripped the railing to see a huge black spider scuttle along the rope toward his fingers. With a yelp, he instinctively jerked away, taking a step back on the bridge.

An earsplitting crack rang out as the board under his feet snapped in two. Shinji plummeted, heart leaping to his throat as he lashed out wildly. He managed to grab on to the planks as he fell and clung to them for dear life as his legs kicked and dangled in empty space.

"Shinji!" Lucy spun, fell to her knees on the boards, and grabbed his arm. "Hang on!"

"What do you think I'm doing?" Shinji gritted out. His fingers slipped from one of the cracks in a board, and he scrabbled frantically at the wood. The wind swirled around his dangling feet, tugging at his legs and trying to yank him into empty air.

Lucy tugged on his arm, and Shinji tried pulling himself up. But the wooden board he was clinging to cracked as well, making Lucy gasp in terror.

A thin, bony hand suddenly clamped on to his other arm. Shinji looked up to see Dr. Ramos kneeling beside Lucy. The spidery fingers curled around his wrist were shockingly strong.

The board supporting Shinji's arms snapped. He let out a yelp of fear as he fell, but something yanked him to an abrupt halt, making his teeth clack together. His legs kicked, swinging out over empty space. The two halves of the board plummeted into the ravine and were lost in the branches far below.

Gasping, Shinji looked up into the faces of Lucy and Dr. Ramos. Both held his arms, their fingers wrapped tightly around his wrists. Lucy's eyes were huge, her jaw clenched in concentration as she tried to pull him up. Dr. Ramos's lips were pressed into a line, his bony fingers digging painfully into Shinji's arm.

Wind swirled around them, tossing their hair and making the bridge sway. As Shinji clung desperately to the boards, something white and papery fluttered past his face. A sheet of parchment soared into open sky, dancing on the wind currents, and went spinning off into the void.

"Hang on, kid!" A shadow fell over Shinji from behind. Oliver Ocean stepped up, grabbed him by the back of his collar, and heaved him out of the hole. Shinji, Lucy, and Dr. Ramos collapsed onto the bridge, gasping, as Oliver blew out a breath and grinned down at them.

"Whew, that was close. You okay, kiddo?" he asked Shinji.

Shinji nodded. His heart was thudding in his ears, his arms shook, and cold sweat was trickling down his neck. But at least he wasn't swinging over an endless drop. Glancing at Lucy and Dr. Ramos, who looked just as shaken, he nodded to them both.

"Thanks," he panted. "For not letting me fall."

Lucy smiled, but Dr. Ramos gave a weird little smirk. "Well, we can't have the bearer of the Coatl's Curse plummeting to his death, now, can we?" he asked. "How are you going to find the font if you break your neck at the bottom of a ravine?"

With a grimace, he pulled himself to his feet, clutching the railings in a white-knuckled grip. "Now, shall we get off this swinging death trap before anything else happens?"

"I'm all for that," Oliver said. "One near-death experience is enough, thanks. Just try to remember the *other* rule of crossing a rope bridge over an endless ravine: always watch where you step."

Lucy frowned at him. "How can we do that if the first rule is never look down?"

"Uh . . ." The ex-pirate scratched the side of his head. "We should keep moving."

Thankfully, there were no more surprises. The bridge didn't snap, the ropes didn't unravel, and they made it to the other side without further catastrophes. Shinji was still sweating, and Lucy's face was white as they stepped off the bridge, Maya and Professor Carrero pulling them to safety. Shinji staggered a few feet from the posts and sat down in the grass, waiting for his heart to stop bouncing around his rib cage. For a moment he considered telling them about the spider he'd seen on the bridge, but he decided against it. They would only think it was a hallucination and worry about him even more. Plus, he didn't want to let on that he'd nearly fallen to his death running from a spider.

"Well, that was fun." Oliver gave a little hop onto solid ground and dusted off his coat. "Rotten rope bridges are always exciting, no matter how many times you cross them.

Have you noticed they *always* seem to break when you're out in the very center?"

"Are you all right, dear boy?" Professor Carrero asked, gazing at Shinji, his eyes wide behind his glasses. "Goodness, you nearly gave us a heart attack. Thank heavens Lucy and Dr. Ramos were there to save you. And Oliver, too, I suppose."

Oliver shrugged. "Sarcasm and timely rescues. It's what I'm here for."

Maya rolled her eyes and strode forward. "Hightower is still behind us," she said, practical as always. "We should get moving."

The rest of the group heaved themselves to their feet, ready to follow, but Lucy put out a hand. "Wait a second," she said. "Aren't we going to cut the ropes?"

Shinji had been thinking the same thing. If they cut the ropes, like everyone in the movies did, Hightower wouldn't be able to cross the chasm. It sounded like a good idea to him. At the very least, it would slow them down.

But Maya shook her head. "No," the explorer said, "we're not."

Lucy frowned in confusion. Maya swept her arm over the chasm. "This bridge was built by the people who live in this jungle," she explained. "If we destroy it, we destroy part of their way of life. It would take them months to rebuild, and who knows how their lives would be disrupted. Bad enough that we already damaged it. The bridge is not ours to take down. We leave it untouched, like everything else."

"But . . ." Lucy glanced at the bridge, then at the machete hanging from Maya's waist. "But Hightower is coming," she argued. "If they catch us, they'll force Shinji to lead them to the temple. And then they'll use the power of the font for their own purposes. If we take out the bridge, we might stop them right there. They might not be able to go any farther." She pointed back to the chasm. "Is one bridge really worth the risk of Hightower catching up with us?"

"Yes," Maya said flatly, and Professor Carrero nodded.

"My dear, I know it might seem foolish to you," he said. "But all members of the Society have taken an oath. To preserve, not destroy. To leave a place in the same state in which we found it, as much as we can, regardless of personal gain or loss. Unless it is a matter of life or death, which it is not—not yet—we try to do the least amount of harm we can."

"Oh." Lucy blinked, a strange expression crossing her face. "You guys . . . really are different from Hightower," she muttered.

"There are other options to lose pursuers in a giant jungle," Maya told Lucy, a faint smile tugging at one side of her mouth. "We don't have to take the easy way out and destroy the bridge. We'll find another way. Dr. Ramos . . . ?" She turned to the man standing under a tree, a safe distance from the edge of the ravine. "Lead on."

"Ah, well." Dr. Ramos hesitated, chewing his bottom lip. "About that," he said sheepishly, avoiding Maya's gaze. "We may have a slight problem. You see, I might have lost the map."

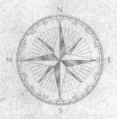

CHAPTER FIFTEEN

"What do you mean, you lost the map?"

Dr. Ramos winced at Oliver's outburst. "When I was trying to keep the boy from falling, the map came loose," he explained. "I couldn't grab it without letting go of Shinji."

Oliver groaned and ran a hand over his face, making the smaller man bristle.

"Would you rather I saved the map instead?" he demanded. "I'm sorry, but I didn't have much time to choose, and between the two of them, I decided that not letting the boy plummet to his death was more important."

"Thanks for that, by the way," Shinji said sincerely. Maybe he'd been wrong about Dr. Ramos. Anyone who saved him from falling into a ravine couldn't be that bad, right?

"Don't worry, good sir, don't worry," Professor Carrero said quickly. "You certainly made the right choice. Obviously saving the boy was the more pressing concern."

"Uh, but now we have no map," Oliver broke in. "And we're in the middle of the Mexican jungle, being chased by the Hightower Corporation, and we have no idea where we're going. Does this not seem like a problem to anyone else?"

"Maybe Zoe could find the temple?" Lucy suggested, glancing at the sky. "She has a better view than anyone else."

Shinji's arm itched. He scratched at it absently and the sensation faded, but there was a weird feeling in the back of his mind. As if something was trying to get his attention.

"Maybe," Maya said, nodding. "I'll tell her to scout ahead and keep an eye out. But the canopy will be the problem; it's too thick to really see through. She could fly right over the temple and not know it was there."

"Well, if the other choice is to wander aimlessly through the jungle until we're completely lost or Hightower catches us," Oliver said, "I choose the drone."

Shinji's arm suddenly throbbed. Wincing, he glanced down at the tattoo, and his heart jumped to his throat.

The Coatl on his arm had moved again. Much like it had in the hotel, its head had swiveled around, and it was now facing off to the left. Shinji drew in an amazed breath and glanced up to see Dr. Ramos watching him.

"The Coatl," the small man whispered, his black eyes

fixed on the tattoo. "It knows. It is pointing the way to the font."

"What? No way." Shinji moved his arm to the right, and the Coatl's head moved as well, though it kept staring in the same direction. He swung his arm to the left, with the same result. The serpent's head continued to face in one direction, no matter how much he moved his arm back and forth.

Lucy, who had been peering at him worriedly, shook her head. "That's impossible," she whispered. "How is it doing that?"

"The magic of the font is calling him," Dr. Ramos murmured, almost to himself. "I was right." His sharp gaze lifted, meeting Shinji's eyes. "You are the compass now. You must lead the way." Maya and Oliver, who had started arguing with each other, stopped and stared at him, too. Oliver blinked as Shinji held out his arm.

"Okay, that's . . . interesting," the ex-pirate remarked, watching the serpent's head swivel back and forth. "Kid, is that thing really telling you which direction to go? Do you know the way to the font?"

"Um . . ." Shinji gazed into the trees, feeling a slight tug in the pit of his stomach urging him on. "Yeah," he answered, glancing back at the members of the Society. "I think I do."

They continued slogging through the jungle, which grew thicker and even more tangled the farther they went. But Shinji's tattoo led them unerringly through the trees, finding spaces in the undergrowth, holes in the endless clusters of vines, and almost invisible paths winding through the rain forest. Sometimes Shinji thought the jungle itself was parting for him, peeling itself back to show him the hidden ways and paths through the undergrowth. He couldn't be certain, of course, but they were moving faster than they had ever moved with Dr. Ramos's map. Shinji hoped this was a good sign. He also hoped the jungle was making it harder for Hightower to follow them. Lucy kept glancing over her shoulder, clearly worried about what would happen should they catch up. Once, Oliver suggested that they deliberately take a different direction from the one that the tattoo pointed toward, just to lead Hightower on a wild-goose chase and maybe get them lost in the jungle. But when they tried, they found their path blocked by thick roots and vines, as if the jungle itself refused to let them go another way.

As they followed a narrow game trail past huge trees that shut out the sky, the path before them suddenly split, going off in two different directions. Shinji stumbled to a halt, looking up from his arm and the jungle floor to find something staring back at him. At the spot where the paths diverged, the statue of a huge moss-covered serpent stared down at them. Its hollow eyes seemed to bore into Shinji.

Oliver peered over his shoulder. "Which way do we go?"

he asked, gazing down both paths before turning to Shinji again. "Kid, what does your tattoo say?"

Shinji glanced down at his wrist. The Coatl's head pointed to the left, but as he watched, it swiveled to the right, then back to the left again. He moved his arm, sweeping it in different directions, but the Coatl didn't stop moving. "I don't know," he finally admitted as the serpent twisted its head around once more. "It can't seem to pick a direction. I think it's confused."

Everyone crowded around Shinji, watching his tattoo swivel from left to right like a weather vane. "Well, that's not very helpful," Oliver commented at last. "I think the magic has gone a bit wacky. Or it's playing a trick on us."

"Hmm." Professor Carrero tapped his chin, looking thoughtful. "No, I don't think this is a case of the magic failing," he mused. "I think this might be some sort of test, as indicated by the snake statue being right at the point where the paths diverge." He gazed up at the serpent, then glanced down each path, looking thoughtful. "So, based on that, I would conclude that one path leads to the temple, and the other does not."

Oliver chuckled. "Brilliant deduction, Watson. So we just have to check out one path, and if that one is wrong, we go down the other."

Professor Carrero's mustache bristled. "It is not quite as simple as you seem to think, my dear boy," he said indignantly. "One, we do not have time to be wrong; Hightower is on our trail, and if we get lost, they might reach the temple before us. Two, I don't believe this will be as easy as choosing one path and turning around if we get it wrong. If this is a test, the consequences for failure tend to be much more severe. We might only have one shot at this, one chance to get it right. So I would take it a bit more seriously, were I you. Shinji . . ." He took off his glasses, rubbed them with a cloth, then stuck them back on his face. "Since you are our compass and the prime mover of this quest, which path do you think is the right one?"

Shinji watched the squirming tattoo a moment, then glanced at each of the paths winding in different directions. One, the path to the left, snaked off into the jungle. The other, the path to the right, headed straight into a tangle of vines and thick undergrowth. Beyond the trees, Shinji could see the side of a jagged cliff rising up toward the clouds. The trail to the right seemed to lead directly toward it.

"Well, if we go to the right, we're going to hit that cliff," Shinji muttered. "And we'll have to hack our way through just to reach it. The trail to the left would probably be the easier one."

"Yes," Professor Carrero agreed. "It would. But look at the statue, dear boy. I believe it is a clue of sorts. You see, the ancient Ximalli were the protectors and guardians of the jungle, but they were also warriors. They valued strength and hard work, and the Coatl itself"—he waved a hand at the statue—"represents tenacity, the will to win the reward through tireless struggle. Therefore . . ." He gazed at Shinji expectantly.

"Therefore . . ." Shinji repeated, and grimaced. "The harder path is probably the correct one."

Oliver groaned. "Oh, come on. Are we really sure this is a test of some kind? I would rather avoid climbing a mountain if I don't have to. I've already had my fill of heights today, thanks."

"We are trying to find an ancient temple that guards a font of magic," Professor Carrero said patiently. "As an adventurer of your renown should know, these kinds of expeditions often come with a set of challenges. It is the whole *prove your worth to pass* scenario. If I had to guess, I would bet that this is only the first of several challenges. And the answer to this type of choice is never *go down the easier path*."

"I'm afraid I agree with Professor Carrero," Dr. Ramos said suddenly. "But if we are going to go, perhaps we should go quickly? Hightower could be right behind us."

A sudden explosion of sharp cries made Shinji jump. Not far behind them, a flock of vivid red-and-gold birds took to the air in a burst of feathers and frantic screeches. Something was coming. And that something was Hightower.

Maya looked at the tangle of vines and undergrowth and drew her machete with stoic resignation. "Right," she announced, and lifted her blade. "Harder path it is. Follow me."

After they hacked their way quickly through the thick undergrowth, the trail did lead them to the base of a cliff. Gazing up at the soaring wall of jagged rock, Oliver groaned once more.

"Go to the jungle, they said. It'll be fun, they said. That does it . . . when we're done here, I'm taking my ship and sailing to the Bahamas. Sun, sand, beaches, and definitely no cliffs."

Zoe's drone suddenly swooped out of the sky to circle them anxiously. "Hurry," she urged. "Hightower is getting closer. Get up that cliff now."

"Easy for you to say," Oliver grumbled. "You can fly."

Maya stripped off her pack and set it down with a thump. Opening the top, she pulled out two coils of bright orange rope, pitons, several carabiners, and a pair of what looked like complicated belts. "Here," she snapped, tossing one of them to Oliver. "Stop complaining and get that harness on the kid. We don't have a lot of time."

"Where's my harness?" Oliver wanted to know, turning to Shinji and motioning him forward. Maya rolled her eyes as she beckoned to Lucy, snapping the canvas belt around the girl's waist when she came over.

"You don't get one."

"What?"

"I only had room for a couple, and I had to make some sacrifices for space. Besides, you've done this enough that you shouldn't need a belt, Ocean."

"I've also flown in Scarlett Blauerhimmel's plane without a parachute; that doesn't mean I like doing it." When Maya didn't answer, Oliver sighed and glanced down at Shinji. "Right. Harness. Ever gone rock climbing, kid?"

"Once," Shinji said. "It was indoors, though. There was a wall with these different-colored handholds that you had to climb to reach the top."

Oliver gave him a smile that was mostly a grimace. "Yeah, well. This is a little different."

And by "a little different" he meant terrifying.

Unlike Oliver, Shinji was not afraid of heights. He'd been atop mountains and city skyscrapers and in the branches of very tall trees. He wasn't scared of flying, and he could stand in a glass elevator as it slid down the side of a building without his stomach jumping to his throat.

Clinging to a side of a cliff wearing a too-big harness attached to a very thin rope, however, put those other scenarios to shame. It was almost as bad as clinging to a rotten bridge that spanned an endless chasm. Except now he was doing it on purpose.

"Keep going, kid!" Oliver encouraged Shinji from behind. Oliver had helped Professors Carrero and Ramos into some SEA-created climbing-assist contraptions and was now showing them how to use the levers and ropes. It didn't seem to be helping them as much as Oliver believed it would. Farther up, Maya led the climb with Lucy behind her. Maya expertly made her way up the cliff face, stopping periodically to shove a piton through a crack in the rock wall, hammer it in place, and snap the safety rope onto the anchor. Shinji's and Lucy's harnesses were attached to this rope, preventing a very lethal drop down the side of the cliff, but it was still slow going. Shinji's arms burned, his hands were scraped, and it was still a long way to the top. He hoped Lucy was doing okay, but he also knew she wouldn't give up.

Pulling himself onto a ledge, Shinji took advantage of the sturdy footing to rest a moment, giving his arms a break from the constant clinging. Far below, the jungle sprawled in every direction, a carpet of trees stretching as far as he could see.

A ripple of movement through the branches caught his eye. Squinting, he peered down through spaces in the canopy and could just make out the place where the path split, the snake statue looming over the trail. A group of men stood before it, dressed in camouflaged clothing. As Shinji watched, they appeared to be debating which direction to go. Finally, they split up, a few of them heading down the path to the left, while the larger force went in the direction of the cliff.

"Come on, kiddo." Zoe's drone floated down, the face on the screen peering out at Shinji worriedly. "Keep climbing. We gotta keep ahead of Hightower, and they're getting close."

"Right." Shinji nodded wearily, and reached for the rock face again.

But as he pulled himself up, his arm pulsed, and an image flashed through his mind. He suddenly saw the group from Hightower, the ones who had gone the wrong way, rushing down the jungle path. Suddenly the ground beneath them crumbled. They fell, tumbling over each other until they slid to a stop at the bottom of a pit full of leaves and vines. Groaning, the men pushed themselves upright, but as they did, the leaves around them moved, and dozens of vipers raised their heads from the vegetation. Baring curved fangs, the serpents lunged with earsplitting hisses, and the image went dark.

Shinji gasped, jerking his head back as a lunging snake filled his vision before blinking into nothing. His hand slipped, and the foothold beneath his sneakers gave way. With a yell, he lost his balance and plummeted down the face of the cliff.

The rope brought him up short, yanking him to a painful halt. Shinji bounced against the side of the cliff and dangled there a moment, gasping, the world spinning around him.

"Shinji!" Oliver's voice rang out below him, intense and alarmed.

"Shinji!" Lucy's panicked voice echoed Oliver's, from the opposite direction. "Are you okay?"

"Yeah," Shinji rasped out. "I'm fine." It was clear from

the way he was hanging that he had a fantastic, if terrifying, view of the sheer drop down the side of the cliff. Oliver's worried face gazed up at him, eyes wide, and Zoe's drone swooped down, shouting instructions he couldn't quite hear.

"Okay, seriously, will you *stop* with the near-death experiences, kid?" Oliver called from below. "Concentrate! You're going to give me a heart attack before this trip is done."

"Like I'm doing this on purpose," Shinji called back. Gritting his teeth, he groped behind him until he found the rope and righted himself on the rock wall again. Panting, he pressed himself to the cliff and waited for his hands to stop shaking and his heart to stop crashing against his ribs.

"That's why we have safety ropes." Maya's voice drifted down from above. "Everyone falls at least once when they're first starting. Come on, Shinji. Don't let it freak you out. You still have to reach the top. Keep moving. Keep climbing."

Keep climbing. Right. Setting his jaw, Shinji started up the cliff once more.

Minutes passed. Or hours, Shinji didn't know. He tried to keep his arms and legs moving, but all he could see in his mind was the image of the men being attacked by vipers over and over again. He didn't know how far from the top of the cliff he was when Maya's voice echoed above them again.

"Wait a minute. There's an opening." She turned her head, shouting down to Professor Carrero. "I found a cave entrance! And it has a pair of snake statues flanking the opening. Do we stop here, or keep going to the top?"

"A cave?" Professor Carrero wheezed. His face was red, his skin drenched with sweat as he glanced up. "I believe . . . that is what we are looking for," he gasped up to Maya. "It might be . . . the entrance to the hidden temple."

A shout echoed far below. Shinji glanced down to see the group of men pushing their way from the jungle and starting toward the cliff.

"Hightower!" he called, causing Oliver to glance down as well.

"Persistent devils, aren't they? Come on, kid," Oliver urged, looking back at Shinji. "We gotta move. Channel your inner mountain goat and climb!"

Shinji climbed, scraping his hands and bloodying his fingers as he scrambled upward. Finally he reached the mouth of the cave, where Maya and Lucy grabbed his arms to pull him onto the ledge. Shinji slumped next to a wheezing Professor Carrero, put his hands on his knees, and concentrated on sucking air into his lungs. Lucy hovered worriedly beside him. She looked dirty and sweaty as well, far from the super-clean neat freak he'd first met in the Hightower headquarters.

"You okay?" she asked. "You looked like you took a pretty hard fall."

"I'm okay," Shinji assured her. His hands were bloody, and there was a gash on his arm where he'd slammed into the side of the cliff. The wounds stung like crazy, but they weren't very deep. "I'm just cut up a little. Nothing's broken."

Lucy wrinkled her nose at the blood. "You should probably clean those," she said. "They could get infected and start to rot, and then you'll have to cut your arms off at the elbow."

"Maybe if I were in a zombie movie," Shinji said with a grimace. "I don't think that's how it normally works."

"Here." Dr. Ramos abruptly stepped forward, handing a roll of gauze to Lucy. "Use that. Infection or no, we can't have him bleeding all over the place; we'll leave a very conspicuous trail for Hightower." His dark eyes watched them as Lucy began winding the bandages around Shinji's palms. "On the cliff," he continued in a softer voice, as if he didn't want anyone else to hear. "Right before you fell . . . you had a vision, didn't you? A hallucination."

Shinji swallowed. He really did not like the way Dr. Ramos continued to stare at him, but he couldn't deny the truth. "Yeah," he said shortly. "I did."

"What did you see?"

"A bunch of Hightower agents following us. Some of them went down the wrong path and fell into a nest of vipers." Lucy gasped, but Dr. Ramos only nodded, looking pleased. Shinji did not share the sentiment. "That could've been us," he muttered, feeling his stomach tighten. "If we had gone the wrong way, we could've all died."

"We didn't, though." Lucy's voice was solemn. "We

passed the first test, thanks to you and Professor Carrero. We can't think about what might've happened; we have to keep going."

"Oof," Oliver announced as he reached the top as well. The ex-pirate dusted off his hands, breathing hard. "Well, that was fun. Though for our next adventure, I propose something a little closer to the ground." He shot a look at Maya, who was busy yanking up the ropes. "You think that will keep those Hightower goons from following us?"

"It will slow them down," Maya commented, peering over the edge of the cliff. "But it won't stop them. And they might have their own climbing gear. We need to keep moving."

Zoe's drone floated down, hovering at the cave entrance. "What about me?" she asked. "I can't follow you guys in there; I'll lose the signal to my drone. What should I do?"

"See if you can find another exit," Maya said. "We don't know if the font is in this cave, but if Hightower is behind us, we won't be coming back the same way. If there is another way out, we'll meet you there. If not, just keep an eye on Hightower. Priya will need to know what happened here."

There was a moment of somber silence as everyone realized what she really meant. Priya would need to know what happened . . . if they never came back.

The drone bobbed in the air. "Got it," Zoe said solemnly. "Lucy, don't you dare get yourself killed; I still need to pick your brain about a million things. Be careful, you guys."

She spiraled into the air and zipped away over the cliff. Oliver watched the drone fly off, then turned and took Professor Carrero's hand, pulling him to his feet. "Oof. Come on, Professor. You heard Maya. We gotta keep moving."

"In . . . deed," gasped Professor Carrero. Straightening slowly, he dabbed his red face with a handkerchief. "Goodness gracious, it has been a long time since I've climbed a mountain. Not like riding a bike at all. But the good news . . ." He nodded to the pair of snake statues on either side of the cave entrance. "I think we are on the right track. What does your tattoo say, Shinji, dear boy?"

Shinji looked down at his wrist. The tattoo was brighter now, glowing with a faint golden light. They all stared at it in wonder for a moment as it flickered and pulsed in the gloom. The feathered head of the Coatl was pointing unerringly into the darkness of the cave.

"Yeah," Shinji muttered as Lucy peered over his shoulder. "Looks like we're still going the right way."

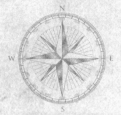

CHAPTER SIXTEEN

Maya handed Shinji a flashlight, and for several minutes they walked through the caverns, following Shinji's tattoo as the Coatl's head twisted this way and that. Despite the humidity outside, the caves were dry and cool. Strange insects crawled along the walls, revealed in the flashlight beams: metallic-green-gold beetles and brilliantly colored centipedes scuttled away from the light as they moved through the tunnels. Shinji was thankful he had the tattoo to guide his group as the cavern tunnels branched off in different directions like a maze or a giant termite mound. Shinji suspected that, without the Coatl guiding them, they would become hopelessly lost very quickly. He prayed the labyrinth of tunnels would slow Hightower down even more than it slowed his own party down.

At first, the floors and walls of the cave were of natural rock, but as they ventured deeper, pillars and statues loomed up from the darkness, and stone tiles began peeking through the dirt. Carvings appeared on the walls: images of people carrying spears and shields, animals like jaguars, monkeys, and, of course, snakes. The cave began to look like an underground temple, though one that was dusty and had been abandoned for centuries.

"Would you look at that?" Professor Carrero paused to gaze at a stretch of wall, raising his lantern to see through the darkness. A mural had been carved into the stone: a pyramid with a huge serpent looming over it, wings outstretched. "Quetzalcoatl, the great feathered serpent. See, now, the Aztecs would have depicted the snake with feathers but no wings. Fascinating how some creatures can show up in numerous cultures and stories around the world. Just think of how many legends there are about dragons."

Shinji gazed at the mural, feeling the eyes of the Coatl staring right back at him. *We're coming,* he told it silently. *We're almost there. I'll get you your idol, and then I can go back to being normal, without a curse hanging over my head. Deal?*

The feathered serpent in the mural didn't answer, though Shinji swore he could still feel its eyes on him as they walked away.

They came to a hallway, a long corridor with worked

stone walls and a stone tile floor. Snake statues, rearing up with their mouths open, lined both sides of the passage. There were dozens of statues, maybe hundreds, stretching to the very end of the hallway. To Shinji, they looked very ominous.

Oliver took a step forward, but Maya suddenly put out a hand, stopping him. "Hold up," the explorer warned. "I've been inside a few different tombs and ancient temples. Long corridor with mysterious snake statues lining the walls?" She snorted. "What does that say to you?"

"That it's a trap," Shinji said immediately. He hadn't been in any ancient temples himself, but he'd played enough video games to guess what was going on. Maya gave him a pleased smile.

"Exactly. At least the kid has been paying attention."

Oliver raised a skeptical eyebrow, but then he bent down and snatched a fist-size rock from the floor, tossing it in one hand as he rose.

"So what do you think it's going to be?" he asked, glancing at the rest of them. "Darts? Poisoned darts? Darts would be my guess, though that's pretty clichéd. Let's hope this challenge is a little more creative." And he tossed the rock into the hallway.

As soon as the stone hit the ground, there was a hiss followed by a roar as columns of flames shot out of not one but *all* the serpents' mouths. Fire filled the entirety of the corridor, bright and searingly hot, making everyone flinch. The flames lasted only a couple of seconds before sputtering out again, but there was no doubt in Shinji's mind: if any one of them set off the trap, they would all be barbecued.

Both of Oliver's eyebrows shot into his hair. "Okay," he said, nodding and taking a rather large step back. "I take back what I said about poisoned darts. Poisoned darts are A-OK in my book. So . . . how are we going to get through this?"

"Look at the ground," Maya said. "The rock triggered the trap when it hit the floor."

Very carefully, Shinji walked to the edge of the corridor, gazing at the rows of deadly arrow traps. He could see the rock Oliver had tossed lying in the very center of the hall and noticed that the ground was covered in stone tiles that stretched all the way down the corridor. All of the tiles had some kind of symbol carved into them. Individually, he could make out a sun, a moon, three squiggly lines that looked like wind, a warrior with a spear, a jaguar, and some kind of strange ratlike creature with a hand on the end of its tail.

Shinji blinked, remembering the picture in Dr. Ramos's office. The fearsome rat-wolf thing with the grasping fingers on its tail looked a lot like the image on the stones.

"Ah, yes." Professor Carrero craned his neck as he observed the hallway, staying several paces back from the edge. "Sun, moon, wind, warrior, jaguar, and . . ." He frowned at the strange rodent creature with the hand on its tail. "I believe that is the ahuizotl."

"An awee-whatsit?" Oliver repeated.

"Ahuizotl." This time, Dr. Ramos spoke up. "A type of water monster found in both Aztec and Ximalli mythology," he went on. "It was an evil creature, one that was often tasked with doing the dirty work of the gods, going after humans with whom the gods were displeased. The extra limb on the end of its tail was said to drag humans underwater so the monster could drown and then eat them."

"How morbidly fascinating," Oliver remarked. "But that doesn't tell us how we're going to get across."

"We have to step on the tiles in the right order," Shinji guessed. "Or, we have to not step on the tiles that are wrong."

"Precisely, dear boy," Professor Carrero said, bending down toward the tiles. "We will have to choose our steps carefully. Just give me a few minutes to study these."

The grinding sound of stone against stone interrupted him. Above them, panels were sliding back, revealing rectangular holes in the ceiling. Things were dropping through onto the floor. Long, thin things that were definitely alive.

"Snakes!" Lucy gasped as a few dozen green-and-yellow serpents raised their heads and slithered toward them. They were vipers, Shinji realized, the same type he'd seen in his vision. And they kept coming, falling through the ceiling holes and writhing about on the ground. The chamber was suddenly filled with hissing and the sounds of scales slithering over rock.

"We don't have a few minutes, Professor," Maya snapped as they all quickly backed away from the rain of venomous snakes. "We need to get across that floor *now*."

"Oh dear, oh dear. I never do my best work when I'm rushed." Professor Carrero glanced back at the snakes, then at the tiles again. "The ahuizotl," he decided. "Of the symbols on the floor, it is the only one that is portrayed in a negative light. We should step on the ahuizotl tiles to cross."

"Is that an educated hypothesis?" Oliver wondered. "Or are you just guessing?"

"One way to find out." Shinji bent down and grabbed another rock. Stepping to the edge of the hallway, he aimed, then tossed the rock at the closest ahuizotl tile. The stone hit the correct tile square-on, and immediately there was a roar as the hallway filled with fire again.

"Nope," Oliver announced. "Not that one. And we don't really have the time to throw rocks at all the pictures. Someone make another choice, quick."

"Snakes," Lucy blurted out. "There are snakes everywhere. It has to be a clue. Is there anything on the tiles that looks like a snake?"

"There are no snake tiles," Maya said. "Choose something else."

The vipers were close now. Shinji hovered at the very edge of the hallway, watching them slither toward him. One huge green viper raised its head and hissed, baring a pair of long, curved fangs. Oliver drew his parrot-head cane, hooked a serpent that had gotten too close, and tossed it back into the nest. This only seemed to anger the others, for they all reared up with furious hisses.

Dr. Ramos snapped his fingers. "Wind," he announced, looking down at the tiles. "The feathered serpent was sometimes called the god of wind. And we have a wind tile right there."

"Unless it's the wrong choice," Professor Carrero said, "and we're all incinerated the second we step into the hall."

The horde of snakes was almost upon them. Shinji jerked back as one viper lunged, the lethal fangs barely missing his leg. "There's no time!" Maya snapped. "We have to move! Everyone into the hall, but be sure to step only on the wind tiles. Go!"

With vipers at their heels, they all sprang into the corridor. Shinji spotted a wind tile near the wall and leaped, holding his breath as his foot came down on the flat stone. For a second, he braced himself to hear the hiss of flame leaving the statue mouths and wondered how badly he would get burned. But no flames shot from the serpent jaws, and back in the room, the horde of vipers had stopped at the very edge of the corridor. Their eyes glittered, and they hissed angrily as they writhed and coiled at the threshold, but they weren't following them into the hall.

"Ah, it looks like wind was the right answer after all,"

Professor Carrero wheezed, balancing precariously on one foot in the center of the passage. "Is everyone all right?"

"I think so," Lucy said shakily. She had landed a few tiles from Shinji, one hand pressed to the wall for support. On the other wall, Oliver stood with his legs splayed wide, each foot on separate wind stones, while Maya, balanced easily on one leg with her arms crossed, looked like a large, somewhat annoyed bird. Dr. Ramos had somehow managed to get both feet on a single stone and now stood ramrod straight, as if he were afraid to move. Shinji was glad they had all found their own wind tile to step on. The hallway was suddenly very crowded.

"Well, the snakes aren't following us," Oliver remarked, glancing back at the angry vipers, which hissed at them furiously but seemed to have hit an invisible barrier. "Thank goodness for that. Did someone spray a line of snake repellent in front of the hall, or did we just meet the world's first trained viper squad?"

"Magic?" Shinji suggested.

Oliver shrugged. "Whatever it is, I'm glad we don't have to play leapfrog down the hall while being chased by serpents at the same time," he said, and glanced at Maya. "How 'bout you get us out of here, fearless leader?"

Maya gave a stiff nod. "Follow me," she said. "Step where I step, and take your time. It's not a race."

"Do be careful, everyone," the professor cautioned as they trailed Maya down the long corridor, making sure to step on the correct stones. "Watch where you put your feet. Some of these stones could be very fragile."

"Yeah," Oliver added, picking his way across the tiles. "We don't want anyone breaking wind while we're here."

Cautiously, they made their way down the corridor, following Maya as she hopped lightly from stone to stone. It was a long, painstakingly slow process. The tiles were all ancient, and some of them were covered in dirt and moss, making them hard to distinguish. Shinji almost lost his balance a couple of times, and once he nearly stepped on a jaguar tile instead of a wind tile because the image was so faded. Thankfully, no one stepped on a wrong picture, and after a few close calls, they were able to reach the other side without triggering any of the statues.

"Well, that was exciting." Oliver dusted off his hands with a grimace. "I love life-threatening puzzles like that. It's always fun when the snakes show up. Or spiders, or centipedes, or scorpions." He glanced at the explorer beside him. "Why do you do this again, Maya?"

"The same reason you go diving with sharks in search of sunken treasure." Maya looked back at the hallway with a smug grin. "Only I don't complain about it."

"Ooh, touché. I'll remember that the next time we sail through the Bermuda Triangle."

Shinji caught up with Lucy as they continued down the tunnel. "Good thinking about the snakes," he told her. "The feathered serpent leading to the wind tile was kind of brilliant. We would've chosen wrong otherwise."

"Thanks." She gave him a shaky smile. "I just figured, snakes are everywhere, and this whole temple was built for a giant serpent god. It would make sense that something about snakes would be the right answer. And not . . . what was the other thing? The ahuizotl. Whatever *that* is, I've never heard of it before."

Abruptly, the tunnel ended, opening up into a large, flooded cavern. The air was still, the only sounds being droplets of water falling from the stalactites to plink into the lake. Statues and broken pillars were scattered throughout the chamber, jutting out of the depths at weird angles. Shinji saw a giant stone head lying half in, half out of the water, one huge eye peering up at him. The surface of the underground lake was pitch-black and as still as glass.

He immediately didn't like it.

"Okay, who wants to guess there's something nasty in the water?" Oliver commented, echoing Shinji's thoughts. Stepping to the edge, the ex-pirate peered into the black depths and wrinkled his nose. "I'd bet money there are snakes in there. Or piranhas. Are there piranhas in this part of the world?"

"There are no piranhas in Central America," Maya said flatly.

"Well, crocodiles, then. Or really big leeches." Oliver

stepped back with a grimace. "Either way, I don't want to go in there. Does anyone see a boat?"

There were no boats anywhere in the room. There were a lot of fallen pillars lying one atop the other, broken pieces of the roof, and shattered statues lying in the water. The stones were slimy and green with algae, but Shinji couldn't see any other way across.

Maya didn't, either. The explorer hopped onto a fallen pillar with the grace of a jaguar and looked back at them. "Come on," she urged everyone. "Follow me, and step where I step. Concentrate on where you put your feet and, as always, be careful. There are no safety lines this time around."

Painstakingly, they made their way across the flooded chamber, following Maya, who always seemed to know the best path to take. She made it look easy, striding along fallen pillars and hopping from stone to stone as if she did this kind of thing every day. Fortunately the broken columns were quite large, and the roots dangling from the ceiling provided something to cling to as Shinji made his way over the still black waters of the lake.

As he hopped from a pillar to a broken snake statue, a chunk of stone crumbled beneath his feet, falling into the water with a splash that made him wince. The sound echoed through the chamber, blaringly loud, making him feel as if a spotlight had flipped on and was shining down on him for all to see. He suddenly felt that, if there was something in the water, it had now noticed him and was staring up from the depths, wondering how best to drag him under.

"Everything all right back there, kid?" Oliver called from his perch atop a boulder. A few broken pillars down, Lucy also turned to watch him, holding tightly to a root dangling from the ceiling. Shinji took a deep breath, wrenched his gaze away from the water, and nodded.

"Yeah," he called back. "I'm fine, I just . . ."

He trailed off, feeling the blood drain from his face. Something was rising from the water behind Lucy. Something long and thin like a snake, with a pale, long-fingered hand on the very end. Before Shinji could yell out a warning, the terrible hand shot forward, grabbed Lucy around the waist, and dragged her under the water.

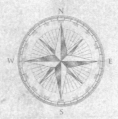

CHAPTER SEVENTEEN

Lucy!"

Shinji didn't think. He didn't wonder what the thing was. He just dove into the water, swimming as hard as he could for the place where Lucy had disappeared. Taking a deep breath, he ducked beneath the surface and swam for the bottom.

It was almost pitch-black in the water. Shinji could barely see the pillars surrounding him. He caught a flash of movement between a pair of statues and kicked toward it, straining to see through the gloom.

Something dark and terrible slid out from behind the statues, fixing him with two beady red eyes. It looked like a cross between a wolf and a rat, with spiky black fur, pointed ears, and a narrow, fang-filled muzzle. Its paws resembled webbed human hands, and a long, naked tail extended behind it.

Shinji's stomach clenched. The pale hand he'd seen was attached to the end of the creature's tail. The long fingers still held Lucy, who was fighting and kicking in its grasp.

The monster stared at Shinji with pitiless red eyes, then curled its muzzle back to reveal sharp yellow teeth. Shinji suddenly realized he didn't have a weapon; he hadn't even grabbed a stick or a rock before he'd leaped into the water. Though what a stick could do to this monster he wasn't certain.

Suddenly there was a splash and an explosion of bubbles as Oliver Ocean dove into the water beside him. Trailing his long coat, he darted in front of Shinji, putting himself before the terrible creature, which was getting ready to attack. Shinji saw a flash of gold as Oliver pulled out his parrot-head cane and brandished it in front of the monster.

The creature snarled. It lunged at Oliver, pointed jaws gaping, and Shinji's heart twisted with fear. But Oliver gripped the handle of his cane and pulled, revealing a thin silver blade. As the monster came toward him, he stabbed out with his weapon, sinking the point into the creature's shoulder.

The monster recoiled with a hiss that made the water in front of it boil. It snapped at Oliver, trying to drive him back, but Oliver's cane flashed out and poked it in the muzzle. Baring its fangs, it tried to flee, its sleek body moving through the water like a shark. But as it did, Shinji reached out and grabbed Lucy's wrist, jerking the monster to a halt. Lucy's eyes were closed now, her body limp and unresponsive in his grasp. Shinji's lungs burned, desperate for oxygen, but there was no way he was leaving her to this monster. The creature spun, hissing and opening its mouth to bite him, but Oliver lunged forward and stabbed it in the nose.

With a shriek, the monster decided that it'd had enough. Releasing Lucy, it turned and swooped away through the water. Gliding between two broken pillars, it vanished into the gloom. The fingerlike appendages on the end of its tail flashed as it went through a beam of light, and then it was gone.

Gripping Lucy's hand, Shinji kicked his way to the surface, pulling her up with him. As their heads broke the water, he took several deep, gasping breaths, sucking air into his lungs, then looked around for the rest of SEA.

"Shinji!" someone shouted. Maya stood on a nearby pillar with her machete drawn, Professor Carrero and Dr. Ramos hovering worriedly behind her. "This way!" she urged. "Get out of the water, Shinji. Hurry!"

Kicking his feet, Shinji dragged Lucy through the cold water to where the others waited, releasing her as Dr. Ramos and Professor Carrero reached down and pulled her onto the rock with them. Lucy's eyes were still closed, her face pale and slack, and Shinji's stomach clenched in fear as they laid her back on the stones.

"Where's Oliver?" Maya asked as Shinji started to pull himself up. "He went in after you, but I don't see him now."

Before Shinji could reply, something cold and clammy like a dead hand grabbed his ankle, yanking him into the water again. He let out a yell as his head went under, and he felt himself being dragged down into the depths. Kicking and squirming, he tried to fight the pull, but the grip on his leg was too strong. Down they went until they hit the floor of the underwater chamber, surrounded by statues and broken columns.

The monster dragged Shinji close, turned, and pinned him down by the shoulders, pressing him into the chamber floor. Its sharp claws dug into his skin, holding him in place, as he writhed and kicked helplessly. The creature was too strong, and he was out of his element. Lungs burning, Shinji stared into the monster's heartless red eyes and felt something inside him grow hot. Raising an arm, he thrust his hand into the creature's face.

His skin pulsed, and a bright golden light flared into existence, lighting up the gloom around them. Strength flowed into Shinji's body, swirling through him like beams of light, and suddenly he could breathe again. For just a moment, he thought he saw scaly golden coils surrounding him and felt the phantom brush of wings against his skin.

The monster—the *ahuizotl*, he suddenly realized—jerked

away from him. Eyes wide with fear, it stared at Shinji a moment before it let out a terrified hiss and darted away into the shadows. As its long-fingered hand-tail vanished into the shadows, Shinji knew that this time, it wasn't coming back.

The light faded, plunging him into darkness once more. As the gloom returned, Shinji realized he was drowning again. His lungs screamed for air, and blackness crawled on the edge of his vision. He kicked his way to the surface as quickly as he could, reaching desperately for the light, but his limbs felt weak, and he was seconds away from gasping underwater.

A hand grabbed his own. Shinji looked up to see Oliver Ocean giving him a half-relieved, half-exasperated look before pulling him to the surface. As Shinji's head broke through the water, he gulped in oxygen, and the black cloud hovering around his vision faded away.

"Shinji!"

Hands grabbed his arms and clothes, dragging him out of the water and onto a fallen pillar. As he slumped, dripping and panting, to the stones, a wet but very much alive Lucy fell to her knees and threw her arms around his neck. Shinji hugged her back, relieved that she was all right, that they had both somehow survived the encounter with the monster of the deep.

Oliver heaved himself out of the water, flinging his hair back as he rose. "You are one lucky kid," he muttered, shaking his head. "Both of you are. Good thing I've grown rather fond of this little group; I don't usually go jumping into monster-infested waters for anything. Well, except for sunken treasure." He gave Shinji a wry grin and shook his head. "Let's not make this a habit, okay? You're ruining my craven coward reputation."

Lucy pulled back as Maya dropped a towel over Shinji's shoulders. "We thought you were dead for sure," Lucy told him. "When the ahuizotl grabbed you and dragged you under, we couldn't find you for a long time. Then there was this glow, this weird light, that came from under the water, and that's when Oliver was able to see you. Are you all right? Are you hurt? What happened? Where's the ahuizotl?"

"I don't know." Unable to keep up with the flurry of questions, Shinji just answered the last one he heard. "Gone, I guess. I don't think it's coming back."

His head felt weird, like there was something else living inside it. Where had that golden light that surrounded him come from? Was it the magic of the idol? Could it have been . . . the Coatl itself saving him from its hated enemy?

"The ahuizotl." Professor Carrero's voice was breathless. He stared out over the water with a dazed look on his face. "It is real. To think we came face-to-face with a creature found only in legend. Well, I suppose you two did," he amended, looking at Shinji and Lucy. "I would have loved to have seen the creature with my own eyes, though I fear it may well have eaten me. Still, this will be a tale for the history books."

A distant shout echoed down the passage they had just come through, making everyone jerk up. Even after the wild encounter with the snakes and the ahuizotl, they still weren't safe.

"Hightower is coming," Maya said grimly. "Break time is over. We need to keep moving."

Wearily, Shinji pulled himself to his feet, dripping wet but happy to get out of the room. As they left the chamber of the ahuizotl, he wondered what other challenges still waited for him before they reached the font, and if he'd be able to get past them.

CHAPTER EIGHTEEN

I see light!" Lucy cried.

Shinji's heart lifted, and he hurried forward. Turning a corner, he saw the mouth of the cave just ahead and a navy-blue sky silhouetted through the opening. Quickly, he checked his tattoo, just to make sure they were still going the right way. The Coatl's head pointed straight toward the exit, and Shinji frowned in confusion.

"Did we miss the temple?" he wondered as Oliver paused beside him. "I swear I followed where the tattoo pointed."

Professor Carrero peered down as well. "Hmm, I wouldn't worry too much about it, dear boy," he stated. "What we went through was likely the trial to get to the temple itself. If we keep following the tattoo, it should lead us to where we're supposed to be."

"Yes," Dr. Ramos added, the look in his eyes almost hungry as he strode forward. "The temple is near. I can feel it."

"Careful now," Maya cautioned as the exit drew ever closer. Shinji wanted to run toward it, but her words made him pause. "The last stretch is sometimes the most dangerous. We don't want to have come all this way and then get shot down at the finish line."

They were all very cautious walking down the final corridor. Shinji was tense, ready to leap back if fire or arrows or poisonous snakes shot toward them out of the wall. When he finally reached the mouth of the cave and the light hit his face, he tilted his head back and closed his eyes, feeling the breeze against his skin.

"Oh . . ." Lucy whispered beside him. "Wow."

Shinji opened his eyes, and his heart jumped to his throat.

A vast clearing stretched out before them, surrounded on all sides by jagged cliffs. Off to the left, a waterfall cascaded into a sparkling pool near the edge of which a herd of spotted deer grazed. Flowers grew everywhere, carpeting the ground, blooming on decaying logs and trees. Swarms of butterflies hovered over them, jeweled splashes of purple, pink, yellow, and blue against the green backdrop of the jungle.

In the distance, over the tops of the highest trees, a massive pyramid rose into the air. Ancient and imposing, it loomed over them like a mountain, its point seeming to touch the sky. Gazing up at it, Shinji felt something stir inside him, a sense of longing and excitement. He wasn't sure if the emotion was his own or the tattoo's.

"Ladies and gentlemen," Professor Carrero declared as they made their way forward. "I believe we have found the ancient temple of the feathered serpent."

"Be on your guard," Maya warned yet again. "We're not there yet. There's always one more surprise waiting for you before you get to the door."

"That's what I love about you, Maya," Oliver said. "You're always so optimistic."

"There you are!"

Everyone jumped as Zoe's drone swooped down in a flash of metal, hovering in front of them. "What took you guys so long?" the face on the screen demanded. "I was getting really freaked out. Never mind, you can tell me later. Right now we have a bigger problem." The drone rose a few feet into the air, turning toward the tunnel they had just exited. "A group of Hightower agents found the cave entrance a few minutes after you guys went inside," she told them. "Unless there was a cave-in or something huge happened, they're not far behind."

"Calm down, Zoe." Oliver raised his hands. "We just

fought our way through snakes, fire traps, a really cold lake, and a nasty water monster out of legend. If Hightower is still on our trail, trust me, they're not going to have an easy time of it."

Zoe looked like she wanted to argue, but Maya waved her hand in front of the drone's screen, bringing its attention to her.

"What's the lay of the land?" the explorer wanted to know. "Anything standing between us and the pyramid?"

The drone swiveled around to face her. "As far as I can tell," Zoe replied, "this is a big flat plateau surrounded by trees and cliffs. The pyramid is across the clearing, and there's a wide-open area right before you reach the steps. But I didn't see anything around it except pillars and some bones."

"Pillars and bones." Oliver winced. "Great. That doesn't sound suspicious at all."

"Whatever it is," Maya put in, "it sounds like we're close. Zoe, stay here; keep an eye on the cave. The second you see Hightower coming, let us know."

"You got it!"

Oliver snorted and glanced at Shinji. "Well, let's get you to the temple, kid." He sighed. "And we'll see if we can get through this last challenge, whatever it is, before Hightower crashes the party."

Carefully they made their way toward the massive

pyramid looming beyond the tree line. The breeze blew gently through the greenery and rustled the branches of the trees as they passed beneath. Birds chirped, butterflies fluttered, and the air smelled of flowers. Everything was very peaceful, but Shinji couldn't shake the feeling that they were being watched.

They stepped out of the trees, and the pyramid abruptly stood before them, silhouetted against the sky. As Zoe had pointed out, a flat, open area lay between them and the temple steps. It was in the shape of a circle, and the ground was made of cracked stone instead of grass, though moss, vines, and roots had pushed their way up through the rock and were spread across the surface. Columns surrounded it, most of the pillars crumbled and broken. But there were a few still intact, and at the tops of these, stone snake heads were perched, mouths open and fangs bared in silent hisses.

As Shinji picked his way over rocks and snaking vines, he caught a glimmer of white buried in the weeds and stopped, nudging it with his foot. A bleached skull rolled out of the grass and wobbled to a stop, seeming to gaze up at him with empty eye sockets. He bit down a yelp.

Lucy peered over his shoulder and frowned. "Is that a skull?" she whispered. "What is this place?"

The feeling of being watched was growing stronger. Shinji gazed around, seeing more bones scattered about, along with bits of weapons and pieces of ancient armor.

Half a spear lay thrust into the stones a few feet from him, and what he thought was a moss-covered rock was really a rusted-out helmet, half buried in vines.

"This isn't just a clearing," he said, his voice echoing into the sudden silence. "This is an arena—"

As soon as he spoke, something flashed from the bushes, barely missing his face as it sped by. A spear clinked off a pillar behind them, clattering to the ground, and everyone froze.

The bushes rustled, and all around them, figures began to step out of the trees, seeming to materialize from nowhere. They skulked into the open, a dozen lean warriors carrying spears in one hand and shields in the other. As they came into the light, Lucy gasped, and Shinji felt his jaw drop open. The warriors wore loincloths, armored breastplates, and bright feathered headdresses, but the faces beneath were of enormous serpents.

Hissing, the snake warriors surrounded them, trapping them all in a ring of spears. Shinji and the others shrank against one another as deadly obsidian tips slid toward them.

"Wait!" Shinji stepped forward, holding up his arms so that the tattoo was clearly visible. "We're not intruders!" he called to the ring of serpent warriors, who turned beady yellow eyes on him. "I'm here to return the Coatl's heart to the temple. Let us pass, and we'll leave as soon as we're finished."

The snake warriors hissed at him, and in their combined voices, he heard words slither into his ears. "Bearer of the mark," they hissed, "you must prove your worth to pass. We are your final challenge. If you wish to enter the temple of the feathered serpent, you must first get past us."

"Get past you?" Shinji gaped at them. "What, you mean, like a fight to the death? One-on-one combat? Will I have to defeat the snake champion or something?"

"No, bearer of the mark. That is not your test."

The crowd of snake warriors parted, and a taller figure stepped forward. Like the rest of the warriors, its face was that of a venomous serpent, a viper, but instead of armor, it wore a cape of yellow, green, and blue feathers. Two bright crimson eyes stared down at Shinji without blinking.

"You," the snake person told him, speaking out loud now, "will be tested. To see if you are worthy to enter the temple."

Shinji gulped. "Just me?"

"Yes. Three trials await you. Three challenges you must overcome on your own. Your companions may not interfere." The serpent's unblinking gaze swung to Oliver and the others. "If they try, if they attempt to help or intervene in any way, we will slay you all."

"Right." Shinji glanced at the others, still surrounded by the ring of deadly spears. "Did you guys hear that?" He tried speaking casually, but his heart was pounding and his throat had gone dry. "This is a test, but no one can help me. I have to do this on my own."

"Ah, the old *chosen one must prove himself worthy to enter* challenge," Professor Carrero said with a nod. "Very traditional. I take it that if we try to intervene or give you any hints, they'll kill us all?"

"Pretty much, yeah."

"Okay, then." Oliver observed the ring of spears around him and raised his hands. "We'll just stand right here and cheer you on." He smiled and gave Shinji a thumbs-up. "No worries. You got this, kiddo."

Lucy caught his eye, looking much more worried than Oliver. "Be careful, Shinji," she whispered.

Shinji nodded, then took a deep breath and turned back to the snake person. He wanted to ask what kind of challenges these were, if he would be expected to run, fight, or solve an impossible riddle, but he was afraid that asking for hints would be failing the test. So he just met the snake warrior's impassive gaze and raised his chin. "All right," he said. "I'm ready. Let's get this over with."

The snake person flicked a forked tongue at him, then raised a scaly arm and pointed to the edge of the arena. "Stand over there," it hissed. "We will see if you are truly worthy to pass. Your first test begins now."

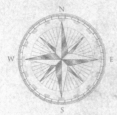

CHAPTER NINETEEN

Shinji did as the snake person ordered, retreating to the edge of the circle, then turning back. When he did, his stomach tightened.

Several snake warriors had broken away from the rest and now stood in a line between Shinji and the cloaked snake person. The warriors held bows and arrows, all nocked and ready to fire. At the end of the line of archers, the cloaked snake raised its head.

"For your first test, you must walk back toward me," it called. "If you stop, you will die. If you run, you will die. There must be no fear and no hesitation. No matter what happens, you must keep walking. Until you reach the end." It raised a clawed hand, beckoning him forward. "Begin."

As the snake person finished speaking, all the serpent archers raised their weapons and drew back the strings, pulling the bows taut. Shinji's heart dropped as a dozen arrows were suddenly pointed at the path he had to walk. Were they going to fire at him? Were they going to shoot him full of arrows before he even reached the end?

Tenacity, whispered a voice in his head. *Don't stop. No matter what happens, keep moving forward.*

Shinji took a deep breath, steeling himself. "Okay," he muttered. "Walking through a firing lane. No problem."

He started walking.

The first arrow flew past his face, zipping right in front of him, so close he heard a vicious buzz. He bit down a yelp and almost stumbled to a halt but forced his feet to keep moving. A second arrow hissed by, this one passing behind his head, ruffling his hair. And a third struck the ground a few inches from his shoe.

Shinji set his jaw and continued walking, trying to ignore the flurry of arrows that zipped all around him. He wanted to stop. Every time an arrow passed an inch or two from his head, he wanted to duck and find cover behind a tree or something solid. But he kept walking, forcing his eyes to stay glued to the serpent in the cape. Once he reached the end of the line, he would be done. He just had to keep moving.

An arrow flashed by his arm, and pain flared as the obsidian tip sliced his skin right above his elbow. Shinji bit back a yelp of pain and nearly staggered to a halt. He could feel blood trickling down his arm and wanted desperately to stop and look at the wound, but he ground his teeth together and kept walking.

Why am I doing this? The thought drifted in before he could stop it, but once there, it wouldn't leave him alone. An arrow flew by his face, making him flinch, but he forced his feet to keep moving. *Why am I even here? I could be killed by crazy snake people in the middle of the jungle, and no one will ever know what happened to me. Aunt Yui will never know what happened. . . .*

He bit his lip. *Aunt Yui.* That was why he was here. He had to see her again, to get back to his life before. He didn't know where she was, but he did know he would do anything to make sure she was safe. Even this.

Okay, Shinji thought. *For Aunt Yui, then. Keep walking.* An arrow zipped past his neck; another almost grazed his nose. *Keep moving.* Another skimmed by his leg, embedding itself in the ground and making him grit his teeth. *Don't stop. Just one . . . more . . . step.*

He came to the end of the line. The gash in his arm was a constant fiery throb, and he could feel blood trickling down his skin, but he was through. The serpent archers lowered their arms, the storm of arrows ceased, and the caped snake warrior regarded him with emotionless red eyes.

"There," Shinji panted, meeting the impassive red gaze of the snake person. "I did it. I kept walking." He held up his wounded arm. "One of your archers has terrible aim, by the way. But I'm here."

He spared a quick glance to Lucy and the others and saw them still being held within the circle of spears. Lucy's face was pale, but Oliver's grim expression shocked him, as if the ex-pirate wished he could be out there helping Shinji through the trials. It lifted his spirits a little, and he gave them all a cheeky grin.

The snake person's tongue flicked out, as if tasting blood, and it gave a slow nod. "Yes," it said calmly. "You have passed. The first test."

As it spoke, it drew the folds of its cape around itself, hiding its upper body from view. "The second challenge awaits," it went on without preamble. "Are you ready?"

"Can I get something for my bleeding arm? The one that one of your snake guys shot with an arrow?"

"No."

Right to the point, at least. Shinji sighed and raised his chin. "Okay, fine. I'm ready."

The warrior drew its arm from beneath the cloak. A

bright yellow viper was coiled around its wrist, lidless eyes staring up at Shinji. It hissed at him, baring long, needle-thin fangs, and Shinji's mouth went dry.

"It can smell fear," the snake warrior continued, unconcerned with the angry, venomous creature it was holding. "If you are afraid, if you give away your fear, it will bite you. Now . . ." It held out its arm, causing the viper to hiss again, staring at Shinji with lidless red eyes. "Take it from me."

"What? Are you joking?"

The snake warrior just continued to watch him. It was, apparently, not joking.

Shinji gazed down at the viper. His heart was pounding, and his stomach felt like a nest of snakes itself. The venomous serpent stared at him and flicked its tongue out, almost daring him to try something.

Courage, whispered that same voice in his head. *True courage is not having no fear. It is being afraid . . . and doing it anyway.*

Shinji swallowed hard. "Okay," he muttered. "If you're going to bite me, snake, do it and get it over with."

Raising an arm, he reached for the viper. Immediately the serpent hissed and coiled its neck into a deadly S shape, ready to strike. Shinji almost jerked his hand back, but he squashed down his fear and gently but firmly wrapped his fingers around the viper's torso.

The snake didn't move. It didn't strike him, but Shinji could feel the steely muscles coiling under his hand. Gathering his courage, he gripped the snake's body and yanked it toward him.

As he pulled it away from the snake warrior's arm, the viper's body suddenly dissolved, making Shinji jump. One second, he was holding a living, breathing snake; the next, it turned into yellow mist that writhed away to nothing between his fingers. Shinji blinked and stared at his empty hand in confusion.

"Excellent," hissed the serpent warrior above him. "You have passed the second test."

"Oh." Shinji watched the last of the mist curl away on the breeze. "Okay, that was easy," he said, feeling a bit foolish. "The viper wasn't real, then? It was just some kind of illusion?"

"It was real," the snake warrior assured him. "Had you hesitated at all, it would have bitten you. And you would have died." It lowered its arm. "But you passed the challenge. Now you face the final trial."

Shinji felt a shiver of both fear and relief run down his spine. *Almost done,* he thought. *This is the last test. That means it's probably going to be super hard, like defeating their best warrior or something like that—*

"Do you see those rocks?" the serpent warrior asked, gesturing across the arena with a clawed hand. Shinji turned and saw three round stones sitting in the grass at the edge of the circle. Except for their sizes, they all looked the same. One was tiny, the size of a baseball. One was larger, almost basketball size. And the last one was the biggest of all, a massive round stone that nearly reached Shinji's waist.

"Retrieve one stone," the serpent warrior said. "Bring it back here, and your final test will be complete."

"That's it?" Shinji gaped at the snake warrior. "You want me to bring you a rock? Just one?"

"Yes."

Shinji grinned. "I can do that." This was going to be easier than he thought. "One rock, coming right up."

However, as he passed the huddle where Oliver and the others were being held, still inside the circle of spears, Lucy caught his eye. There was a warning in her gaze, as if she were trying to tell him something without words. It made him pause. *Be careful,* he thought she was saying. *There is more to this challenge than you think.*

He reached the trio of stones and stared down at them. They didn't look like anything special, just normal round rocks. There were no markings on any of them, no pictures or carvings or anything that set them apart from one another. They were, to Shinji's eye, just rocks.

I just gotta bring one back? Shinji crossed his arms, observing the three stones. *Lucy is right; this seems too easy. There has to be something I'm missing.* Frowning, he directed his next thought at the voice in his head. *Any cryptic hints to help me out?*

This time, the mysterious voice was silent. After a few moments, Shinji shrugged and reached for the smallest of the rocks, the baseball-size stone on the end. If he was going to bring back a rock, he'd go for the one that was easy to pick up. The one in the middle looked heavy, and the biggest one on the end looked like it would take forever to roll. . . .

Shinji stopped, his fingers an inch away from picking up the stone. It *would* be easy to grab the smallest stone, he realized. That was the point. What had Professor Carrero said about the values the Coatl represented? Tenacity. Courage.

Hard work.

Shinji straightened, pulling his arm back. This was the test. It wasn't about just grabbing a stone and bringing it back. The real test was to see if he would pick the easier task, or if he would choose the one that was the most work.

Shinji looked at the biggest rock and winced. It looked really, really heavy. Moving up behind it, he put both hands against the rough stone and pushed as hard as he could.

It moved maybe an inch.

Yep, Shinji thought. *This is going to suck.*

For what felt like hours, Shinji struggled to move the heavy stone. He tried pushing it, rolling it, using branches and other rocks to leverage it across the ground. It was slow going. The hot sun beat down on him, and sweat poured off him in waves, seeping into his cuts and making them sting like crazy. He scraped his hands raw trying to move the giant stone, tore open his knees as he crawled over the vine-covered stone floor, and bruised his shoulder trying to shove it across the ground.

Finally, gasping, sweating, and bleeding, he gave the stone one last push and rolled it in front of the snake warrior, who had waited motionless in the same spot the entire time of Shinji's struggle. As Shinji collapsed beside the boulder, trying to suck air into his lungs, the sound of applause echoed around him. He looked up to see Lucy, Oliver, Maya, and Professor Carrero all clapping for him. He gave them a weak grin and a wave before struggling to his feet and turning to face the snake warrior.

Those red serpent eyes stared down at the boulder for a moment, then up at Shinji. Shinji's heart thumped in his chest. Had he chosen wrong after all? Had he moved that gigantic rock for nothing?

The snake person stepped gracefully around the rock to loom in front of Shinji. "You . . . have passed," it finally hissed, making Shinji's knees buckle in relief. "You have shown the ideals of the feathered serpent—tenacity, courage, and hard work. You have proven yourself worthy to enter the temple."

"And my friends?"

"The tests were only for you." The snake warrior cocked its serpentine head at Shinji. "If you had failed, their lives would have been forfeit. But since you passed, they are free to enter as well."

It raised an arm, and the ring of serpent warriors surrounding the members of Shinji's group drew back, lowering their spears.

"Now," the snake warrior continued, glancing down at Shinji, "Chosen One of the feathered serpent, you must—"

Suddenly it jerked its head up, red eyes widening. The snakelike jaws opened, and it let out a furious hiss. "Intruders!" it snarled, and the rest of the warriors jerked up. "Intruders in the feathered serpent's jungle. Warriors, fall back!"

Immediately the rest of the serpent warriors sprang into action. Hissing and baring their fangs, they drew away and melted into the trees. In seconds, every snake warrior had vanished into the jungle like they had never been there, leaving Shinji, Lucy, and the Society members standing alone in the center of the arena.

"Okay." Oliver gazed around cautiously. "Any idea what that was about?"

Before Shinji could even catch his breath, a shout echoed in the jungle, sounding dangerously close. In a flash of metal, Zoe's drone swooped through the trees and zipped toward them. Shinji's relief at seeing her again was cut short as the drone circled them, its movements quick and frantic.

"Hightower!" Zoe cried, making Shinji's blood run cold. "Hightower is here! Shinji, Lucy, run!"

Branches snapped in the jungle, bushes rustling madly, and Lucy gasped as a dozen people spilled from the trees and leveled very large guns in her and Shinji's direction.

CHAPTER TWENTY

Don't move!" A large man stepped forward, pointing his weapon, first at Shinji and then at each member of the group in turn. Shinji recognized him instantly: the same blond man he'd met in Abenge marketplace, who had grabbed him on the deck of the *Good Tern*. What was his name again? Kraus? "Hands where I can see them," the agent barked. "Now!"

Lucy quickly raised her hands. Oliver and the others did the same. After a moment, Shinji reluctantly followed their example. His heart pounded in desperation and anger. So close! They had come so far, passed all the tests, found the hidden temple and everything, only to be caught by

Hightower in the end. He could feel the Coatl tattoo moving on his arm, urging him toward the steps of the temple. But if he moved now, Lucy and the others might be hurt or killed.

The Hightower leader gazed around, then gave a nod of satisfaction. "It's clear, sir," he said over his shoulder, making Shinji frown in confusion.

Something floated up behind the agent: a small machine with delicate propellers, very similar to Zoe's drone, but smaller. This one hovered in the air a moment; then a blue light flicked on, and a transparent image of a man appeared between them and the Hightower agents. A man Shinji recognized.

"Well," Gideon Frost said, gazing down at them imperiously. "And here we are. I suppose I must extend my thanks to the Society of Explorers and Adventurers. Not only did you lead me right to the font, you solved all the riddles and challenges so we didn't have to. Plus you kept both the key"—he glanced at Shinji—"*and* my wayward daughter safe. You have my gratitude."

Oliver's mouth dropped open. "Daughter?" he sputtered, glaring at Lucy.

"Oh, didn't you know?" The holographic image smiled nastily. "Did my darling Lucy neglect to mention that little fact? Yes, she is my very talented wayward daughter, and she has been very naughty of late. But now that I have the location of the font, she can come home and forget this foolishness." He turned that sinister smile on Lucy. "Isn't that right, my dear?"

Lucy glared at Frost. "Don't do this, Dad," she snapped through gritted teeth. "This is one of the last places of magic left. Hightower doesn't need to come exploit it like they do everything else."

"Listen to her, Frost," Oliver called. "If Hightower builds on the font, they'll destroy the jungle and everything that lives here. All the wildlife and the people who call this jungle their home will suffer because of the corporation's greed. You don't have to do this."

"It is already done." Gideon Frost waved a careless hand. "Now that we have the boy and the font, nothing will stop us. Kraus, have your men secure the members of SEA. Once they are dealt with, take the boy up to the temple; if my predictions are correct, he is the key to getting inside. Oh, and someone please bring me my daughter—"

"No!" Lucy yelled, surprising them all. The drone whirled on her as she stepped forward, her voice as cold and final as Hightower's. "If you do this, Dad, I will never return to Hightower," she said firmly. "I will never help you or the company with their goals ever again. I'll stay with SEA and fight you and Hightower every chance I get."

"Don't be ridiculous," Frost responded with his signature iciness. "You are descended from greatness, from the blood of Harrison himself. Your fate is with Hightower; it has *always* been with Hightower. You cannot deny who you are."

"I don't have to be what you want," Lucy returned. "You told me that the only way to survive is to be ruthless and to take what you need, but that's not true. We should be protecting the sacred places of the world, not exploiting them. Look around you." She gestured to the jungle surrounding them all. "The magic belongs here, not in the hands of any corporation. Would you really destroy this place just to make Hightower more powerful?"

"Power," Gideon Frost said coldly, "is the only thing that matters. If we don't take it, someone else will. And if you cannot see that, then I have not raised you as I should have. Perhaps all this is my fault." He paused, as if struggling with himself, then held out a transparent hand. "Come, Lucy," he urged. "You cannot stop what is happening here. We *will* take the font, and we will use that magic to make our dreams come true. You can be a part of it, if you stop these foolish games and realize your destiny. You are the heir to Hightower; it is time to come home."

"No." Lucy raised her chin, eyes flashing. "Enough is enough. I won't be a part of this."

"I'm not giving you a choice!" Gideon Frost roared, finally losing his composure. "Kraus, have your men bring my daughter and take the boy up to the font. Make sure SEA does not interfere. We *will* have the font, and nothing—"

A spear tipped with green-and-yellow feathers suddenly flew from the trees, striking the Hightower drone square-on. The machine jerked, sparking and buzzing, before dropping to the ground in a puff of smoke. The image of Gideon Frost sputtered once, the look on his face one of shock, then winked into nothing.

The rest of Hightower's men jumped and pointed their weapons at the surrounding trees, searching for attackers. For a moment, everything was silent, the jungle seeming to hold its breath. Then, with furious hisses, the bushes around Hightower parted and a group of snake warriors leaped into their midst.

Hightower's men gave shouts of alarm as the serpent people swarmed them. Shots rang out, echoing over the trees and sending flocks of birds into the air. Spears flashed, howls of fear and pain mingled with the sounds of battle, and everything descended into chaos.

"Shinji!" Oliver's voice made Shinji jump. The ex-pirate stabbed a finger toward the top of the pyramid. "Get to the temple," he told him. "Return the heart. We'll keep Hightower busy."

Shinji looked at the raging battle with Hightower and the serpent warriors and swallowed. There were too many Hightower agents, and they had guns. SEA, even with the snake warriors helping them, didn't stand a chance. "But—"

"Don't worry about us, dear boy," Professor Carrero interrupted. "We're the Society of Explorers and Adventurers; I daresay we know a few things about handling ourselves in a fight." He raised two fists in front of his face. "In my younger days, I had quite the mean right hook. We'll take care of these hooligans; you just get yourself to the font."

With a whoop, Oliver flung himself across the arena, into the group of Hightower agents. His parrot-head cane whipped out, striking limbs and knocking weapons aside. Maya joined him, her machete flashing in the sun, and Zoe's drone swooped down out of nowhere, striking a Hightower agent in the back of the head. Even Professor Carrero waded into the fight, his fists raised before him like a boxer.

Dr. Ramos, Shinji noticed, was nowhere to be seen.

Lucy took his hand. "Come on, Shinji," she urged. "We can't help them now; we have to reach the font."

With one last look at the battle between SEA, Hightower, and the temple guardians, Shinji turned and sprinted toward the pyramid. He heard Kraus shouting after him, telling his men to "get those kids," but he didn't dare look back.

The tattoo on his arm pulsed when they reached the stone steps, and Shinji could feel the Coatl squirming beneath his skin as they climbed. Behind them, the sounds of battle faded. Shinji and Lucy kept climbing, feeling the wind tug at their hair and clothes, until they came to the very top of the stairs. A massive doorway stood before them, a solid slab of carved stone blocking the way into the temple. The image in the stone was a familiar winged serpent, mimicking the pose of the tattoo on Shinji's arm.

"I think we're in the right place," Shinji said.

"Yes, but how do we get inside?" Lucy wondered. "There's no lock, no keyhole, nothing."

A shout echoed behind them. Shinji and Lucy turned to see one of the Hightower agents who had somehow broken away from the battle and was jogging up the steps toward them. Lucy gasped, and Shinji glared at the barrier blocking their way.

"No time left. We have to get inside, now!"

They rushed to the door, pushing and shoving as hard as they could, but the enormous stone slab didn't budge. It felt to Shinji like they were straining against a solid wall.

"The Coatl tattoo," Lucy exclaimed. "Dad said it was the key. Quick, Shinji, hold it up to the door!"

Shinji stepped back and raised his arm, turning the tattoo toward the stone slab. But a couple of seconds ticked by, and nothing happened. The door remained firmly shut, and the Hightower agent's footsteps sounded ever closer.

Long, cold fingers wrapped around his wrist. Stomach clenching, Shinji jerked back, but it wasn't the Hightower agent who had grabbed him. It was Dr. Ramos.

"Dr. Ramos? What are you doing?"

"Not like that, fool," the small man whispered harshly. His grip like iron, he pressed Shinji's arm to the carving of the winged snake in the door.

The second Shinji's skin touched the slab, the eyes of the carved snake lit up with a green glow. A rumble shook the pyramid, the stones beneath them trembling, as dust and loose pebbles plinked down around them. With a deep grinding sound, the slab opened, two sides sliding away to reveal a gap just large enough for a person to slip through.

"Go!" Dr. Ramos spat, throwing Shinji forward. "Get inside. The door won't stay open long."

Shinji stumbled into Lucy, who caught him with a worried look. Frowning, Shinji turned to shout something at Dr. Ramos, but at that moment the Hightower agent reached the top of the steps. With a yell, he lunged for them.

Shinji and Lucy dove through the crack, hearing the grind of stone on stone as the door began to close. At the last second, Dr. Ramos scuttled through as well, moving so quickly, Shinji almost thought he had imagined it. Then the stone door shut with a boom, cutting them off from the outside, trapping them within the temple of the feathered serpent.

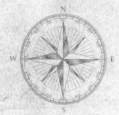

CHAPTER TWENTY-ONE

For a few seconds, Shinji was frozen, waiting for his heart to calm down. Waiting for something to leap out and attack. Nothing happened. The air was completely still, the noises outside vanishing like someone had flipped a switch.

Then Lucy drew in a slow breath and took a step forward.

"Oh, wow," she breathed. "Shinji, look at this. It's beautiful."

Carefully Shinji turned around and felt his own amazement rise up to join hers.

They had stepped into some kind of inner sanctum. The room before them was large and opened to the sky, letting beams of sunlight filter through the chamber. Ancient moss-covered statues of warriors with animal heads were scattered throughout the room, interspersed with a forest of pillars. The air was still, and motes of light danced on the air like fireflies.

"I can feel the magic here," Lucy whispered as they edged farther into the room. She kept her voice low, as anything louder felt wrong in the somber silence of the chamber. "I can feel it drifting through the air and flowing through the ground. We are definitely in the right place."

"Yeah, but . . ." Shinji gazed around, searching between the shadows and rays of sunlight, trying to see through the glare. "If this is the font, then where's the Coatl?"

Dr. Ramos took a few steps forward, pointing a thin, sticklike finger toward the center of the room. "There."

Shinji followed his gesture, and his heart sank.

In the very center of the room, a ring of mossy stone steps led down to a shallow pool. Sparkling motes, like multicolored fireflies, drifted up from the basin before fading away. The rippling water within glowed faintly, throwing spiderwebs of light over the walls, illuminating the bones of a massive snake that surrounded the entire pool. The skeleton was enormous, three times bigger than the biggest pythons at the zoo, its stark white skull the length of Shinji's arm. Shinji felt his stomach tighten as he stared at the dead serpent, not because of its size, but because the creature he was hoping to find, the great Coatl itself, seemed to have faded into extinction. For some reason, he almost felt betrayed. They had come all this way, faced the challenges, and made it to the temple and the font only to find the creature he thought had been calling to him was long dead. *There is no more Coatl,* Shinji thought, staring at the skeleton. *So what was the point of any of this?*

"The Coatl," Lucy said in a whisper. "It's real. Or, it was." She turned to him, eyes shining. "We've found it, Shinji. This is the font."

"Yes," said Dr. Ramos behind them. "This is the font. At last."

His voice was hungry. Shinji felt a chill, like an icy finger trailing all the way down his spine. Dr. Ramos stepped around him and Lucy, and walked slowly to the edge of the glowing pool. "Years of planning," he whispered, raising his arms as if to embrace the serpent. "Decades of pulling the strings, tugging the future in the direction I wanted, manipulating the webs of fate. I am finally here. I feel the magic once again. And now I will finally claim what I have lost!"

He spun to face them, and as he did, his appearance changed. His hair grew long and straight, the wrinkles on his face smoothed out, and his clothes changed. In the time it took him to turn around, he transformed from Dr. Ramos into a beautiful woman. She was small and slender, with pale skin, jet-black hair, and a billowing crimson-and-black robe.

"Shinji," she crooned, and with a start, Shinji recognized the voice. The same voice as the one he heard in his dreams, the one that threatened to destroy everything he cared about. "Thank you for bringing me to the font. I had almost given up hope that you would ever reach it."

"Who are you?" Shinji demanded, and the woman arched a thin, inklike brow at him. "I've . . . I've heard you before, haven't I?" he went on. "You've been in my head, messing with my dreams. What do you want?"

The woman chuckled.

"My name is not important," she purred. "I doubt your human tongue would be able to speak it anyway. You may call me the Weaver. And I do know you, Shinji." She laced slender hands, like pale spiders, below her chin. The nails on the end of her fingers were two inches long and as red as blood. "I have watched over you for years, guiding you down the path you needed to go. All the events that have led up to this moment were designed by me. All to bring you to this spot. I made certain you and the statue would find each other. I allowed Hightower to know the location of the statue in order to force the confrontation that would bond you with the idol. The 'creepy' security guard that allowed you to escape? That was my puppet."

Shinji gave a start of realization. "You're the mole," he

said, pointing an accusing finger at her. "The one who has been sending information to Hightower, telling them where we were. It was never Lucy. It was you all along."

"Very good, Shinji." The Weaver chuckled again. "Yes, of course it was me. I needed the Society of Explorers and Adventurers to get you here safely, but I knew they would be problematic once we found the temple. Having Hightower catch up to them would ensure they stayed out of the way when the time came. It worked out quite well, don't you think?"

"And Dr. Ramos?" Lucy demanded. "The real Dr. Ramos? What did you do with him?"

The Weaver smiled. "My last meal."

Lucy cringed, but Shinji crossed his arms. "You're just trying to scare us," he accused.

"Am I?" The Weaver gave him a smile that stretched her lips from ear to ear. "Poor Dr. Ramos," she crooned. "So terrified he had picked up some terrible curse that would doom him. I suppose it did, in a way. His fear made him quite stringy."

Shinji recoiled in horror.

"You're a monster," Lucy whispered.

Shinji narrowed his eyes. "What are you?"

"Oh." The woman's bloodred smile grew even wider, and her eyes gleamed in the darkness. "Be careful what you wish for, little mortal. You might not like what you see. But here, let me show you . . ." She raised her arms away from her sides. "What I really am."

Eight slender, shiny legs erupted from her sides, curling to the floor. The Weaver started to grow, swelling in height until she towered over them. When she finally stopped growing, Shinji had to force himself to stand his ground, to not turn and run, screaming, from the room. The torso and upper half of the Weaver were unchanged: a slender woman with long black hair. She still wore her fancy robe, but what emerged from beneath the cloth was the stuff of nightmares. From the waist down was the monstrous body of an enormous spider banded in yellow and red. The bloated thorax was shiny and black, not hairy, and the segmented legs came to impossibly thin points, like she was walking on needles.

Lucy let out a shriek.

The Weaver laughed, a terrible hissing chortle that Shinji recognized instantly. It was the same laugh as the one he'd heard in his dreams. "How do you like me now, little humans?" she crowed, throwing out her arms and rising up to her full, terrible height. "Do you not like what you see? People used to love me, you know. I was once a guardian of a font, just like the Coatl. I had a beautiful shrine in Hokkaido, built on the spot where the magic flowed, and the priests who lived there worshiped me as a protector spirit. I was perfectly happy in my shrine, watching over the land and its people. Until one day when members of SEA arrived."

She pointed an accusing fingernail at Shinji that had somehow grown to six inches long. "Those people," she hissed, "those *explorers and adventurers*, broke into my shrine and took my sacred relics without any thought of who they belonged to. Granted, by that time, all the priests had moved on and the shrine was abandoned. But *I* was still there. And the magic was still there. SEA just moved in and started building on my font. And by doing so, all the nature spirits who lived around the shrine fled or disappeared. Eventually I was forced to leave as well. Because of SEA."

The Weaver's mouth curled in a snarl, her eyes glittering with hate. "Now the font, *my* font, lies in the hands of those same thieves, bringing them undeserved prosperity. They stole my magic without even knowing its value, depriving me of my power and forcing me to leave. I am the shell of what I once was, weak and unimportant. But all that is about to change." She took a few steps forward, her legs clicking over the stone floor. "Because *you* are going to give me the heart, Shinji. You, the descendant of those priests who once protected the shrine with me. It took me years to track down a direct bloodline, and once I found him, I wasn't about to let him go. I needed you to lead me to this font, one of the last in the world untouched by man. Only you could have bonded with the Coatl; it recognizes you as a friend of the guardians. Only you could have gotten through the door."

"But what about the curse?" Lucy asked, and the Weaver scoffed.

"There was never a curse," she said flatly. "It was a lie, a legend propagated to make certain the idol was returned to the font. Make no mistake, there *are* artifacts with ancient curses attached to them; the idol of Shiriki Utundu, for example. But the heart of the Coatl, while it did make you yearn for the jungle and the font, was never going to kill you."

"But . . ." Shinji's mind spun with confusion. "But SEA told me . . ."

"Was it SEA who told you it was cursed?" The Weaver smiled. "Or was it Gideon Frost, the man who wanted the idol for himself, who would've said anything to acquire it? Or Dr. Ramos, who saw curses in every shadow, who told you exactly what I wanted him to say?" The spider woman chuckled. "Granted, it was easy enough to manipulate you; a few spiders here and there, a few whispers in your dreams, and you swallowed the legend of the curse just like everyone else."

There was never a curse. Shinji didn't know whether to be relieved or angry. *It was just a trick to bring me here. Everything was an elaborate scheme conjured by a creepy spider woman to get the heart to the temple. And we played right into her plans.*

"In any case, it matters not," the Weaver went on, gesturing to the chamber around them. "We are here. We found the font, and now you are going to give me the heart, Shinji Takahashi. Finally I will be restored to my full power."

Shinji settled on anger. He backed up, taking Lucy with him. "Why should I?" he asked her. "What do you plan to do with the magic if you get it?"

"I will take my revenge upon those who dared steal my font from me," the Weaver said calmly. "Not just the members of the Society, but *all* of humankind. Humans are a plague upon the world. They steal and pillage and take and consume. And if they cannot have something, they tear it down so that no one else can have it. Mankind's greed and destruction are unlimited. The only thing they know how to do is destroy."

"That's not true," Lucy protested. "Yes, some humans are greedy and destructive. But we can change, too. We don't have to follow the path laid out for us."

"That's right," Shinji broke in. "Lucy is proof of that. She's part of Hightower. She was brought up to be greedy and ruthless like the rest of them. But she chose not to be like that. She's here, helping us return the heart to the font because it was the right thing to do."

"Insufficient," the spider woman said flatly. "A few individuals are not enough." Her lips curled in a grimace of contempt. "Humans are a force of destruction. They have spread across the world like a virus, leaving nothing in their wake. Cities stand where there were once forests. Many animals are gone, hunted to extinction. The jungles have been razed, the trees chopped down, even the oceans are being fished clean. Humans have sucked the magic of the world dry; only a few tiny pockets remain. And I will not allow this one to slip through my fingers. Mankind will pay for what it has done. So, Shinji . . ." She turned her full attention on him, her smile like a crimson knife. "I will ask one more time, and then I will stop being polite. Please, give me the heart."

Shinji's heart pounded, but he set his jaw and took another step back. "No," he husked out. "No way. I get it, I do. Humans are jerks sometimes. We're greedy and selfish, and we destroy what we don't understand. But not all humans are like that. There are some of us who are really trying to do better." He remembered Priya and how she spoke of righting the wrongs of their past. And Maya, refusing to destroy the bridge. And even Oliver, trying to reason with Gideon Frost. "You talked about the members of SEA," he told the Weaver. "They know they screwed up. They realized their mistake, and they're trying to make things right. You can't punish all humans for the crimes of a few."

"Can't I?" The Weaver's smile was cruel. "Just watch me. I wonder how humankind will fare when poisonous spiders infest every part of their world? Their buildings will become giant cocoons, their cities wastelands of webbing and silk. My children will feast upon their blood and lay their eggs in their flesh. Humans will finally sit at the bottom of the food chain, where they belong, and my children will rule this world."

Lucy shuddered, and Shinji felt his skin crawl. "No way," he snarled. "I'm not gonna let that happen." He clenched his fist, holding his left arm close to his chest, as the Weaver turned toward him. "You can't kill me," he warned as the huge spider woman stepped closer, casting him in her shadow. "If I die, the magic dies, too. You'll lose it forever."

"That is true," the Weaver agreed. "But you're forgetting something, Shinji. I might not be able to hurt *you* . . ." She gestured, and suddenly thick white silk threads descended from the ceiling, wrapped themselves around Lucy, and dragged her into the air. Lucy cried out, fighting and kicking, but she could only dangle like a puppet as the threads lifted her higher.

Shinji's heart dropped to his toes, and the Weaver smiled. "But your little friend has no magical protection, does she?" she crooned.

"Let her go!" Clenching his fists, Shinji whirled on the spider woman, who chuckled.

"I warned you, didn't I?" the Weaver went on, unconcerned with Shinji's anger. She clicked toward him, her movements unhurried, encasing him in her terrible shadow. "I told you in your dreams, if you did not return to me what was stolen, I would destroy everything you care about. Starting with your little friend. And, also . . ."

She paused, reaching into her sleeve and pulling out something small and white. A cocoon, Shinji realized, the clump of webbing no bigger than a golf ball in her palm. Turning, she raised her hand and stuck the cocoon on the wall of the temple. As she did, it began to grow in size, becoming as big as a human. Someone's head poked out of the top of the cocoon, their mouth covered in webbing like a gag. As Shinji watched, the figure opened its eyes and raised its head, and Shinji gasped.

"Aunt Yui!"

Aunt Yui's eyes widened, and her head thrashed back and forth, shaking the cocoon, but she couldn't break free of the spider's web. The Weaver laughed, moving in front of Shinji as he started forward, blocking the way to his aunt.

"So easy," she mused as Shinji spun on her furiously. "You left your aunt all alone on that boat, unguarded and defenseless in the middle of the river. After Hightower kidnapped you, I climbed aboard and helped myself. Now," she continued, narrowing her eyes, "I will ask you one last time before I start tearing limbs from bodies and hearts from chests. You know what I want, Shinji Takahashi." She stepped forward and held out her hand, long fingers opening like spider legs. "Give me the heart, or I will start eating people in front of you. Starting with your aunt." She gave him a chilling smile. "You do not want to lose any *more* family members, do you?"

Shinji glared at the Weaver. "What are you talking about?"

"Do you think your parents' death was an accident?" The woman's smile grew wider as an icy hand gripped Shinji's stomach. "How do you think you ended up with your globe-trotting aunt? You should thank me, Shinji. Your parents would have held you back. They were perfectly boring, ordinary mortals who would have given you a perfectly boring, ordinary life. I needed you to travel the world, discover new places, and eventually come face-to-face with an ancient statue in a dusty little shop in Abenge."

Shinji clenched his fists so hard, he felt his nails bite into his palms. "You killed them," he whispered, anger and disbelief a twisting knot inside. "Just to make sure I would find the statue. You *are* a monster."

"Do not attempt to make me feel guilt, boy." The Weaver made a dismissive gesture with one hand. "They were human, and the world is infested with them. It is time to cull the herd before they do even more damage. Now . . ." She took a menacing step forward. "Give. Me. The. Heart."

Shinji's breaths came in short gasps. He felt trapped, like

a fly caught in a web. He knew he couldn't give the Weaver the heart, but if he didn't, Lucy and Aunt Yui would suffer for it.

Desperate, Shinji glanced at Lucy, hanging like a marionette directly over the font. Light motes danced around her, little swirls of magic that coiled away into the air. She met his eyes, gave her head a small shake, and mouthed the word *stall*.

Shinji frowned. Stall? How? What was she going to do, and how was he supposed to stall a centuries-old spider woman with a serious grudge against humans?

"I am growing impatient, Shinji Takahashi." The Weaver stepped very close, her bloated, shiny thorax and multiple legs filling his vision. As Shinji stumbled back a step, she smiled at him, a pair of black fangs curling from her lips. "And when I grow impatient, I grow hungry. Tell me, what part of your aunt do you want me to eat first?"

"Okay, okay!" Thinking fast, Shinji held up both hands in surrender. "You win. I'll give you the heart, just don't hurt my aunt or Lucy."

"See? Was that so hard?" The Weaver relaxed, lacing her claws together. "Now, hand over the heart, and we can put this whole unpleasant experience behind us."

"One problem, though." Shinji held up his arm, displaying the Coatl tattoo, which hissed and bared its fangs at the spider woman. "I'm not entirely sure how this comes off."

The Weaver rolled her eyes. "The magic has bonded to you," she explained. She shifted a step closer, her attention riveted by the colorful image on Shinji's arm. "To release it, you must simply will it out of your body."

Shinji glanced over the Weaver's shoulder and saw that Lucy had gone limp against the ropes. Her head was bowed and her eyes were closed. His worry spiked, but she suddenly raised her arms, and around her, the motes of light started to swirl.

She was calling on the magic of the font. Maybe all was not lost. Quickly Shinji turned his attention back to the Weaver, who was watching him impatiently. "Uh, just *will* it out of me?" he repeated, frowning. "You mean, just think: *Okay, magic, now jump out of my body*, and it'll happen? Why couldn't I have done that any time before?"

The Weaver tapped one long leg against the stones in exasperation. "Because you needed to find the font first," she said. "That was the entire point of the magic bonding to you; it needed to be returned to the font, and it needed you to take it there. Now that you are here . . ." She gestured back toward the pool, and Shinji's stomach twisted. Thankfully the Weaver didn't turn her head, so she did not see Lucy surrounded by swirling bits of color and sparkles, hanging in the center of the light. "The magic recognizes it is in the place it's supposed to be. It will want to leave you and return to the font. All you have to do is tell it where to go. And you will tell it to go to me."

"Really?" Shinji looked down at the tattoo and found the Coatl staring right back. *Help us,* he thought to it. *We can't let the Weaver take the heart. I can't let her hurt my family again. Please, do something.*

He wasn't sure if he was seeing correctly or if his eyes were playing tricks on him, but he could've sworn the Coatl winked.

"Yes," the Weaver encouraged. "All you have to do is release the magic and it will respond. So give me the heart, Shinji. You don't have a lot of time left. I am getting . . . very hungry."

"Okay," Shinji muttered, keeping his arm held out before him. "Give you the magic. You mean, like . . . this?"

He squinted, and the Coatl tattoo flared its wings, wiggled its tail, and abruptly slithered up his arm.

"What? What are you doing?" the Weaver said, scowling as the tattoo vanished under his shirt. "Bring it back. Give me the heart."

"I'm trying," Shinji said. "But it doesn't want to listen." There was a tickle across his skin as he felt the Coatl slide up his neck and coil around his ear. "I don't know what it's doing," he told the spider woman as the Coatl bared its fangs and hissed at her. "I can't seem to stop it."

Behind the Weaver, the lights continued to dance around Lucy. Shinji spared a split-second glance at her and saw a tiny creature with copper ears poking its head out of her pocket, nose twitching.

Tinker!

The Weaver let out an angry hiss. "Enough!" she spat, and curled her talons around Shinji's neck. Lifting him off the ground, she brought her face very close to his, close enough for him to see his reflection in her black eyes. "I have grown tired of this game, mortal," she snarled, baring her fangs in his face. "Give me the heart! Right now, or I swear, I will start peeling the skin from Lucy's bones until you do."

Shinji clamped his fingers around the Weaver's wrist, but it was like an iron bar beneath his palm. He couldn't breathe, but he knew he couldn't give up the magic. As his vision started to swim, there was a flash of movement across the ground. A glitter of something tiny and metallic skittered up the spider's back as Tinker raced across the stones and vanished down the collar of her robes.

"What!" The Weaver jerked up, flailing her arms.

Shinji dropped to the ground, gasping. Looking up, he saw the Weaver spinning and flapping her arms, trying to dislodge the tiny creature that had scuttled into her clothes. He looked past her and saw Lucy hanging by the ropes and his aunt still trapped in the cocoon. And surrounding the pool, he saw the bones of the giant snake, the guardian that had once protected the font.

Shinji's heart raced. He knew he only had a few seconds to act. Taking a breath, he reached deep inside himself, finding the glow, the pulse of magic that had always been there. His heart raced, and he felt the Coatl tattoo stir in response. As the Weaver cursed and thrashed above him, he leaped to his feet, dodged a leg that tried to trip him, and sprinted to the pool. To the giant skull lying motionless in the water.

His arm grew warm. Holding out his hand, Shinji concentrated on releasing the magic, letting it flow from his body into his palm until he held a ball of soft golden light.

This is yours, he told the ancient guardian. *You are the true protector of the font, and now I return its magic to you.*

As soon as he thought the words, the orb of light left his palm, rising into the air. It hovered over the pool for a moment, spinning in a tight circle, then plunged straight down toward the water.

"No!" the Weaver snarled. "No, it is mine! The magic will be mine!" Baring her fangs again, she turned and scuttled toward him, arms and gleaming talons outstretched. Lunging forward, she swiped desperately at the ball of light, but the sphere passed between her claws and hit the water without a sound. There was a brief flare as the orb vanished beneath the surface, but then the light faded, and the pool looked normal again.

With a howl of rage, the Weaver turned and struck Shinji in the chest, sending him crashing into one of the pillars. Shinji gasped, pain exploding through every part of his body as he crumpled to the ground. It felt like he had been hit with a baseball bat. Coughing, he tried to rise, but the room spun around him like a carousel, and he sank to the floor again.

"You will pay for that, Shinji Takahashi." The Weaver's voice was tight with fury. Her legs clacked against the stones as she came toward him, flexing her curved talons. "You will suffer for your defiance. Would you like to hear what I am going to do to you now that you have no magic?"

"Not really." Shinji tried to get up but had to slump against the pillar to keep from falling. Behind the Weaver, the pool was starting to bubble and glow. He saw Lucy, still hanging suspended over the water, bathed in the sudden light. Her eyes widened, and her mouth dropped open.

Then the Weaver was in front of him, kicking him to the floor with one long, pointed leg, and he couldn't see anything but her.

"I will pull your limbs off one by one," the spider woman hissed down at him. "Like the wings of a fly or the legs of a beetle. It is all an insect like you deserves. But you won't die, oh no. I'll wrap you up nice and tight in my web, and you'll just stay like that. Forever. I am a patient monster, as you'll soon discover. But once I've got you wrapped up, you'll see everything I'm going to do to your aunt, your friends, and everyone you care about. For years and years to come. I hope it was worth it. So . . ."

She raised one pointed leg and stabbed it down, barely missing Shinji's foot. "What limb would you like me to pull off first? An arm or a leg?"

Shinji's body ached. He felt nauseated, and his side felt like someone had stabbed a pencil between his ribs. But he managed a hoarse chuckle, and the Weaver frowned. "What is so funny, human?" she hissed.

"Just the irony," Shinji replied, smiling up at her. "That something with no arms or legs is about to put the hurt on you right . . . now."

"What?"

A rush of wind. A ringing, piercing cry. And then something long and bright swooped through the air and struck the Weaver from the side. She tumbled over the rocks, legs curled under her belly, before bouncing upright with a hiss.

Mouth agape, Shinji stared up at the creature before him, his heart racing. A giant serpent with shimmering emerald eyes turned its head and peered down at him, an eerie intelligence shining from its gaze. The scales covering its serpentine body were dark green, the color of the jungle, and banded with yellow and crimson and blue. Its belly plates looked like molten gold, and a magnificent feathery hood extended from the sides of its skull. A pair of enormous wings, white and gold and almost too bright to look at, framed its lithe form, casting Shinji in their shadow.

Shinji released a slow breath, a feeling of awe and genuine happiness filling him as he stared up at the guardian. "It took you long enough."

The Coatl's tail twitched. For a moment, it almost looked amused. Turning back to the Weaver, it raised its wings with a roar of challenge that echoed through the chamber. The Weaver drew herself up, flexing her talons, and the two legendary creatures flew at each other with ringing battle cries.

"Shinji!" Lucy's voice snapped him out of his daze. He started toward her, but she shook her head. "Don't worry about me," she told him. "Tinker will get me down. Help your aunt."

Looking up, Shinji saw the little mouse clinging to Lucy's threads above her, gnawing them through with tiny metal teeth.

Shinji hurried to the cocoon on the wall, where his aunt's face watched him, wide-eyed, from the top. Pulling out his pocketknife, he began slicing through the webs that held his aunt in place. The white strands were tough and sticky at the same time, clinging to his skin as well as the knife edge. Finally he cut through the wall of the cocoon, and Yui stumbled out into the open.

She staggered, nearly falling, and Shinji helped her sit against the wall. Reaching up, Yui peeled the webbing gag from her lips, took a deep breath, and glanced at Shinji.

He managed a weak grin, though his vision was getting slightly blurry. His aunt smiled back and pressed a hand to his cheek.

"Hey, kiddo." Yui's voice was faint and raspy. "Crazy times. You doing okay?"

Shinji nodded. "Just dealing with a megacorporation, an ancient curse, and an angry spider monster; nothing I can't handle. How was your day?"

"Smart aleck," Aunt Yui muttered, and pulled Shinji into a crushing hug. Closing his eyes, Shinji hugged her back and, for just a moment, let himself believe everything was going to be fine.

"Shinji!"

Lucy's voice jerked him out of his moment. He opened his eyes as she rushed up, Tinker clinging tightly to her shoulder. "We have to get out of here," she announced, just as a roar echoed through the chamber. The Coatl and the Weaver were still rampaging around the room, snapping and slashing at each other. As the Coatl lunged at the Weaver, she hissed and spat a stream of yellow venom into the serpent's face. The Coatl recoiled as its muscular body slammed into a pillar, and the tower of stones went crashing to the ground in a roar of dust and rock. Shaking its head, the serpent reared up and gave its wings a mighty flap. A miniature tornado formed, swirling into existence between the Coatl and the Weaver. It caught the spider woman and flung her back into the wall, crushing stones and causing another pillar to tumble to the ground.

"They're going to tear this place apart," Lucy cried. "Shinji, do you think you can open the door again?"

"I don't know." Shinji looked down at his arm, and his stomach twisted. The Coatl tattoo was no longer there. He'd expected as much, but still. After all this time, he'd become so used to having the winged serpent stare back at him. Now that it was gone, he felt almost empty.

Aunt Yui gripped his shoulder. "I'm not sure what is going on," she said in a surprisingly calm voice. "But I do agree with your friend, Shinji. We should find a way out before Godzilla and Mothra bring this whole place down on our heads."

Shinji glanced at the fight between the Coatl and the Weaver, and a chill crawled down his arms. He couldn't tell who was winning or even who had the upper hand. The Coatl was bigger, but the spider woman was quick. She scuttled over the walls and leaped between the pillars, trailing shimmering white strands behind her. Darting between a pair of broken statues, she disappeared.

Shinji gasped, suddenly realizing what the Weaver was doing. "It's a web," he muttered, gazing around the room. He could see it now. The almost-invisible lines of webbing strung throughout the chamber. The Weaver was baiting the winged serpent into a trap. The Coatl, soaring gracefully around the room, searching for its enemy, did not see the trap spread for it, but once it was sprung, the serpent would be caught like a fly in a web.

Shinji scrambled to his feet. "We have to help the Coatl," he announced. "We have to get rid of those webs."

"Get rid of them?" Lucy gazed around the room in disbelief and shook her head. "There are dozens of them, maybe hundreds. How are we going to cut through them all?"

In a blur of darkness, the Weaver scuttled up the wall and leaped atop a broken pillar in the center of the room. Raising herself up, she opened her arms in the universal gesture of *come get me*. Swooping gracefully around a column, the Coatl caught sight of its enemy and streaked forward with a ringing cry.

The Weaver smiled. As the feathered serpent came swooping through the pillars, she yanked her hands down like she was pulling several threads at once. Around the room, dozens of white strands tightened, snapping into place and forming a giant web in the center of the chamber. The Coatl flew right into the middle of the web and became stuck, tangling its wings and binding itself in place. Hissing, it thrashed, giant coils writhing about as it struggled to free itself but succeeded only in tangling itself further. The Weaver cackled in triumph.

Lucy gasped, looking at Shinji in desperation. "What can we do?" she asked. "There's no way we'll be able to free it in time."

Shinji jerked up with a sudden breath. "Wind," he

muttered, remembering something Professor Carrero had said. "The feathered serpent was worshipped as the god of wind. We can use that."

"What?" Lucy repeated, sounding confused. "How?" Ignoring her, Shinji glanced around and spotted one of the ancient torches set into a snake bracket on the wall. Snatching it up, he turned back to Lucy and thrust the torch at her.

"Tinker, can you light this?"

Lucy still looked confused, but she held out her arm and Tinker leaped to the torch. Scurrying up the handle, the robot mouse reached the top, opened his mouth, and breathed a tiny flame onto the cloth wrappings. After a few moments, the wrappings caught, and fire crackled to life on the end of the torch.

"Take this," Shinji told Lucy, holding the torch upright and out to her again. She did, still wearing a puzzled frown. "Set everything that you can on fire," he told her as the flames flickered bright. "Everything. Light all the torches, set the bramble on fire, burn all the grass. Burn everything, especially the bushes around the pillars and statues."

"How is that going to help the Coatl?"

"Trust me, just do it."

"Hold on just a second, Shinji."

Shinji looked at Aunt Yui, hoping she wouldn't tell him to stay put, that whatever he was planning was too dangerous. "If you want something that will burn fast," she said, and nodded to the massive cocoon sitting against the wall, "I bet that thing will go up like paper."

A piercing hiss echoed through the chamber. Shinji jerked his gaze to the Coatl and saw it still trapped in the web, thrashing wildly as the Weaver crawled up the pillars and stepped onto the strands.

Shinji clenched his fists. "Lucy, Aunt Yui, light the fires," he told them, and took a step back. "I'll try to buy you some time."

Lucy frowned. "Shinji, wait. What are you going to do?"

Shinji gave her a lopsided smirk. "What I do best," he said. "Be a smart aleck." And he sprinted away, toward the forest of pillars and the two ancient guardians in the center.

He heard the Weaver's laughter as he approached the giant web, her gaze riveted to the tangled form of the Coatl. "You can't fight forever," she told the serpent. "There is no escape. Give up and make it easy for yourself."

"Hey!" Shinji yelled, and hurled a rock at the Weaver. It sailed through the air, passed harmlessly through a hole in the web, and the spider woman turned her head to glare at him. "Is this how you always fight your fights?" he called. "With dirty cheater moves? Too scared to face anything yourself? I didn't think the guardian of a font would be such a coward. Oh, sorry," he added as the Weaver scowled. "*Ex*-guardian. Since you lost your own font."

"Insignificant insect." The Weaver narrowed her eyes. "You are like a mosquito, buzzing and whining in my ear. After I take care of the Coatl, I will be sure to kill you slowly."

From the corner of his eye, Shinji saw Lucy and Aunt Yui dragging the giant cocoon across the floor. Unfortunately the Weaver turned her head and saw them as well, raising one bemused eyebrow.

"Interesting," she said, sounding amused. "And what, exactly, do you think that will accomplish? This is my world," she announced, gesturing to the webs and strands all around them. "I can turn anything into my kingdom, even the lair of the feathered serpent. I control all. Nothing escapes once I've spun my webs. I may not have the heart, but once I kill the Coatl, this will be mine. Even a small font is better than none." Her eyes narrowed, and she leaped off the web, landing in front of Shinji with her claws raised. "After I dispose of one last pesky fly!"

A sudden whooshing sound filled the air. The Weaver turned, and Shinji saw the hollow cocoon directly below the Coatl and the giant web. It was on fire, and the flames rose up rapidly, snapping and crackling in the still air. The spider woman laughed.

"Fools, what do you think you are doing? Do you think a few brush fires will stop me?"

"Not usually," Shinji muttered, and met the eyes of the

Coatl peering down from the web. "Call the winds!" he told it as the Weaver spun back. "Fan the flames! Burn all the webs and set yourself free!"

"That is enough from you," the Weaver hissed, and plunged her talons into his chest, sinking them deep.

Shinji jerked. He opened his mouth, but nothing came out. Somewhere far away, he thought he heard Lucy scream and Aunt Yui cry out his name. In a daze, he looked up at the Weaver, who gave him a smug smile.

"Now, little insect, you can finally die."

She yanked her claws from his body. Shinji swayed on his feet a moment and glanced down at the front of his shirt, which was now covered in red. Then his legs gave out, and he collapsed to the stones.

A roar echoed through the chamber, and a gust of wind tore at his hair and clothes. It didn't die down, but grew in ferocity, howling through the temple with the force of a maelstrom. The flames burning beneath the web flared up with a bellow, spreading rapidly to grass, roots, and bramble. Tongues of fire licked the stones, turning the air scalding hot, and the Weaver recoiled in the broiling heat.

With a sizzling hiss, the enormous web ignited, bursting into flames that roared up and consumed every strand of webbing in the chamber. In seconds, the entire spiderweb burned away, turning to cinders that spiraled away into the smoke. Slumped on the ground, Shinji watched the Weaver face an enraged Coatl surrounded by an inferno. A brief look of fear crossed her face just as the serpent lunged, wrapping its coils around the bloated body. The spider woman shrieked, flailing in the Coatl's squeezing embrace, her legs scrabbling against its hard scales. But then the serpent's great golden wings swept down, hiding her from sight, and that was the last Shinji saw of the Weaver.

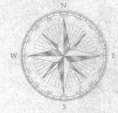

CHAPTER TWENTY-TWO

Shinji passed out for a few moments, for when he opened his eyes again, the flames had died down and the world was darker. He was lying on the stones near the pool, so someone must've moved his body away from the pillars. Glancing up, he saw Lucy's tear-streaked face peering down at him and Aunt Yui hovering on his other side, looking distraught.

"Will he be all right?" Lucy whispered, apparently not seeing that Shinji was awake. She looked up at Aunt Yui, her voice pleading. "He'll be all right, won't he?"

Aunt Yui made a noise that sounded like a sob. "I don't know," she whispered. "He's lost a lot of blood, and we don't have any way to get him to a hospital. He might already be . . ." She trailed off, and Lucy sniffled loudly.

"Stupid Shinji. Why did you have to be a hero?"

I'm right here, Shinji wanted to tell them. *I can hear you, you know.* But for some reason, his voice wasn't working. He couldn't make a sound. He could only lie there, listening to Lucy and his aunt talk about him like he wasn't there.

Like he was already dead.

A shadow fell over them, somehow dark and bright at the same time. Shinji gazed up, past Lucy's head, until he met the piercing emerald eyes of the Coatl.

The great winged serpent towered over them, its magnificent wings spread to either side. Looking over her shoulder, Lucy gasped, and Aunt Yui stiffened, but the Coatl ignored them both. Its gaze was focused solely on Shinji. Slowly, it lowered its head.

"What is it doing?" Aunt Yui's voice, seeming to come from a great distance away.

"I don't know," Lucy replied. "But I don't think it will hurt him. Maybe . . ."

She didn't finish the thought. The Coatl's reptilian face hovered only a couple of feet from Shinji's own, so close that he could see his reflection in its slitted green eyes. A large forked tongue flicked out, tasting the air between them. Shinji forced a weak smirk.

Are you trying to figure out what I taste like? he thought at the ancient creature.

The Coatl's stare didn't waver. *Mortal who returned the heart of the font,* said a voice in his head, as clear as if it were speaking to him out loud. *You have journeyed far to reach this place, faced many trials and challenges, battled a great evil, even sacrificed your own existence in order to return the heart to the font. You have my gratitude and the gratitude of the jungle. You are worthy to be called guardian.*

Oh, Shinji thought. *Good. Does that mean I level up?*

From the corner of his eye, he saw Lucy edge forward. "Help him," she told the Coatl. "Please. You have to save him. Don't let him die here."

Die? Shinji tried to frown, but it took too much effort. *I'm not dying. Am I?* His gaze sought the Coatl's. *Am I dying?*

Your light grows dim, the Coatl said in a solemn voice. *The Weaver's talons missed your heart, but only barely. I can save you,* it went on as Shinji stared at it numbly, *but not without cost. Snatching a soul from the jaws of death requires the full power of the font. If I do this, the magic will fade, and the font will disappear. Forever.*

No, Shinji thought immediately. *That can't happen. We came all this way to return the heart and restore the font. If the magic dries up, everything we did will be for nothing. The font has to stay here and protect the jungle.*

The Coatl's expression didn't change, but gazing into its intense emerald eyes, Shinji was almost certain it smiled at him. *And that,* it said quietly, *is exactly why the world cannot lose Shinji Takahashi. Magic is important, but life is precious.*

And a life like yours will have a greater impact on the world than a hidden well of magic in the middle of the jungle. But there is another choice, Shinji Takahashi. One that requires just as much sacrifice. I can transfer the magic of the font directly to you, and you will become the new guardian.

But I thought the magic of the world was almost gone, Shinji said. *If the font dries up here, what will happen to the jungle around it?*

The magic will not be gone, the Coatl told him. *It will be inside you, Shinji Takahashi. Without the font, the jungle will continue. Life will go on as it always has. But you will be able to subtly influence your world in small, or maybe not so small, ways. It depends on what you do with the magic. Be warned, though.* The serpent edged even closer until all Shinji could see were those eyes staring down at him. *This means you are taking on an even greater responsibility. You will become a true guardian, dedicated to protecting this world and the hidden wonders within it. You might come up against creatures like the Weaver, hungry for your magic. Or you might stand in the way of those like the Hightower Corporation, who are concerned only with power and their own gain. Wherever you go, you will have enemies, but know also that there will be those who stand alongside you. Who are dedicated to preserving the world and doing the right thing, even if the right path is not the easy path. Find them, and you will never be alone in your purpose, if you accept. So, Shinji Takahashi . . .* The Coatl pulled away but still continued to watch him. *Do you accept the mantle of guardian?*

Shinji hesitated. The choice hung in the air before him, and for a few seconds, he felt torn. If he refused, he could have his normal life back. If he said no, everything would return to how it was before. Playing video games and sailing with Aunt Yui to far-off places. Homeschooling. Doing normal kid stuff without having to worry about magic and monsters and secret organizations.

But if he refused, he might never see Lucy again. Or the members of the Society of Explorers and Adventurers. And he had seen so much; he had fought villains and creatures of legend and had been on a real-life quest to save something important. Could he really give that up to become normal and ordinary again? Now that he knew what was at stake, how could he close his eyes and pretend it didn't exist?

In the end, he understood that it was only fear that was stopping him. But he knew what he had to do. Closing his eyes, he gathered himself for a second, making sure his mind was clear before he looked into the eyes of the ancient creature waiting for his response.

Yeah, he told the Coatl, as clearly as he could. *I accept.*

The Coatl opened its golden wings. *The battle with Hightower still rages,* it told him, making his stomach knot. *I can hear my warriors being driven back and the jungle crying out in fear. Stop Hightower and save the jungle, Shinji Takahashi. The power of the Guardian is yours.*

With a cry, the great serpent flapped its wings and rose up, sending dust and grass swirling around Shinji, Lucy, and

Aunt Yui. As Shinji watched the creature spiral above him, it started to glow, like sunlight was seeping out between its scales, filling the room with light. As it swirled through the air, going faster and faster, the light grew brighter and brighter until the Coatl was a band of sunlight swirling overhead. Then, with a last ringing cry, the ribbon of light dove right at Shinji, filling his vision. There was a blinding flash, and for a moment, everything went white.

Shinji gasped and opened his eyes.

Above him, Lucy let out a yelp and grabbed the front of his shirt. "Shinji," she exclaimed, "you're awake. Are you all right? Can you hear me?"

"I'm fine," Shinji croaked, struggling to sit up. He could hear it now, what the Coatl was talking about. He could *feel* the battle outside, hear the shouts of men and the hisses of the snake warriors. The gunshots scarring the trees and the ground, slamming into the walls of the temple. "SEA is in trouble," he panted, clawing himself to his feet. "We have to help them! I have to help them."

"What? What are you talking about?" Aunt Yui grabbed his arm, her face white. "You almost died, Shinji. I thought you *had* died. Where do you think you're going now?"

"I'm sorry." Shinji pulled out of her grasp. "I have to do this. I promised the Coatl. I can't let Hightower win."

With Lucy and Aunt Yui following, Shinji raced across the chamber to the place where the door had first opened. It looked like a solid wall again, but as Shinji approached, a shudder went through the rock, and the huge slab began grinding open.

As he slipped out, a bullet struck the wall a few feet from his head, spraying him with grit and rock shards. Wincing, he looked down on the battle, and his stomach churned. Oliver, Maya, and Professor Carrero all knelt on the ground with their hands tied behind them, a pair of Hightower agents standing over them with guns. Only a few serpent warriors stood between Hightower and the temple, hissing defiantly and brandishing their spears. As Shinji stepped into the open, one of the Hightower agents glanced up and saw him. It was Kraus, who smiled evilly as their eyes met, then turned and pointed a finger up the temple steps.

"There's the kid. Grab him!"

The soldiers started forward. The serpent warriors hissed and leaped to attack, spears at the ready. Shinji started to cry out for them to stop, but his voice was drowned in the bark of gunfire as the Hightower agents raised their weapons and fired. Several serpent warriors fell, and as they did, their bodies turned into dozens of colorful snakes that slithered away through the grass.

"No," Shinji growled, glaring at the men charging up the steps toward him. They didn't stop, and he felt the power within him boil. Heat flooded his veins like a ball of sunlight had erupted inside him, and anger tinted his vision red. "That's *enough!*"

Light exploded from his skin, golden and intense, filling the clearing. The Hightower agents near the bottom of the steps cried out, flinching back in the searing glow. Shinji glanced down at himself and saw the Coatl tattoo blazing gold on his skin, a faint nimbus of light surrounding him. He could feel the jungle around them all; he could sense the life that flowed through its very roots, in every breath and movement and heartbeat. He inhaled deeply and felt the jungle rise up in response.

Near the bottom of the stairs, the Hightower agents squinted up at him, shielding their faces. Shinji looked down and saw Kraus climbing the steps, his eyes hard with determination. The Hightower agent raised his arm, shouting to his men, and Shinji flung out a hand.

With an ear-piercing shriek, a blast of wind swept down the temple steps. It caught the Hightower agents and sent them tumbling backward, rolling down the stairs until they came to a graceless stop at the bottom. Shinji raised his arms, power and light flaring around him. As Kraus and the Hightower agents struggled to their feet, the trees began to shake, vines and bushes writhing madly about. For a moment, it seemed like the entire jungle had come to life.

Creatures stepped from the undergrowth, emerging into the light. Small animals like armadillos and opossums scurried out of the brush, and flocks of birds, including an enormous harpy eagle, soared down to perch on the broken columns. Monkeys dropped from the branches, hooting. Tapirs shoved their way into view, grunting in their pig-like voices. A pair of jaguars, one spotted and the other as black as night, stepped silently from the trees. And from the undergrowth, hundreds of snakes—vipers, pythons, and more—spilled into the open.

The Hightower agents paled, gazing around in growing fear as more creatures emerged from the jungle. None of the animals paid any attention to the members of SEA, who were still kneeling on the ground, though Oliver shifted uncomfortably as a large python slithered past him. The animals' gazes were riveted to the Hightower agents huddled together at the foot of the temple steps. At the edge of the arena, the horde of creatures paused, staring at the soldiers with hundreds of glowing eyes. Shinji gazed down at the Hightower agents and raised his voice.

"Get out of here," he told the agents, his words seeming to echo through the trees. "Before the entire jungle turns on you. Leave now, and don't come back!"

As he spoke, the mob of creatures surrounding them roared, hooted, screamed, hissed, shrieked, and howled, lifting their voices in one unified cry that made the ground shake. Even the members of SEA winced, squinting their eyes and turning their heads as the cacophony rose into the air and swirled around the clearing.

The Hightower agents trembled. They seemed to be on

the verge of fleeing, but Kraus glared up at the top of the steps, his eyes hard with anger. Setting his jaw, he turned and swung the barrel of his gun toward Shinji.

Shinji felt the power in him erupt. A beam of light surged out of his body, becoming the image of an enormous serpent with massive golden wings. Baring its fangs, the Coatl lunged, and Kraus vanished into those gaping jaws. His gun clattered to the steps, and the Hightower agent was gone.

The rest of the agents panicked. Dropping their weapons, they fled, nearly falling over one another to get away from the temple. Shinji watched them go, parting snakes and monkeys as they tore out of the clearing and vanished into the jungle.

The glow around Shinji faded, and the image of the Coatl flickered and died. He swayed on his feet, felt Lucy's and Aunt Yui's arms around him, and then knew nothing for a little while.

He woke up surrounded by friends. Lucy and Aunt Yui were there, and Oliver's worried face peered over their shoulders as well. Shinji turned his head and saw Maya, Professor Carrero, and a very battered-looking drone hovering beside him. Lucy let out a gasp as he opened his eyes.

"Shinji? Are you awake? Can you hear me?"

"No," Shinji croaked at her. "I'm just sleep-talking. This

is my corpse, talking to you from the great beyond—ow." He winced as she pinched his shoulder, then gently helped him sit up. Gazing at the relieved, slightly awed faces surrounding him, he offered a weak smile. "Looks like we did it. SEA one, Hightower zero."

"Shinji . . ." Oliver blew out a breath, shaking his head. "I've seen a lot of crazy stuff," he admitted. "Weird places and treasures and creatures that will turn your blood to ice. But today pretty much tops them all." He reached down, resting a palm atop Shinji's head, and the smile that tugged at the corner of his mouth was almost affectionate. "You are one lucky kid."

Shinji grinned, and Oliver shook his head again. "Though I have no idea what just happened here," the ex-pirate went on, dropping his arm. "And I have so many questions. What happened to the font? Where did Dr. Ramos go? Why is Shinji's aunt suddenly here? I assume that's who you are, no offense," he told Aunt Yui. She smiled at him.

"None taken," Yui said. "I am indeed Shinji's aunt, though I don't have the pleasure of knowing who *you* are."

"Aunt Yui," Shinji broke in, and gestured to the rest of them, "this is Oliver Ocean, Maya Griffin, Professor Carrero, and Zoe Kim. They're part of the Society of Explorers and Adventurers."

Her brows shot up. "The Society of Explorers and Adventurers?" she repeated, gazing around at them all. "You are all . . . members of SEA?"

Professor Carrero blinked. "I take it you have heard of us?"

Aunt Yui nodded. "In my travels around the world, I heard rumors of the existence of the Society," she explained, "but I didn't know if they were true or not. Sometimes, I wondered what would happen if I actually met them. They sounded like kindred spirits." She blinked and shook herself, putting a hand on Shinji's shoulder. "Thank you for helping my nephew," she said sincerely. "I know he can be surly and a smart aleck, but he's all the family I have left."

"Hey," Shinji said. "I wasn't *that* surly."

Oliver smiled and offered a dashing bow. "Happy to help," he said with a grin. "And it was truly a pleasure to be part of this adventure. I would do it again in a heartbeat. But there is something else I feel I'm missing, something big. What was it again?" He pondered for a moment, then snapped his fingers. "Oh, yeah! The giant mythological winged serpent just deciding to pop in! I feel that needs a bit of explanation. So, kid . . ." He gave Shinji an expectant look. "This is your story. Maybe you should start at the beginning."

Shinji felt a smile stretch across his face. Glancing down at his arm, he was unsurprised to see the Coatl tattoo standing proudly against his wrist, still looking like a golden football as it stared back. He was part of something bigger now. An enormous responsibility had been draped over his shoulders, but he wasn't worried. He had friends. People he could trust, who believed in the sanctity of life and protecting what was important. As the Coatl had said, he wasn't alone in this. He would be just fine.

"It's a really, really long story," he said to the bemused looks all around him. Standing up, he put an arm around his aunt and held out a hand to Lucy, who grasped it firmly as they turned toward the steps. "I'll tell everyone the whole thing on the way home."

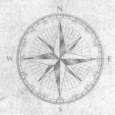

EPILOGUE

"Are you sure *this* is the place?" Aunt Yui said, peering through the windshield at the tiny shops lining the road. The Discovery Trading Company stood across from them, its single door propped open with a large book. "It's so small. Doesn't look like the entrance to a secret organization to me."

Shinji snickered. "Right, I'm sure they just forgot to put out the arrow sign that said SEA'S TOP SECRET ENTRANCE HERE."

Aunt Yui shared a look with Lucy in the rearview mirror. "Lucy, dear, I can't turn around. Pinch him for me, would you?"

"Sure."

"Ow!" Shinji slid away from Lucy's grasping fingers and quickly opened the door. Rubbing his arm, he stepped onto the sidewalk. It was early evening, and the air was balmy and warm. As he gazed up at the Discovery Trading Company, nerves prickled his stomach.

Lucy stepped up beside him. "What do you think the Society wants?" she asked quietly.

"I dunno," he replied. "I hope everything is all right."

It had been several days since they had returned from the jungle, and life was finally starting to return to normal. Shinji and Aunt Yui had returned home to the Lost River Outfitters, and the Society had helped them get everything back in order. They had even found and returned Aunt Yui's boat, the *Good Tern*, though the ancient trawler would need several weeks of repairs before it was seaworthy again.

Lucy had been there, too, staying with Shinji and his aunt and refusing to return to Hightower. She had shown great interest in the Lost River Outfitters and had delighted Aunt Yui with her interest, sharp mind, and willingness to learn all she could. She and Aunt Yui had spent many hours talking about Yui's travels, what she had seen, and future trips in the *Good Tern*. Shinji might've found this girl-bonding thing annoying, but honestly, he was glad Lucy was there. He'd tried to get back into video games, picking up where he had left off with his quests and levels. But the online adventures just didn't compare to the real thing. He had seen *real* monsters and magic. And he knew there was more out there.

More to see, more wonders to experience. Sometimes he thought he could feel the tattoo moving on his skin, though whenever he looked down at it, it was always the same. He wished he could talk to the Coatl again; ask the million questions swirling around his head. He had the magic of the font inside him, but did that mean he could use it? Would he be able to cast spells, summon creatures, heal the sick? Or would things just *happen* around him? What did being a guardian actually mean? Shinji didn't know the answers to any of these questions. And since the Coatl hadn't left behind an instruction pamphlet on how to be a new guardian of the font, he guessed he'd have to figure it out himself.

But at least he could talk to Lucy about it. She had been there; she had seen all the crazy, scary, unbelievable stuff, too. And the Society had as well. Oliver Ocean, Maya Griffin, Professor Carrero, and Zoe Kim. The Society members had also returned to their own lives and adventures, but Oliver had promised Shinji that they would see each other again.

"We gotta go, kiddo," he'd announced one morning. "Priya is waiting for us back at headquarters. She's *very* interested to hear about our little adventure in the jungle, and she gets cranky when she's impatient. So I'm afraid we're going to have to part ways for now."

"Will we see you again?" Lucy wanted to know.

"Of course, dear girl!" Professor Carrero exclaimed. "We have been on quite the adventure together. The Society doesn't forget its friends."

"Not to mention Shinji now has a magic tattoo granted by a flying serpent that proclaims him the guardian of one of the last fonts of power." Maya's voice was as dry as ever, though she was smiling as she talked. "That kind of thing isn't something the Society can ignore, especially if organizations like Hightower find out about it. Expect to see us again, probably sooner than you think."

Apparently it would be "sooner" rather than "later," but that was okay with Shinji. The Society was part of his life now. Just knowing they were out there made him feel less afraid.

Gazing up at the Discovery Trading Company's sign, he shrugged. "No one's coming out to meet us. Guess we'll just have to go in and see what they want."

Inside, the place was the same as Shinji remembered, aisles and shelves full of all the things an adventurer could want. Aunt Yui got very distracted by the various displays, and Shinji had to pull her away in the end, claiming the shop was going to close soon and the Society was still waiting for them. Molly waved them through the door into the back room, and Shinji paused a moment in front of the bookshelf, staring at the different titles.

"Which one was it again?" he muttered, reaching for the spine of *The Congo Queen*. "I know it was on this shelf. . . ." He pulled the book down, but it toppled off the shelf and fell to the floor. "Okay, so not that one."

"Move." Lucy reached past him, to the shelf above, and

pulled down the spine of *The Jungle Book*. There was a creak, and the bookshelf swung backward, revealing the tunnel beyond.

"Oho," remarked Aunt Yui. "Now *this* is a proper entrance to a super-secret hideout. The revolving bookcase? Classic. Shinji, don't forget to put the book back; we don't want SEA thinking you're rude."

Shinji replaced *The Congo Queen*, and together they stepped through the door into the long hallway beyond. The bookshelf creaked shut behind them, plunging the hall into darkness.

"Does it seem darker in here to you?" Shinji asked Lucy as they walked down the narrow corridor. He tried to recall the last time they had been through this space with Oliver, so long ago, it seemed. "Weren't there more lights on last time?"

"I don't remember," Lucy replied. "Maybe?"

A low growl was all the warning Shinji received before a large black shape came hurtling out of the darkness and slammed into him. He hit the floor with a grunt as Aunt Yui let out a shriek and two massive paws pressed down on his chest.

"Hi, Kali," he wheezed as the bear rumbled and settled herself on him more firmly. "Nice to see you, too. Maybe next time we could try a greeting that doesn't snap my ribs?"

The bear slapped his face with a very large, wet tongue and pushed off him as a chuckle went through the hall.

Wincing, Shinji sat up, meeting the gaze of Priya Banerjee a few feet away. Kali went to sit beside her, huffing and looking rather smug, and the woman gave Shinji a smile.

"Congratulations," she said as Lucy and Aunt Yui pulled him to his feet. "You have passed the Kali test. It appears that she thinks you are, in fact, okay."

"Oh," Shinji muttered, wiping bear spit from his face with the back of his sleeve. "Great. So that's the *I guess you're okay* greeting. I'd hate to see the *I don't like you* one."

"Yes, you would," Priya agreed, and turned away, beckoning them down the hall. "If you would all follow me. We have a surprise for you."

Curious now, Shinji trailed Priya and the black bear down the hall, Lucy and Aunt Yui close behind. He wanted to ask what was happening, what the big secret was, but Priya didn't pause or look back. Finally she stopped at a familiar door. With a smile, she opened it for him and beckoned him through the frame. "Go on," she said quietly as he hesitated. "Everyone is waiting."

Shinji stepped through the door, into the same room where he'd first met the members of SEA. Only this time, the central table was gone, and the room was filled with people. They stood in a semicircle facing the door, watching him as he entered the room. Some were seated on the few couches along the walls, elbows and legs bumping each other, but nobody looked uncomfortable. Oliver Ocean lounged against the wall with Maya and Professor

Carrero beside him and Zoe beaming at Shinji from her chair. Whatever this was, the members of SEA were fully aware of it.

The room broke into applause as Shinji and Lucy walked through the door, making Shinji gaze around in confusion. From the corner of his eye, he saw Aunt Yui discreetly slide away, taking a spot near the far wall, and realize she, too, was in on whatever was happening.

"Shinji, Lucy." Priya came to stand before them, smiling. "This is a special day, and I have gathered our members of the Society, as many that could come, to witness it. By now, we have all heard of your exploits with Hightower and the Coatl's Curse. And, Shinji, I personally want to say that I am so proud of you. Your decision to become the new guardian of the font could not have been easy. We know what a huge responsibility you've taken on yourself, and we want to help as much as we can. To that end, three days ago the Society held a vote to make both you and Lucy members of SEA, and the outcome was unanimous. Your aunt has also given her blessing, so all that is left is to make this official."

Shinji's heart started thudding in his ears. He glanced to where Oliver, Maya, Zoe, and Professor Carrero watched them in the crowd and found all four were smiling at him. Oliver, especially, had an enormous proud grin on his weathered face. He winked at Shinji as their gazes met, and Shinji couldn't help but grin back.

"Lucy Hightower. Shinji Takahashi." Priya clasped her

hands in front of her, her gaze intense as she faced them. "Driven by purpose, you are more than meets the eye, and you are not alone. For your outstanding courage, strength of character, and upholding of the ideals our organization stands for, you have been granted membership to our little family. It is my honor to personally welcome you both into the Society of Explorers and Adventurers."

ACKNOWLEDGMENTS

First and foremost, a huge thank-you to my editor, Kieran Viola, who not only has been my biggest cheerleader for *Shinji*, but who was also responsible for bringing me onboard Disney Hyperion and introducing me to the awesome and amazing world of SEA. To my agent, Laurie McLean, for all the agent-y things she does that I cannot. To Mark LaVine, Kiran Jeffery, and the incredible and talented Imagineers at Disney Parks: Thank you for sharing your insights, your vision, your imagination, and for making this whole experience completely magical.